THE KOBRA MANIFESTO

'I'm in this trade to prove myself. I'm frightened of pushing things to the point where they might blow up – so that's what I go on doing, to prove I'm not frightened.'

Conscious as always that he is living on borrowed time, Quiller allows the London Bureau to throw him into a mission that seems already to be running out of control as one agent after another is reported missing or dead, out there in the field.

On the French Riviera a defector from behind the Curtain crash-lands his plane, uttering only one word before dying: the name of Kobra . . . on Rome Airport a fuel tanker explodes as a dead man's car loses direction . . . in Cambodia a man sipping his coffee under the palm trees goes crashing back in his chair as a bullet shatters his skull . . . until there is only one executive left to carry the mission, and Quiller is ordered in.

But Kobra – an international group of terrorists – counters every attempt to penetrate its operation: in the White House the scream of an ambulance siren is heard as Quiller's rendezvous is blown . . . in the jungle night along the Amazon a woman fires six slow shots, and each time shoots to kill . . . on a U.S. Air Force base a jetliner stands isolated as a young girl is offered up as hostage . . . until Quiller sets the scene for his final throw, where only a ghost of a chance can get him through as a time-bomb ticks towards its detonation.

In his mission against the Kobra group, Quiller comes closer than ever to 'pushing things to the point where they might blow up . . .' and only those readers with strong nerves will want to go all the way with him.

THE
KOBRA
MANIFESTO

Adam Hall

COLLINS
St James's Place, London
1976

William Collins Sons & Co Ltd
London · Glasgow · Sydney · Auckland
Toronto · Johannesburg

First published 1976
© Elleston Trevor 1976

ISBN 0 00 222487 9

Set in Monotype Baskerville
Made and Printed in Great Britain by
William Collins Sons & Co Ltd Glasgow

For Bob and Florence Schiffer

Contents

I

Zarkovic

This year they'd added another layer of Armco on the out-side of the bends and joined the two bottom rows with mass-ive steel flitch plates to stop people forcing the rails apart and this must have saved a lot of injuries when Hans Strobel came round three laps from the finish and hit one of the uprights and bounced off it and spun twice and caught fire.

There wasn't a lot of noise from the crash itself, just a low roaring as the flames bannered back in the slipstream; but some people down there had started screaming and there was a kind of whimpering noise as the first of the emergency vehicles wheelspun on the hot tarmac as it pulled away from the pits.

'Oh God,' Marianne said and buried her face against me.

'He's all right,' I told her, but of course she knew he wasn't. He'd been hurled clear but the flames had caught him and he was rolling over and over like a small quiet fire-ball along the guard rails with no one to help him.

Up to now we'd all been cheering him on. This was Strobel's third year at Monaco and he'd been steadily getting the hang of the gear ratios and the characteristic front-end problem as the weight came off past the Casino, and in practice he'd notched up a diabolical 1 min. 25.35 sec. just before he came in, and for most of the time it had looked like his race and in another few minutes we would have heard the corks popping but now he was rolling along the guard rails, orange and black and flickering, *le pauvre*, the man next to me kept saying monotonously, *oh mon Dieu, le pauvre*, till he got on my nerves.

The B.R.M. wasn't in the way and the rest of the field were coming past in a strung-out line, slowing under the brakes and losing some of their traction on the hot tarmac. Rizzoli and Marks had begun shunting and one of the team Ferraris lost the back end and did a complete spin and tore off its nose aerofoil and that was about all I saw because Marianne had gone dead white and I wanted to get her away from the stands before the shoving and pushing began. People were standing on the benches to get a better view of the mess down there and that made it easier for me and we were going down the steps to the harbour car park as the P.A. system began sending out its near-unintelligible echoes round the circuit.

They didn't mention Strobel but just said the race was being abandoned and this wasn't surprising because even if he were still alive they couldn't bring the thing to a decent conclusion with wreckage and fire-foam all over the finishing-straight. A lot of people were already coming down from the stands, because there'd only been three laps to go and they wanted to avoid the traffic jam.

'It looked worse,' I said, 'than it really was.'

'Yes,' Marianne said, 'yes of course.'

She clung to me as far as the entrance to the harbour car park and then freed herself and walked apart from me for a little way, as if ashamed of her behaviour. I didn't know her very well but I knew she had pride. She walked very straight but with her head down, the snakeskin bag swinging from her tanned hand, the gold bracelet sparkling in the sun. In a minute I put an arm round her and she brought her head up and we walked in step to the line of cars along the harbour's edge where I'd left the Lancia.

'*Vous avez vos papiers, m'sieur?*'

Two Monegasque *motards*, their bikes heeled over on their stands, one in front of the Lancia and one behind. I showed them my passport and driving licence and left them reading the things while I opened the door for Marianne. She looked up at me and managed a slightly lopsided smile.

'*C'est la vie,*' she said, and I nodded. She was talking about Hans Strobel, and she probably meant, *c'est la mort.* The loudspeakers were still echoing around the buildings but I couldn't make out what they were saying because the Radio Monte-Carlo helicopter was making some low passes across the circuit where the crash had been. A whole crowd of people were moving into the car park now and the traffic police were taking up stations.

'*Merci, m'sieur.*'

He gave me back my papers and it occurred to me that the whole thing was a bit odd because you can't break many regulations leaving your car parked in a nice neat row with the others; but I wasn't really interested because I wanted to start battling a gangway through the traffic till we got to a quiet bar where I could give Marianne a cognac.

'*Eh bien, m'sieur,*' the big one said, '*il y a un Monsieur Steadman qui vous attend à l'Hotel Negresco, à Nice. C'est assez urgent, et vous n'avez qu'à nous suivre, vous savez?*'

'Okay,' I said, and got into the Lancia.

'What is happening?' asked Marianne.

'They're going to give us a hand getting through all the traffic.'

She kept her green eyes on me for a moment and then looked down and didn't ask anything else. I'd told her I was in the diplomatic corps, one of the routine covers when we're hanging around foreign parts between missions. There was the prescribed plate on the back of the car and I'd telexed the number to London and that was routine too. We're never asked to report at intervals or tell them where we're staying because we're meant to relax between missions but we have to tell them the country we're in and the car we're driving, so that they can get their hooks on us if something blows up.

The two *motards* had got their hee-haws going and the whistles began shrilling ahead of us as the traffic police began pulling the line of cars to one side to let us through. Marianne lit a cigarette and leaned her head back and closed her eyes and we didn't talk until the cops had taken us in a loop along the Boulevard des Moulins to the frontier by the bus terminal. A pair of French *motards* were waiting for us there with their bikes ticking over and the Monégasques peeled off and left us to it. The main street through Beausoleil was almost deserted because everyone was down there by the sea, and the French cops put on a bit of speed, using their klaxons on the rising hairpin bends to the Grande Corniche.

3

'Will you have to go?' asked Marianne. She was leaning her dark head sideways, watching me.

'Probably.'

Because London doesn't grab you just for a giggle. I didn't know who Monsieur Steadman was because it'd be a code name and it could be Ferris or Loman or Comyngs or anyone at all: it didn't have to be a director in the field at this stage; it could simply be a contact. During the last few hours something had come up on the board and they'd flown this man out and asked Interpol in Paris to pick up the driver of the car with the number I'd given them and tell him where the rendezvous was: the Negresco, Nice.

'That is a shame,' Marianne said.

She always tried to speak English to me, because I said I liked her accent.

'Yes.' I turned to look at her, then away again.

We'd planned three more days together before she had to go back on duty handing out trays at thirty thousand feet and I wouldn't have let anything bust into a situation like that in the ordinary way, but this wasn't the ordinary way: it looked as if the Bureau had a mission for me and all I could think about now was what I was going into and whether I was going to get out.

'They've got some trouble,' I told her, 'in French Guinea, and the U.K. has been asked to mediate.' We were going through La Turbie at the correct speed and there wasn't any traffic so they weren't using their klaxons, which was a relief. 'It just means they'll want me back in Paris.'

'*Merde*,' she said.

'Are you on the metropolitan flights?'

'No. I will be in Durban.'

She opened her eyes and looked at me for a minute and then curled her bare brown legs up on the seat and closed her eyes again and we didn't talk any more till we were rolling along the Promenade des Anglais, one *motard* still ahead of us and one behind. They'd taken us through most of the Corniche at a hundred k.p.h. and all we'd met were the La Turbie bus and a couple of *deux chevaux* but they'd used their hee-haws on sight and the indications seemed to

4

be that London had sent a real phase-one priority to Interpol with the end result that these two *anges de la route* had been given instructions to get me through fire and water if it were necessary. It hadn't been necessary but they'd at least tried to show they were right on the ball in case any questions were asked later.

London doesn't normally fidget like that.

Marianne had an apartment in the Gustave V and I turned off the sea front and dropped her there, the rear-guard *motard* following up and the front one meeting us from the opposite direction when he found out we'd made a deviation. She told me not to come up.

'All right,' I said.

She'd been quiet for most of the time since we'd left the Principality, because the Strobel thing was still on her mind. Also I think she'd been looking forward to the three days we'd planned, and probably thought I should ring Paris and tell them I was down with the *grippe* or something; and that was what I would have done, if it had been Paris.

I got out of the Lancia and opened the little rusty iron gate of the Villa Madeleine, breaking another tendril of the morning glory that was twined round the hinges.

'Are you ever in Durban?' She gave a little *moue* and turned away and went up the tiled steps, finding the key in her bag; and when I was back in the car she'd gone, Marianne, with her slim brown legs and her smoky eyes and the way she made you feel it was the first time and never-ending.

Steadman had left a message at the desk saying he'd be in the Rotunda, and I saw him on the far side sitting alone at a table with a tray of tea. He looked at me over the cup.

'Took your time,' he said.

We went through the code-intro for the month, inter-national and unspecified, and he ordered me some tea.

'I had a fast police escort,' I said, 'what more do you want?'

He looked faintly surprised. 'I was just joking.'

He was a small man with sideboards and a huge tie and

suede shoes and I wondered where they'd got him from. He wasn't Bureau. I looked around and saw it was all right: there aren't any bugs in the Rotunda at the Negresco and the dome doesn't throw any echoes because of the carpet and all those gilt-framed copies of Little Lord Fauntleroy.

'Where are you from?' I asked him.

'Liaison 9.'

That explained it: we call them the Wet Look. The thing is they spend their time liaising with the major services and therefore know a lot more than we do and we resent that. Our only consolation is that we know one or two things they can never hope to get their hands on because they're filed in a heat-proof box with an all-eventualities cutout circuit and a bang-destruct and they'd never get near the thing, even if they took off their little suede shoes.

'All right,' I told him, 'what's the form?'

We spoke just above a whisper, because people could go past on the other side of the pillars to look at the onyx ash-trays in the display windows.

'There isn't any.'

He sipped his tea.

I didn't say anything. If I said anything it would get his back up and there wasn't any point in doing that because he wasn't anyone important: he was just a contact thrown in to early-warn the executive, that was all; and once the mission was set up they'd give me a first rank director in the field I'd have to live with and like it. He'd have to be different from Steadman.

'You're on stand-by,' he said, and brushed his lips with the napkin.

'What phase?'

He gave a little laugh, displacing a lock of hair.

'Oh, it's nothing like that.'

Sometimes they try and shove a between-mission executive straight into a middle-phase or an end-phase assignment that's come unstuck and we all squeal like hell but never refuse it because we can hear the sound of distant bugles and we want to get in there where the bloodied banners are reeling through the fray. And there's another reason: we know

6

there's always the chance that someone's managed to put most of an important mission in the bag before he caught a stray shot or hit a wall, so we can go in and tie up the end-phase and reach the objective and come out alive and take the glory for the poor bastard who couldn't quite make it – listen, if we weren't people like that we wouldn't be in this trade, work it out for yourself.

My tea came and when the boy had gone I said:

'Is it a mission?'

'It has all the earmarks, old boy.'

So he'd been getting the lingo wrong, that was all: trust Liaison 9. He'd told me I was on stand-by and they only use that term when they want to throw you into the fire to look for the chestnuts and that's why I'd asked the obvious question, to find out what phase they'd got the thing running at. When you're down for a mission they don't put you on stand-by, they put you on call; and maybe it doesn't sound very different but it is: a full-scale mission is your very own little toy to play with and you take it very seriously indeed and that was how I was taking it now.

The nerves were on edge.

'What time are they calling up?'

He sipped his tea.

'No special time.'

I sat back and looked at Little Lord Fauntleroy. Under the big glass dome of the Rotunda the silence was peculiar, made up of tiny sounds that ticked or scratched or bumped and then died away before you could place them; but they weren't the ones I was listening to. Up there on the far side of the Channel there were doors opening and closing along those dim-lit passages, and the gibberish was crackling through the static and out of the scramblers in Signals while a phone rang and was picked up and someone in Monitoring sent a memo to Egerton or Mildmay or Parkis and everyone waited for the word that would start this whole thing running. Somewhere in Beirut or The Hague or the Azores they were looking for the hole, and when they'd found the hole they were going to put the ferret down, and the ferret was me.

7

From where we sat in our plush chairs in this sepulchral calm we could hear the telephone, faintly, at the desk in the foyer. I listened to that sound, too.

'You must have some idea,' I told Steadman.

Sat cursing myself. Perfectly normal for the executive to be on edge when he's on call but we always try not to show it and we always try not to show it especially to little ticks like this one.

He looked at the shine on his nails.

'There's someone trying to get across.'

I sat forward an inch.

'Where from?'

'We don't know.'

'Oh for Christ's sake, you must know where the – '

Stopped.

He looked around him, terribly casual, hamming it. The executive is requested to keep his cool and not shout the place down so that strangers can hear.

'Correction,' he said blandly, his gaze passing across my face as if by accident. 'For "we" don't know, read "I" don't know.' He let three seconds go by and added gently: 'Possibly that's why they're going to phone.'

It was twenty-five past six and at ten past seven the little bastard got up and wandered about looking at the costume jewellery in the display windows and the brass plates at the bottom of the picture frames and then came wandering back. I'd counted twenty-three calls to the desk out there.

'*M'sieur Steadman?*'

'What? Oh, yes.'

They never got used to their cover names.

'A telephone call for you.'

'Thanks.'

The waiter took him to the foyer and came back to get our trays.

'*Vous avez terminé, m'sieur?*'

'*Bien sûr. Dites-moi, il y a des nouvelles de ce pilote, Hans Strobel, à Monté Carle?*'

His waxed eyebrows lifted slightly in a gesture of desolation.

8

'*Il est mort. Dans l'ambulance, vous savez. Eh, oui.*' The delicate porcelain tinkled as he stacked the cups, gilt and rose-buds and tea-leaves. '*Je crois que c'est le destin qu'ils cherchent, hein, ces types-là?*'

'*C'est possible.*'

A fireball rolling along the guard rail. Death or glory, make up your mind because you can't have both.

I got up and went over to the line of windows, Cartier, Chanel, and then some Hermes scarves like the one Marianne was wearing, reminding me of the bars of sunlight and shadow thrown by those peeling Venetian blinds across the white carpet, across her gold body. But already she seemed a long time ago and in a distant place, because the moment you know they've sent for you it's like dropping over a brink and into a void, and the memory tends to blank off.

His reflection came against the window glass.

'What about a little stroll along the promenade?'

'All right.'

When we left the hotel I checked and got negative and checked again after we'd crossed the two roads to the sea front and got negative again and felt totally satisfied because anyone trying to tag us across that hellish traffic would never make it alive. He'd probably picked up some ticks in London because the Liaison 9 people can hardly avoid it: their routine travel pattern takes them from one intelligence base to the next and they're fair game, and when they board an aircraft for anywhere abroad they're liable to be overtaken by signals and find someone on the peep for them wherever they land. But he'd obviously flushed them, and I could believe he was clever at it because people like Steadman dislike human contact.

'It's for tomorrow morning,' he said.

'They can't do that.'

'I think they can, old boy.'

There was something wrong and I didn't like it because there just wasn't enough time to set me up overnight: they had to brief me and push me through Clearance and drop me into the target zone and set me running with everything I needed – communications, access channels, escape lines, so forth. And there wasn't enough time for that: I couldn't even make London before midnight unless there were a flight with a delay on it.

Then I saw I was missing the obvious, too bloody impatient to think straight. This was local.

'This chap's going into Istres,' he said.

Local.

'You know where that is?' he asked me.

'Bouches du Rhône.'

'Yes. There's an airfield there. Have you got a Michelin 84 in your car?'

'I've got the whole set.'

'Well I never, they don't do that at Hertz.'

We stood for a minute watching the rollers breaking white across the stones, the spindrift catching the light of the tall lamp-standards.

'His name is Milos Zarkovic, and he – '

'Name, or cover name?'

'What? I don't know. I'm just repeating what they told me on the phone, so please try not to interrupt, or I might forget something.' He gave a little smile with his chin tucked in. 'I'm only joking, of course. This chap is using a Pulmeister 101 single seat interceptor, which is apparently the longest-range machine he can pinch without anybody noticing too much.'

'Where's he coming from?'

'One of the satellite air force bases near Zagreb. Ostensibly he'll make for Madrid but the weather's going to take him off course slightly and he's going to run out of fuel and do a belly flop near the airfield at Istres.'

We reached one of the car park kiosks and turned back, walking slowly. He was very good: he'd checked the two men over by the rail and the one sitting on the bench reading *Nice Matin* and they hadn't made a move.

'How do I get him out of Istres?'

'That's up to you.' He glanced at me sharply. 'If you want any kind of backup laid on you'd better tell London right away. But they're expecting you to handle it solo. Up to you, as I say.'

I thought about it. London knew I didn't want any back-up: I work solo or not at all and they know that; but there were things like communications and alternative action and the availability of a safe-house. The area around Istres was nearly all marshland and that made it perfect for the forced-landing cover story but Marseille was close and Marseille is one of the nerve centres for half a dozen major networks with permanent agents-in-place, and this was a daytime oper-ation. It wouldn't be more than ten minutes before the first people showed up at the landing site, but I didn't have to get the aircraft away: all they wanted was Milos Zarkovic.

'All right,' I told him. 'They want him in London?'

'Yes.'

'How soon?'

'Soonest.'

'Will he be carrying papers?'

'Oh yes. Yugoslavian passport, Communist Party member-ship, everything quite above board – I mean there won't be any trouble from the local police if you can manage to get him out of sight straight away, not till the news gets around that he's wanted in Yugers for pinching the plane. It's the spooks, you see, that you'll have to contend with; Marseille is rather like a fly-paper, as doubtless you're aware.'

We waited by the traffic lights and he pressed the button.

'What time is he coming in?'

'As soon as it's light enough for him to see the ground. The idea is that there won't be a lot of people about at that hour.'

'How far's the landing site from Istres?'

'I'm going to show you.'

The little green man flickered into life and we went across and opened the Lancia and got in and took Section 84 out of the glove compartment. He had a red felt pen in his hand.

'Just here, okay? A kilometre south of St-Martin-de-Crau.'

The place would be visible from the tower at Istres air-field through a pair of 7×50's but that wasn't critical be-cause the minor road ran north and then west behind a low elevation and that was where I could lose people.

'All right,' I said.

'You want to recap?'

'No.' I wanted to find a phone and tell London they could screw the Pulmeister 101 and screw Milos Zarkovic because this wasn't a mission they were handing me, it was a contact and escort operation and they could have used Coleman or Matthews or Johnson or anyone from the general facilities pool: they didn't need a first-line shadow executive for this thing and they knew it. But I was between missions and not far along the coastline from Istres and they thought they'd save the expense of flying someone else out from London and risking the operation through lack of experience so they'd winkled me out and sent this little jerk to local-brief me and sell me the thing about 'handling it solo' to give it the look of a first-line penetration job.

His cologne was rather heavy and I folded the map and put it back with the others and got out of the car and stood watching an Air France Boeing sliding down to the airport across the bay.

'You don't seem very happy, old boy.'

Screw Steadman too.

'If London wants this character, I'll bring him in.'

Soon after Aix-en-Provence I began hitting the Mistral, touching the wheel to correct the steering as the gusts came broadside-on. The Mistral is a strong and steady wind, blowing down the Rhône Valley and bending the cypresses and unnerving the people in its path; it blows for three, six or nine days and by Napoleonic law if it blows for longer than that, murder is not a capital charge.

I didn't know how long it had been blowing this time. If it hadn't dropped by dawn, Zarkovic would have to make a half circuit to bring his plane up-wind because a belly flop would be tricky enough without dead-air conditions. The Mistral turns eastward when it reaches the coast, and that would be Zarkovic's approach direction.

By midnight I was in St-Martin-de-Crau and drove straight through and pulled the Lancia into cover alongside a vineyard, dousing the lights and sleeping on and off for the next five hours. The last time I woke up I was aware of the silence: the Mistral had died and the pre-dawn air was still.

By 05:15 I was positioned to receive the contact, halfway along a narrow road that led south to the coast. The wind had got up again and I stopped trying to work out which way he'd be coming in. There wasn't a lot of room between the railway to the east and the Rhône Basin to the west, but if he managed to come down precisely into the wind he'd be sliding towards me at this point and finish up within a hundred metres of the car.

There are never clouds when the Mistral blows, and I could make out the tower at Istres, black against the pale dawn sky. Within minutes the reeds at the edge of the marshland were turning from blood red to silver as the sun lifted from the low horizons, and the wind tugged at them, curving them into scimitars. Gusts hit the side of the Lancia, shifting it on its springs; I leaned away from it and settled the binoculars on the skyline in the east.

06:00.

He was overdue because Steadman had told me he was coming in at first light and the sun was already five or six diameters high and the waves of heat were floating horizontally across the lens where the railway embankment made the skyline. He could have mucked it, of course. I didn't know anything about his background: he could be a major element in something big the Bureau was running or he could be coming across with the blueprints of the Russian fleet, but even if he were only a contact or a courier he had to get a front-line interceptor airborne out of a military base and he had to go like hell through a gauntlet of radar stations that would trigger off signals to every air police unit along the north Mediterranean before he was across the Italian Alps. He could be chased and intercepted and ordered to turn back by pursuit squadrons of the Yugoslavian air arm, and if they managed to interest the Italians in this thing he'd have to move faster than the decision-makers at a dozen military airfields along his course.

That was his problem, not mine.

06:30.

The heat shimmered against the lenses. I lowered the glasses to rest my eyes and then put them up again. The sky to the east was a blinding sheet of white.

It occurred to me that I'd missed a couple of points because it had looked as if they'd thrown a full-scale mission at me and it had triggered the normal degree of first-night nerves and I'd been jumping gaps. The thing was this: there hadn't been any need for Steadman in this picture. London could have just signalled Interpol to get me into communication, and all those Monegasque cops had to do was tell me to phone the Bureau; then the Bureau would have told me to go and pick up this character at dawn, Bouches du Rhône, so forth.

But they hadn't done that. They'd sent Steadman. Or Steadman had been down here in the field and they'd told him to stand by and brief me. One possible answer was that some other service like D.I.6 had got on to this Zarkovic thing and found it too hot to handle and shunted it through Liaison 9 for the Bureau to look after, because the Bureau doesn't exist. Another possible answer was that London was still in the middle of sorting out a mass of raw intelligence that had started hitting the fan up there, but there wasn't time for me to think about that because a quick black dart was crossing the lenses and I swung them to keep it centred.

He was moving from east through south and standing on his starboard wingtip as he came round again and dropped very fast across the skyline to the west. I began running because his approach path looked like half a kilometre north of the mark Steadman had made on the map and I couldn't get the Lancia there. The only available detour would take me five or six kilometres and rather close to the airfield buildings and I didn't want to expose the image because in an hour from now the Lancia with the CD plate could be the subject of an all-points bulletin if the gendarmerie decided that Yugoslavians ought not to drop out of the sky and jump into cars and disappear.

The ground was soft and I kept away from the reeds and the bright areas where the sun was reflecting off stagnant

14

water but it was sticky going because the surface was inconsistent and I kept stumbling over firm patches and then wallowing in the troughs. A lot of white birds were crowding into the air not far away because they'd seen the plane. Vision was jerky and I stopped and stood still and tried to get some kind of a fix on the spot where he'd be coming down. From this oblique angle the front-end configuration was like a bent dart, with a very small wing area that would make for a high stalling-speed: he couldn't stay airborne much longer and I worked it out that if I ran like hell I could finish up at a point where I'd be close enough to make the rendezvous without fetching the thing on top of me.

Began running again. Heard the whine of the twin jets, then they cut off and there was only the buffeting of the wind: he was keeping to his cover situation and going through the motions of running out of fuel; either that or for some very good reason he'd been loafing about over the sea to use up the reserve tank to the point where he'd have to come in, to give the whole thing credibility if anyone decided to take a look at the fuel gauges.

He was coming in very low indeed and I had to veer a bit without breaking my run because he wouldn't be able to avoid me if I got it wrong. There was the smell of kerosene as the wind shifted and the light shone bright on the silver-grey fuselage and I could see the nose wheel turning very slowly as the airstream caught it, then he was alongside and I veered again into the wind and got a rear-oblique view of him as he reached the stalling-point and dropped tail first and bounced and tilted and bounced again and then bucked forward and dug the nose in and flipped over in a wave of mud. I kept on running.

2

London

The momentum hadn't been completely exhausted when the Pulmeister had flipped over, and the razor-thin trailing edges of the tail unit had been thrust into the soft earth like a dart driven backwards with force. The front end of the thing was sticking up at something like twenty degrees from the horizontal and of course it was upside down. It looked as if he'd tried to get out because the cockpit hood was open and I could see part of his head and one elbow.

The wave of mud had sloshed upwards into the cockpit and it was difficult to see any detailed objects against the glare of the sky but I knew one thing: if I couldn't pull him out very soon the weight of the front end would prise the tail unit out of the mud and bring the cockpit down on both of us, so I crawled underneath and felt for the release clip of his helmet. He didn't move.

The whole thing was smothered in mud and I couldn't find the clip, partly because my fingers didn't know the precise shape to feel for. Some kind of fluid was dripping from a severed pipe somewhere behind the instrument panel and the wind kept slapping the side of the fuselage: I could hear the sucking sound as the tail unit flexed in the mud. I didn't think I had more than a few seconds to get him clear. My hands began moving in a kind of controlled frenzy, feeling for whatever they could find: clips, buckles, fasteners, anything they could release, worming their way in the mud and the half-dark while the tail unit flexed, steadied and flexed again.

'Zarkovic,' I said to the helmet.

He didn't move.

'Zarkovic.'

A basic form of communication designed to inform him that his identity was known and that I must therefore be an ally, even a saviour. He didn't answer.

The restrain harness seemed to be free and it looked as if he might have released it too early, having to make a critical decision between staying in place with the harness on to minimize the impact forces, and trying to jump clear. It couldn't have been easy to make up his mind because a lot of the data was unavailable: he didn't know what the Pulmeister was going to do when it hit the ground. If he stayed in place with the harness still on he could be trapped upside down in the cockpit in total darkness and with no incoming air and the risk of something catching fire; and if he tried to jump clear he could get fouled in the loose harness and risk the edge of the cockpit coming down on him.

'Zarkovic.'

My voice was beginning to have no more meaning than the wind.

The buckles seemed to be free but he wasn't able to drop out of the cockpit and I squeezed my body higher, making a decision of my own that was as critical as his because I was too far inside the thing now to get clear if the tail came out of the mud. It wasn't possible to work out what would happen if six tons of metal came down on us but I didn't think there'd be enough room to stay alive.

The wind buffeted, screaming faintly through the reeds outside. I could feel the movement very distinctly as the aircraft yawed to the gusts, and my hands slowed, taking their time, because in a shut-ended situation the organism must resist panic if it wants to survive. The harness was indeed free but his legs were twisted awkwardly and his feet had got trapped by some sort of equipment that had come unshipped on impact: the whole thing had taken somewhere in the region of fifty or sixty g's and it was now clear that he'd decided to jump and hadn't been able to.

My leg was against the padded edge of the cockpit and I could feel it lift and fall every time the tail unit flexed, lifting a little less, falling a little more, till the point was reached when I had to ask whether London wanted one live agent or two dead ones because if the thing came down on me now I was going to get crushed and so was Zarkovic. But I'd

17

started something and I wanted to finish it, so I decided to give it sixty seconds more and then get out.

Bloody stuff was oozing down from the cockpit floor, some of it running into my eyes before I could shut them and wipe it away. Some kind of instrument ticking steadily in the quietness, the chronometer or a timed alert system; with one eye I could see the ghostly phosphorescence of the instrument dials. Still couldn't free him because his flying-boots had been wrenched around as his body had twisted, and I thought that if I ever got him out of here he might not walk again.

'Zarkovic.'

Nothing.

Zarkovic, my friend, will you ever walk again?

Oh come on for Christ's sake, the whole bloody thing's going to blot us both out and you've given yourself sixty seconds and you've got thirty left so *come on for Christ's sake, get this poor bastard out.*

Unlace the boots. Get his boots off.

Another thing was that they must have seen the Pulmeister from the tower at Istres and if there were anyone on duty at this hour they'd send emergency crews and the distance was less than four kilometres by road and I didn't want any emergency crews or gendarmes or anyone like that – all I wanted was to get this man's *bloody* boots off.

A wind gust came and the whole thing shuddered and I worked very hard and he dropped half across me as I got the first boot off but he didn't say anything or make any movement because he'd taken a beating through those fifty or sixty g's and he'd been hanging here with the blood accumulating in his head and maybe I was wrong: maybe we *did* want the emergency crews here and as fast as they could make it.

Another wind gust and then everything happened at once: the Pulmeister shook itself as the tail unit began coming out of the mud and I ducked low and pulled him down with me and tried to roll him clear and didn't manage it because my feet and knees were slipping across the mud and I couldn't find any purchase, it was no go. Tried again and got my heels dug in and pulled him backwards like a rope in a tug-o'-war and kept on going while the fuselage came slowly down till the edge of the cockpit reached the mud and the thing became a trap but that didn't matter now because we were clear and I saw where the clip was and snapped it open and took off the helmet, easing it gently, easing it, because he must have suffered some degree of whiplash.

'Zarkovic.'

The wind blew across us, whining faintly through the reeds. It was a good face: young, sharp, with a hooked nose and thick dark eyebrows and a scar running from one ear to the chin. His eyes were coming open but there wasn't much intelligence in them.

Emergency klaxons, from the direction of Istres. They were closer than they sounded, because of the wind. I knelt in the mud beside him, watching his eyes and waiting; but their dull glaze remained. One leg was badly twisted and he was holding his head awkwardly and it occurred to me that he'd broken his neck. The blood was slowly receding from his face, leaving it translucent white, like the flesh of coconut.

Klaxons.

'Zarkovic,' I said. 'Can you talk?'

Intelligence came into the narrowed brown eyes and they watched me without blinking.

'I was sent to meet you,' I said, 'from London.'

He watched me, a spasm passing across his face. He didn't take his eyes off mine. Then his thin mouth moved.

'What?' I asked him. It had sounded like 'coder'.

His eyes squeezed shut and I waited.

A flash of light sparked from the reeds on the horizon, then another. They would be the emergency vehicles along the road beyond the marshland, the sun striking reflections from their windscreens.

'Listen,' I said against the cuffing of the wind, 'I'm going to – '

'*Cobra.*'

'What?'

I watched his lips.

'*Cobra.*'

Another spasm came and I waited but it wasn't any good because the eyes were losing their intelligence: they were staring at me but I wasn't there any more. Nothing was there.

The klaxons sounded urgently as the wind shifted and I tugged at the zip of his flying-suit and found his wallet and felt for other things like that, flat things, any kind of papers, documents. Nothing. Only the wallet. I took it and pulled the zip shut and got to my feet and began running. They were coming from the south and would have to leave their vehicles on the road and bring their equipment here on foot across the soggy ground. The Lancia was standing beyond the fringe of reeds north-west of here and I could reach it in ten minutes if I tried and I was going to try. In any case they wouldn't take any interest in me till they'd examined the body, so I had plenty of time.

But London wouldn't be pleased.

It was raining hard and they had the gas mains up from one end of Whitehall to the other and I left clay all over the floor of the lift. Matthews was trudging along the corridor with a wad of papers, which is the only thing I've ever seen him doing.

'Oh hello, Q – how was the Grand Prix?'

'Bloody awful, where's Tilson?'

'What? Monitoring, the last I saw.'

There were only three people in Monitoring and none of them was Tilson. They were sitting there like waxworks and I picked up a spare set and heard a lot of Asian coming through, probably from Laos. Everybody was worried about Laos these days, which made a change from Ireland. I went along to Incoming Staff and knocked and opened the door. They've got a man there now, instead of the two women clerks, because Incoming Staff is the place where you report first thing at the end of a mission or at the end of whatever phase of a mission you managed to reach before the whole thing blew up in your face. We don't always look very well-groomed when we come in here, and some of us have to go on to a head shrinker or a nervous disorders ward or somewhere like that; and finally the two women clerks couldn't stand it any more and I don't blame them.

'Interim debriefing,' I said, 'who wants me?'

He looked up with a swing of his big square head. I didn't know his name because in the Bureau we never know the names of people below active rank because it isn't necessary; as a matter of fact we don't know anybody's name at all, because they're just convenient labels thought up in Personnel. The Bureau doesn't exist, and that allows it to take on operations that no one else wants to be seen dead with: and that's not a bad metaphor. The intelligence lords on the top floor run the place as if it were a secret munitions ship moving at dead slow through a minefield by night: they like there to be a hush over everything, a permanent blackout, reducing to a calculated minimum the risk of an odd spark sending the whole outfit into Kingdom Come.

'Where from, sir?' the big man asked me.

'Istres, south of France.'

'Ah, yes.' He checked the board that would tell him which mission I was on, and who was running it. He didn't find anything because no one had given me a mission yet, so he opened a drawer and moved his colourless eyes twice from left to right.

'Room 6,' he said and shut the drawer. 'Just let me tell him you're here.' He picked up a phone.

They've put numbers on some of the doors now: their lordships went a bit too far in the beginning, when even the doors had to be anonymous; it had worked up to a point but there'd been a couple of cases where a visitor had wandered into Codes and Cyphers without an escort, scaring the day-lights out of us all; and they kept having to haul Thompson out of the Ladies, though God knows what he was doing in there because most of the ladies at the Bureau have brogues and rimless bifocals.

'Yes sir,' the big man said into the phone and put it down and looked at me. 'Would you care to wait five minutes?'

'All right.'

So it wasn't going to be Parkis, and it wasn't going to be Egerton. Parkis always keeps the executives waiting for half an hour because he's paranoid on the subject of status; and Egerton is too courteous to keep anyone waiting, though it comes to the same thing in the end because no one can ever find him.

'How did it go?' the big man asked.

'Got a negative.'

'Ah.' He eyed me without looking at me, in the way ex-Scotland Yard men have learned, but he couldn't see any cuts or bruises or anything wrong with my nerves, only some clay on my shoes and that wasn't too bad because five months ago Bateman had come in from a nasty one in Tangier and been told to wait and couldn't manage it: he just went along the corridor and dropped over the banisters into the stairwell before anyone had a clue what was in his mind. These cases are mostly when there's been some kind of implemented interrogation by the opposition, leaving the nerve-ends bared; but nobody comes off a mission or an interim phase feeling very jolly.

We listened to the rain pattering on the windowsill, and the distant hammering of a road drill where they were doing the gas mains.

'Smoke, sir?'

'No thanks.'

'Trying to give it up myself.' He lit one and dropped the match into the ashbowl and hit the chrome knob.

'Who is it,' I asked him, 'in Room 6?'

'Couldn't say, sir.'

He said it so fast that I knew it was routine.

It could be Mildmay. Or Sargent. The rest of them had something on the board, I knew that. In any case I was reaching the point where I didn't give a damn who was going to run me: all I wanted to do was get into the field and start moving. The Zarkovic thing had left me feeling hooked and I wanted to know more. There'd been nothing in his wallet, not a damned thing: passport, medical card, Communist membership papers, picture of a dark-haired girl smiling with the tip of her tongue between her teeth, nothing

22

else, nothing to go on. Whatever Milos Zarkovic had brought over from Yugoslavia he'd brought in his head.

I'd taken the Lancia to Marseille and used the phone and they'd told me to come in by air through Paris and here I was, hanging around this bloody office talking to a man I didn't know.

'Looks like setting in, sir.'

'What?'

'The rain.'

'Yes.'

I gave it another five minutes and told him I was going along to the Caff, so if anyone wanted me they knew where to find me.

'Okay sir, I'll tell – ' then the phone rang and he asked me to hold on. I tried to recognize the voice at the other end but all I could tell was that it wasn't Parkis and it wasn't Egerton.

'They're ready for you now, sir, in Room 6.'

It was the next floor up and I took the stairs and met Woods coming out of Signals with his tie under one ear and a cigarette in his mouth and a cup of tea in his hand.

'Jesus Christ,' he said, 'three changes in the last twenty-four hours!' He limped along to the Gents. God knew which current operation he was doing the signals for, but anyone having to change his code three times in twenty-four hours was running it very close.

Room 6 was along in the briefing complex and I knocked and went in.

'Who are you?'

'Quiller.'

'Ah yes. Sit down, won't you?'

He was behind the desk, sliding a ruler across some paper in a series of angled jerks, presumably making a graph. He was slightly rumpled-looking, with black hair and a grey face and sooty bags under his eyes. I'd never seen him before. His ruler went on sliding and I watched the deft working of his hands. He sat very still with his head angled down to look at the desk, and I took no notice when one of the telephones buzzed. After a while I got the impression that he was a remote-controlled robot with orders to fiddle here while some kind of Rome went burning down.

'Yes.'

He slid the ruler to one side and looked across at me. It was the first time I'd seen his eyes; they were the same unhealthy grey as the rest of his face, and gave away nothing.

'We haven't long,' he said, and got up and began walking about. 'I'm sending two of you people across to Lisbon by the first available flight – direct, of course. They are Pritchard and Mailer. Have you worked with them before?'

'No.'

'They are exceptionally talented. You will be making covert rendezvous with them tonight at 21:00 hours and the code introduction will be concomitant with the third series.' He stopped walking for a moment and stood looking down at his shoes with his hands tucked behind his back and his grey face intent. It was perfectly genuine: he'd forgotten I was here. I waited.

'You speak Portuguese?'

'Yes.'

'Very good. Pritchard is fluent, and Mailer has been swatting up a handbook of phrases for tourists. The three of you will be working close together, you understand. Communication will be via open channels unless there is a need for a code, in which case you will of course signal through Crowborough.'

He was telling me about access lines when I got up and went out and looked for Tilson and found him in Firearms.

'Who's that bloody fool in Room 6?'

'Oh my God,' he said, 'when did you get in?'

'Twenty minutes ago and the only thing that's happened so far is that I.S. pushed me into Room 6 for debriefing and some idiot tried to sell me a lot of crap about working with two other executives in Portugal.'

Tilson put down the sub-machine gun and looked for a phone.

'I wish someone had told me, old horse.'

'Oh for Christ's sake, can't they get their records straight?'

'There's a flap on,' he said, and pushed the button again.

'Does that mean the whole system's gone on the blink?'

He started talking to someone and I went back into the corridor and walked up and down for a bit, getting control by degrees and finding it difficult and not liking it: when we're called in for a mission the nerves react because this branch of the trade is the tricky one and it's like playing Russian roulette. There's an ambivalent attitude towards the situation that pulls us both ways: we're desperate to get back into some kind of action because that's the way we tick and if we didn't tick that way we wouldn't be here, but at the same time we know what we're doing – we're sticking our neck out a bit farther every time and one day we're going to get the chopper. It's a question of watching the odds stack up against us, mission after mission.

But I shouldn't have lost my cool so easily.

They note things like that.

The bulbs glowed yellow in the stairwell and I leaned on the banisters for a minute, listening to the raindrops hitting the skylight in the roof. Someone had made a mistake, that was all: the character in Room 6 was running a minor operation in Portugal with the local telephone for communication and a code series no one had used since I'd got back from Tunisia – it hadn't been blown anywhere but C and C had worked out some rather more sophisticated matrices with a computer for the mainline operations and these days the first-to-fourth series were given the trainees to play with.

'It's all right now,' Tilson said.

He was shuffling along the corridor in his plaid slippers, his round pink face radiating reassurance.

'Who is he, anyway?'

'Who is who, old fruit?'

'That bloody fool.'

He gave a slight wince, and looked back along the corridor for a moment, lowering his voice. 'He's from upstairs.'

Now I got it. At the Bureau 'upstairs' is the rarefied territory where Administration has its offices. Normally their lordships leave us alone but sometimes one of them asks the directorate if he can run a minor operation to keep his hand in, and of course the directorate can't refuse. I suppose there's a point in it somewhere but that kind of thing can get out of hand: we could find one of those amateur heroes running a mission the wrong way round and getting the poor bloody executive caught in the works. We don't appreciate that sort of thing: it's our life, not theirs.

'All right Tilson, get me debriefed.'

'Of course,' he said comfortingly. 'What about a spot of tea first?'

'Listen, will you, they told me to make contact and escort on the French coast and the poor bastard killed himself and I've got his papers for whoever wants them and all I'm asking for is some service and I'm asking you to get it for me.'

The tone of my voice was pitching up again and I heard it and was warned. There wasn't anything to worry about: they must have a mission lined up for me or they wouldn't have sent me to Istres like that, through a Liaison 9 cut-out: they'd have told those Monegasque cops I had to telephone London. And if they had a mission lined up for me I'd be sent into the field within a matter of days and then I'd be all right.

Tilson was shuffling along beside me.

'Where the hell are we going now, Tilson?'

'Debriefing,' he said, 'then briefing.'

I could feel the subtle rise in the pulse rate throughout my body. 'They've got something for me, have they?'

'That's right.' He turned a bland smile on me. 'Thought you'd be pleased.'

We went down the stairs.

'Who's my director?'

'Mr Egerton.'

I slowed. Egerton was a mainliner, one of the top echelon people in the London directorate. So it was something big.

'Look,' I said, 'this isn't the way to – '

'I do wish you'd take your foot off, old fruit, just till I can get you sorted out. The thing is, he's not in his office. I tried, from Firearms.'

'Where is he?'

'I don't know. I've told everyone to ransack the entire building, and I can't do more than that for you, can I?'

We walked under the yellow bulbs, passing the grimy windows where the rain was leaving streaks. There was nothing along here except the Caff and some storerooms.

'Something big, is it?'

I wanted to know more. I wanted to know *everything*. But I wouldn't know anything at all, until they found Egerton.

'To judge by the size of the flap,' Tilson said, 'yes.' He wasn't normally communicative: he didn't like committing himself. His job was to shunt people from one department to another, make sure they never got lost in transit, and occasionally brief them on behalf of a director.

'There's a flap?' I said.

'Rather an understatement, old boy. I don't mind telling you, we've got four people out there trying to find access for the executive, and one of them is playing it so close that he's keeping Signals up all night changing codes.' We went through the door at the end of the passage and he said above the clatter of crockery: 'Meanwhile I thought you might like a spot of tea. My treat, of course.'

3
Briefing

It was no go.

For fifteen minutes Egerton had sat behind his cluttered desk in the room right at the top of the building, giving me a rough outline of the mission, his voice quiet and modulated, his dull brown eyes wandering about behind his glasses as he sketched in the problems with access, the lack of direction, the uncertainty about objectives. He didn't make apologies for anything, and he didn't try to persuade me. He just hoped, with that wistful smile of his, that I might want to 'have a go'.

I didn't.

'It's not my field,' I said, 'you know that.'

'Of course.' He gave a shrug of resignation. 'It's just that I didn't feel like handing this operation to – well – someone who might drop it.'

I got out of the Louis Quinze chair and moved about, feeling trapped. The room was claustrophobic, part of the servants' dormitories at the turn of the century when the place was built; and he'd crammed it with trophies from Petticoat Lane – old bulb horns and a stuffed owl and a whole rack of Coronation mugs. The rain beat at the high dormer window, and I could hear pigeons scratching along the ledge below.

'The point is,' I told him, 'there's no mission lined up. I mean nothing with any shape.'

He knew my field. I'm a penetration agent. We've all got our speciality: Heppinstall likes a difficult objective with a complicated access so that he can work like a slide-rule and use positive and negative feedback to take him to the target. Vickers is a socialite and likes keeping his hands clean: put him in pinstripes and send him into a Palace garden party with white gloves and a carnation and he'll bring out the K.G.B. man we've been hunting for months, and none of the guests will know it's happened. I happen to be a ferret: I want them to specify the target zone and the objective and send me down the hole and leave me alone in the dark. Then I can do something: but only then.

'There's no access,' I told him. 'And no objective.'

'Not yet, no.'

I looked down at him, leaning against the fireplace; he'd covered it with some French tapestry but I could still feel the draught. 'How long will it take?'

'Not long,' he said. His dull brown eyes surveyed my face.

Egerton was a good man to work for: you couldn't hope for a better Control if a wheel came off halfway through a mission and you needed support from London to get you through. He was slow, calculating and ruthless, and if he had to throw you to the dogs he wouldn't do it because he didn't value you or because he'd lost patience with your lack of progress: he'd do it because he had to, because if he left you alive he'd expose the Bureau itself to hazard. I've worked for Egerton quite a few times and come out with a whole skin and a bit of pride still left; but I don't work for anyone who can't give me access, an objective and a free hand.

No go.

'What I should be unhappy to see,' he said gently, 'would be your taking on the next mission that comes up, and missing this one that we are all working hard to put together. Because it's rather substantial.' He blinked twice, still watching me. 'And frankly there's no one I'd prefer to control. No one.'

I knew one thing about Egerton: he'd get me into this thing if he could, provided he wanted me enough: he'd done it before and now he was trying again – it wouldn't 'take long' to find the access; this operation was 'rather substantial' and there was nobody he'd 'prefer to control'; so forth.

But this time I didn't think he could do it because there was nothing about it I liked, nothing at all.

'Can't you put me on call?'

'I could,' he said. 'But I'm not going to.'

Fair enough. It could be for a week or two and I'd have to

report in every day and hang around and hope the mission was going to break at any hour and within twenty-one days I'd be a nervous wreck and he knew it.

'Zarkovic,' I said. 'Didn't he have any contact in Zagreb?'

'None that we know about.'

'What about "Cobra" then?'

He looked into the middle distance. 'We've got some people working on that. The only thing we know about it at the moment is that it's spelt with a "K".'

'Big deal.' But I watched him because if he knew that much then he must know more. 'What about this man in Tokyo?'

'We are working on him, too.' He leaned across the desk suddenly, looking up at me. 'We have four people out there, you see, all working very hard. Tonight we are sending a fifth, dropping him into the countryside near Beirut. You must admit, at least, that the opening phase is simple enough? There are five men apparently converging upon a given focal point, and we already have four of them under remote surveillance, and by tomorrow the fifth will be located. With any luck, our five targets will converge very soon, and we shall be able to send in a penetration agent with the access and objective known and integrated. I don't see why you are so – ' he moved a long thin hand despairingly – 'uninterested.'

I went and sat down again.

The situation he'd given me wasn't uninteresting as such: one of our people had picked up an isolated bit of info in Alexandria quite by chance and checked it with Shin Bet, the Israeli Intelligence Service, and drawn blank. Then he'd checked it with our top contact inside Sovinformburo and got an instant lead. Then there were a couple more blanks: the S.D.E.C.E. in Paris knew nothing, nor did K.Y.P., Athens; but two separate sources in Berlin began putting odd bits of raw intelligence through the monitors and finally Egerton was told to send a man out there to try analysing it. It took him six days.

The picture was now reasonably clear. Five international terrorists had started making their way to a predetermined rendezvous from Taipei, Beirut, Cairo, Naples and Tangier, and they were taking a lot of trouble to cover their tracks, doubling back and feinting and leaping gaps. Egerton had now put four men into the field and was sending a fifth, and any number of them – from one to five – would show up at the rendezvous and keep very strict tabs.

'My conjecture,' Egerton had told me, 'is that once the group has come together, it will then move directly to whatever may be the objective.' He'd given one of his quiet sighs. 'I had very much hoped you would want to join them there.'

I saw the point but didn't like it. I want to know what the objective is before I start because I'm a fast-burn operator and I can keep up a lot of heat for a short period but then I'm done. You can't expect it both ways: some people are sprinters and some are long-distance; and I'm a sprinter. Egerton knew that, and he was trying to push me into a cross-country marathon and I wasn't having any.

'It's not on,' I told him.

He stood up rather wearily and watched the rain trickling down the window above him. It wasn't shifting any of the grime and it occurred to me that if the thing ever got cleaned he wouldn't have to use his glasses any more. He didn't say anything for two minutes but I didn't fidget because that was what he was waiting for.

He turned round and sat down again, piling himself behind the desk like a heap of dead sticks.

'What you might care to consider,' he said in hushed parson's tones, 'is being placed on a five- or six-day call, and – '

A phone buzzed and it was the one on the end and he picked it up without even finishing. It was the yellow one, direct from Signals.

'Yes?'

He listened while I shifted my haunches around on the seat of the Louis Quinze chair: there's a spring that catches you, and one fine day I hope he'll have the bloody thing re-stuffed.

'I see.' He sagged a little, gazing without any expression at

31

all at the dented bugle hanging from the shelf of Coronation mugs. 'Yes, very well.' He put the phone down and picked up the one nearest him.

I heard Macklin's voice come on. Macklin is in Briefing, crack at his job. Egerton said in a still voice: 'Harrison won't be returning. Naples, yes – he got as far as Milan.'

A chill came into the room and I looked away from him. He'd told me that Harrison was one of the four people he'd put into the field on the Kobra thing. Now there were three.

Harrison had got too close.

'I want you to send Moresby.'

Macklin said something I couldn't catch, but it sounded like an objection.

'Very well,' Egerton told him. 'What about Perkins?'

Something about 'okay'.

'Perkins, then. Brief him as soon as you can.'

He put the phone down.

'They must be sensitive,' I said.

'Yes.' He studied his knuckles, whose skin was calloused with the scars of winter chilblains. 'The entire situation is sensitive.'

I didn't say anything else. He was a dismal man, a case of chronic melancholia, perhaps because his wife had taken an overdose during a seaside holiday, or perhaps because he was just born dismal, with some kind of acid in his soul. And he was ruthless, because his career demanded it: or possibly it was the reverse – he'd been attracted to this kind of work as an outlet for his ruthlessness. But he wasn't totally without feeling, and I knew from experience that he didn't like losing an executive. Even when it was their fault, through clumsiness or lack of judgement, Egerton saw it as his own failure, and was sobered.

Harrison hadn't been terribly good. He'd been short on nerve when it came to the crunch, and some of his security work was unimaginative (he seldom checked for bugs, and would open a parcel without getting it checked by Firearms first, that sort of thing). Without damning the man out of hand, I'd say it had probably been his fault, in Milan. But Egerton felt diminished.

I had some thoughts of my own: he wasn't exaggerating when he said this entire situation was sensitive. These days the major intelligence services were as impenetrable as anyone could make them, and we didn't often try to get inside someone else's preserves. If we had to, and if we succeeded, nobody took it too hard, because there's a certain camaraderie among spooks and it keeps a lot of us alive, except of course when there's a mainline operation in full swing and someone gets in the way.

No one would normally despatch a surveillance man. They'd flush him, bring him in, rough him up a little, try to get something out of him, then let him go. They wouldn't kill him, as these people had killed Harrison. So the Kobra group must be operating wildcat, without any kind of intelligence support or directive. They must be precisely what Egerton had called them: terrorists. They're not usually our game.

'So be it,' he said at last, and got out of his chair and looked at a moustache cup and blew the dust off it and put it back on the shelf.

I didn't know whether he was talking about Harrison or my refusal to take on the mission, and I wasn't interested.

'Do we have a man in Milan?' I asked him.

He turned a blank look on me.

'I mean,' I said, 'in place.'

'Oh. No.'

'Christ, you mean you've got *directors in the field* looking after those people?'

It was the only way Signals could have known about Harrison.

'Of course.'

He went on looking at me.

I got up again, feeling restless. I knew he was trying to trap me, get me into this bloody thing, and I wasn't having any. He was trying to sell it to me on its size alone: it had to be something pretty massive for the Bureau to put local directors out there with the executives before they'd even found out the objective. But it was the size of the thing that was turning me off: I've told you, I'm a ferret and I want them to put me down the hole and leave me alone.

'What the hell are you trying to sell me, a world war?'

He tilted his head, regretfully.

'In any case, I appreciate your having considered the mission.'

'Hope it goes off all right.'

'Thank you, yes.'

I went to the door and a phone rang and he stretched his thin hand down to take it. I could hear the voice at the other end, but not the words. It wasn't a voice I knew. Egerton glanced at me once, then looked away again. When they'd finished he sat down slowly with the phone in his hand. His tone was courteous, as always.

'Quiller is at present engaged in my services, and is unable to report to you. Please allow me to add that the Directorate would appreciate being left to pursue its affairs without interference of this nature from the Administration.'

He lowered the phone and looked at me.

'I assume you unwittingly offered some kind of – provocation.' He gave a wintry smile.

'They got it ballsed up,' I said. 'Someone in Room 6 thought I was a trainee.'

'In that case the provocation was surely theirs.'

'No hard feelings.'

I turned to go again.

Sometimes you do things you never mean to do. You work it all out, size it all up, make a decision and then go and do the very opposite, either because you've got some kind of obsession or because you're being run by gut-think instead of brain-think or because some totally irrelevant factor gets suddenly in the works and sends you the other way.

He needn't have done that. He could have just said: 'They want to see you in Administration.' Their lordships had sent for me because an executive doesn't just turn his back on them and walk out and leave the door open: he's expected to say excuse me, sir, but I think there's some little mistake, so forth. They'd wanted me up there for a lecture. But Egerton hadn't known that. He didn't care in the least what they wanted me for. He'd just realized they wanted me on the carpet, and he doesn't like his executives inter-fered with by the non-active staff.

So he'd told them to go and screw themselves.

And this was a totally irrelevant factor.

I came away from the door.

'I forgot to ask. Who was Harrison's local director?'

He lifted his eyebrows slightly.

'Dewhurst.'

I stood looking at one of the mugs. *God Bless Our Glorious Queen.*

'Who are the others?' I asked him. 'You don't mind if I – '

'Not at all. They are Hunter, Brockley and Smythe. I'm sending Ferris out to look after the fifth executive.'

In a minute I said: 'All top rankers.'

'Oh yes.' He looked slightly deprecating: there's a degree of modesty about this ruthless and brilliant man that almost shocks you, sometimes. 'As I explained, this is quite a sub-stantial undertaking.'

I sat down slowly in the Louis Quinze chair.

'Feel like telling me a bit more?'

Macklin got up and wandered across to the cabinets and got out a file and kicked the drawer shut and came back, lighting another cigarette.

'Didn't imagine you'd be accepting this one,' he said.

'Why not?'

'Not quite your style, is it?'

'That's none of your bloody business.'

He gave a lopsided smile.

'Fraction touchy today, are we?'

'Come on, for Christ's sake get me briefed.'

Now that I'd made up my mind, I wanted to get out of here.

Macklin opened the file and I waited, trying to cool down. He wasn't going to let me rush him so it was no good trying: he was a topliner at this job and when he sent me out of here I'd be briefed to perfection.

The fluorescent tubes sizzled faintly across the ceiling,

35

casting an ashen light and leaving a tracery of shadow across his face where the tissue didn't quite match. He'd been one of our best executives until a couple of years ago, when something had blown up; and now he was one of our best briefers.

'All right,' he said, and squinted at me through the smoke of his cigarette. 'How much did Egerton tell you?'

'Not much.' I went through it for him.

He nodded, spreading the file flat.

'These five men. One: Ilyich Kuznetski, freelance saboteur, mercenary, guerilla. Set up the bombing of the Simplon Tunnel, worked three months with French counter-espionage, arrested last June in Rome and shot his way out of gaol, disappeared. Smythe is now with him, last reporting from Cairo. Two: Carlos Ramirez, terrorist, explosives expert, worked for half a dozen groups and now takes on anything that appeals to him politically. Three: Satynovich Zade, undercover agent for Palestinian factions, once ran with a group affiliated to the Fourth International, at present wanted by the Dutch police on homicide charges. We have Brockley with him. Four: Francisco – '

'Harrison was watching Ramirez, is that right?'

He looked up. 'You didn't tell me Egerton had briefed you on that.'

'Didn't I?'

I suppose you don't talk about what you'd rather forget.

He looked down.

'Number Four is Francisco Ventura, once a member of the Basque *Euzkadi Ta Askatasuna*, now operating freelance for anyone who'll pay him enough, including Black September and the *Fuerzas Armadas Rebeldes* of Guatemala. Connections in Moscow and strong sympathies with the Arabs. Hunter is local-controlling the surveillance, last signals from Geneva. Five: Sabri Sassine, trained in Palestine and now an international, twice called in by the F.L.Q. in Canada, spent five years in prison in Argentina until released as a political prisoner in exchange for a Ford Motor Company vice president. Ferris will local-control Perkins on that one.'

He picked up a telephone.

'Who kidnapped the Ford man?' I asked him.

'Splinter group, believed to be the Argentine Trotskyite Organization.' He said into the phone: 'Have you located Perkins yet?'

I couldn't see how any group made up of these widely differing agitators could find a common cause – or seek a common rendezvous. There'd have to be something that triggered an identical response in all of them.

'It's no good beating your gums about it,' Macklin said into the telephone. 'He's down for priority briefing and I want him, so please get him.'

He put the phone down and looked at me.

'Who would he be with, do you think?'

'Corinne. Or maybe Laura.' Possibly both, knowing Perkins.

He scribbled their names down.

'Okay so far?'

'Satynovich Zade,' I said. 'Wasn't he the one they found in Paris a couple of weeks ago?'

'Yes. Shot an informer and two *Deuxième Bureau* men when they knocked at the door. Anything else?'

'No.'

'Fair enough.'

He went into the routine phase of the briefing: probable access, communication modes with agents-in-place, signals facilities through Crowborough, liaison with directors in the field, fallback systems, security, suggested cover, suggested identity, so forth. He'd be passing a lot of this on to Clearance, as soon as I'd indicated preferences where the area was flexible: the drawing of weapons, agreement on codes and things like that. He already knew most of my preferences but he wouldn't take anything for granted because we're a nervy and superstitious lot and have a tendency to change our minds about something quite radical: Perkins is a case in point – for a long time he never drew a cyanide capsule because it gave him the willies just to think about it; then he saw what they did to Fawcett under interrogation in Leningrad prison hospital and he's drawn a capsule ever since, won't go into the field without it.

'We come to general theory,' said Macklin, and shut the file. 'As Egerton told you, we believe the Kobra group will start moving in a specific direction soon after it's come together. Excuse me.'

The yellow telephone was buzzing and he took it.

General theory my arse. They don't put out five executives into the field and five top rank controls to run them unless they've got a pretty accurate idea about what's going to happen. Possibly Macklin didn't know, but if he knew anything he wouldn't necessarily pass it on to me. Except for operations with strong political overtones the executives are sent in without a lot of material stuffed into their heads, and this is particularly the case with penetration agents: we want to go in and do the job and get out so fast that nobody has time to stop us, and we can't concentrate if we're thinking about all the ramifications in the background: it'd put us right off our stroke.

'What time was that?'

He was talking to Signals. Every senior member of the active staff has a yellow telephone on his desk, among others, and he always picks it up the instant it buzzes.

'All right, will do.'

He put it down.

'There's another one.'

'Another what?'

He was making notes.

'Objective for surveillance. Tangier says he's just got in from Teneriffe.'

He picked up a telephone.

'Put Whitaker on immediate call, will you?'

He put it down. I said:

'Who's this one?'

'They think it's Fogel.' He made another note.

'Heinrich Fogel?'

'Yes.' I began counting the seconds and he got it on four, looking up quickly. 'He was your opposition in Budapest, wasn't he?'

'Yes.'

'Old times.'

38

'Yes.'

The bastard had lined up a very long shot that had smashed a hole in the wall an inch from my head. I wished Whitaker luck.

'General theory,' Macklin said.

'Wait a minute. They only *think* it's Fogel?'

'That's right.'

'When are they going to find out?'

'As soon as they can find someone to identify him. For the moment he's gone to ground.' He got up and put the file back into the cabinet and kicked the drawer shut and stubbed out his cigarette, lighting the next, cupping his hands round the match. There wasn't any draught: he liked people to think they were steady. 'Right. I've no specific instructions for you but Egerton won't be leaving the building until you're through Clearance: he'll probably go and sit in with Signals. All I know for the moment is that Perkins will be going out as soon as we can find him, with Ferris local-directing in Milan –'

'*If* they can pick up Ramirez again.'

He squinted at me through the smoke. 'You know, one of the most encouraging things about this situation is that we only really need to keep tabs on *one* of these objectives, on the reasonable assumption that they're converging on a fixed rendezvous.'

'You're talking a lot of cock, Macklin. Look what happened to Harrison: you'd have lost the whole bunch.'

He drew in smoke, his face twisted into a half-smile.

'Just making sure you know the score, old boy.'

'You're not putting me into surveillance, so you can stop wasting your time.'

'Wouldn't dream of it.'

'That's good.'

'Any questions?'

'Yes. Who's going to direct me in the field?'

He hooked his leg over a stool and dangled one foot, trying so hard to look unconcerned that it had me on edge. He and Egerton knew such a bloody sight more than I did about this operation and they'd both got gooseflesh and I didn't find it terribly reassuring. The mission wasn't even running yet and there was one man dead: two, if you counted Milos Zarkovic.

'We shan't know,' he said, 'until we know the field.'

'It could be anywhere. Right?'

'Right. Anywhere.'

There was a knock on the door and it opened and one of the security guards put his head round.

'Mr Perkins has just come in, sir.'

'Thank God for that.'

Macklin got off the stool and went over to the cabinet.

'I'll go and get cleared,' I said.

'What? Yes. You do that.' He pulled open the drawer and then turned his head suddenly, looking at me over his shoulder, the bleak light on his face and one eye squinting over the cigarette. 'If I don't see you again before you go,' he said, 'take care.'

4
Alitalia

I always go through Firearms like a dose of salts because a gun is more trouble than it's worth: you've got to conceal it across frontiers and get it through the airport peep-shows and look after it in strange hotels and you finish up baby-sitting for the bloody thing right through the mission. Some of the front-line executives carry them but don't often use them, so maybe they look on them as a suitable fetish for their trade, like garters for tarts.

I don't draw a capsule either.

Because if you're firing correctly on both frontal lobes you can often convince the opposition that you don't know anything of interest; but if they find one of those things on you they'll understandably believe you've got a headful of information more valuable than your life and they'll put you through the whole roller-coaster from electrodes to heroin-deprivation and you'll die with your hair white and only yourself to blame. It's strictly no go.

'Sign here sir, will you?'

No weapons drawn.

I wasn't long in Accounts either: *Nothing to bequeath, no next of kin,* so forth. The routine thought crossed my mind: at any given moment I'm not worth much in cold cash but why not leave it to Moira? But the routine answer came up: she got a quarter of a million in sterling for her last film so the only gesture I could make would be to put down on this form: *Five thousand roses for Moira, to be delivered at dawn by six white horses from Harrods.* But these arthritic old bags would only talk me out of it because their pet charity is the Salvation Army and they'd send the cheque round on a bike.

'Your medical card has come through.'

I took it over to one of the windows where there was a bit of light. String of normals, vision 20/20. *Remarks: 12 lbs below ideal weight for height. Vitamin and mineral deficiencies.*

Suggested supplementary intake daily as follows – 500 mg Vitamin C organic and 100 mg Calcium. They might as well print that last bit because in our trade we live on the nerves and the adrenals are under constant pressure and there's nothing we can do about it except drink more milk and orange juice and see a bit more of the girls.

'When did this medical card come through?'

One of them looked up from her knitting.

'Last night.'

This is the sequence: when we come out of a mission we're sent to Norfolk for various tests including a medical and it normally takes a month to come through to London, and this is well in time for clearance on the next mission because the leave period is a standard two months. During these two months they can drop on us if something urgent comes up and we have the right to tell them to buzz off if that's the way we feel. In most cases we rally to the call because that's what we live for and the only reality is when we're working. The point is that I'd come off my last mission precisely seventeen days ago and they must have rushed the medical analysis in Norfolk so that I could get cleared for a new mission in record time.

Typical Egerton. He'd got me into his office and I'd dug my heels in and told him no, repeat no, and I'd come out saying yes and I do *not* know how that bastard does it. There's always a reason but it's never the kind of reason he could possibly have manufactured: on this occasion some bloody fool in the hierarchy had made a mistake and set up a chain reaction that ended when Egerton picked up that phone. I think he would have told them what he did in any case: he doesn't like those people throwing their weight around where his executives are concerned. But this time he'd done it at the precise psychological moment: and I was into the mission.

No, you don't take on a job that's not in your particular field just because a director puts in a good word for you: if it's not in your field then you'll be uncomfortable and that can be dangerous and sometimes fatal. I'd taken on this one because Egerton had reminded me by pure chance that he always looks after his executives. I probably hadn't thought about it consciously: it had been civil of him, and that was about all. But the data had hit the organism on the subliminal level and got an emphatic response, because all the time the forebrain is driving you through a mission against grievous and increasing odds the organism is kicking and yelling somewhere down there inside you, desperate to stay alive.

In that priestlike scarecrow with the dull brown eyes my organism had sensed a friend. If I were going out on a new mission, this was the one where I stood a chance. And there was another reason, appealing this time to the forebrain: whatever kind of mission Egerton was cooking up it didn't look like anything in my field because I'm a penetration specialist: the hole, the kill and the get-out. But that man is highly intelligent and he wouldn't want a misfit in anything he was running and I therefore supposed that somewhere along the line in Beirut or Cairo or Tangier he was expecting the operation to take on the character of a penetration job and that was why he wanted to get me in.

Well he'd got me.

I took the medical card back and dropped it on to the desk.

'Get Sam along here for me, there's an angel.'

'My name is Miss Robinson.'

'All right, but for Christ's sake get Sam here, I'm on a count-down.'

I think they spray the air with carbolic after I've gone.

The security guard met me outside and took me along the corridor to Codes and Cyphers and unlocked the door for me and left me there.

'What've you got?'

'The new seventh,' she said, 'or you can stay on one of the series.' She touched her blue-rinsed hair.

I tried out the new one but it was too complicated: you could commit it to memory inside half an hour including the inverted radicals and the alert numerals but if you got one of the prefixes wrong you could throw the whole pattern out and finish up with gibberish.

'I'd have to keep this on me, Harriet. You got a sixth

43

series, acid-destruct?'

'With or without abbreviations?'

'Without.' They can trip you unless you're phrase-perfect.

I finished up with a short, flexible pattern designed to pump crude intelligence into the network without any frills, embossed in high relief on fifteen-second acid-soluble plastic.

'Be good, Harry.'

She looked up from her work.

'When are you going?'

'Any time.'

'Look after yourself,' she said.

'You know me.'

Credentials: Paul Wexford, overseas representative of Europress, London Division; passport with extensive frankings and selected western visas including Portugal; independent assignments, letters of introduction, continental references, so forth. It was light cover, unsophisticated and convenient at frontiers, with a press pass in five languages and some invitations to public seminars and grand openings. You could blow a hole right through it with a peashooter and as soon as the operation began taking on some kind of shape there'd be a directive from London to change it; but for the moment they couldn't provide me with viable specifics because even Egerton didn't know what I was going into.

Four American Express guest cards and the usual mnemonic aids, *Paul Wexford* running from the first line to the tenth in ten separate lists of names, so forth: the only thing they don't give you in Credentials are alphabet bricks. Driving licence, worn Polyphoto of current girl friend (not unlike the one Milos Zarkovic had carried in his wallet, and my scalp contracted for a moment).

'Keys?'

She dropped a bunch on the desk: two Yales and a tumbler model, two car keys and a Jaguar tab. They wouldn't ever open anything but you can keep the opposition fiddling about for hours if they snitch them on what they think is your home ground.

Going down the staircase on my way to Travel I saw

Perkins coming out of Briefing and thought he looked a bit off colour: we're always superstitious about replacing a deceased executive in the field. I didn't talk to him.

In Travel they fitted me out with currency and credit cards and told me that Mr Egerton was in Signals and would be glad if I'd go along there as soon as convenient: typical Egerton again, courteous to a degree. I found him hitched angularly across a packing-case of new electronics with a set on his head. He saw me come in but went on listening, his eyes wandering forlornly from wall to wall. In this section of the room, currently reserved for his operation, one of the sets had gone dead and I knew it had been beamed on Milan.

'If you need to repack your things,' Egerton said at last, 'I think you might do that.' He got off the packing-case and hung the set on the hook.

One of the Signals wallahs across the room was bent over a speaker, monitoring some stuff that had come off the unscrambler a few minutes ago: I could hear the interposed time slips.

Surveillance secure . . . aid requested from local police and granted . . . discreet forces deployed in area Riff Hotel . . . will come in at ten-minute intervals . . .

Tangier. And Egerton was pushing him hard, asking for ten-minute intervals on a gone-to-ground situation: the poor bastard could be on the air all night. He must have our man-in-place working with him: Glover, at the Oasis Bar.

Egerton was half-listening to the monitor tape.

'What am I on,' I asked him, 'immediate call?'

'Yes. Oh yes.' His eyes wandered over my face. 'You may have to leave directly from your flat, of course.' He was holding out a thin knuckly hand. 'I'm really most grateful, you know, most grateful. I didn't want anyone else, you see, not for this one.' He smiled wanly and turned away, forgetting my existence.

There was a break in the overcast and the sun was coming out for the last hour of the day as I reached Knightsbridge and sent up a wave from the gutter with the nearside wheels of the Jensen.

Fox to 15.

Base acknowledged and I cut the switch and clipped the mike back and got out and opened the boot. There are one or two obligations when you're on immediate call and one of them is to keep them informed of your travel pattern so that they can pick you up at once when they want you. Another obligation is that you remain on readiness at all times and that means you can't see a film or go along to the Turkish baths or visit a girl friend: most of our girl friends have telephones but the directors have agreed not to ring us unless there's something urgent and since any kind of signal is designated urgent when we're on immediate call we tend to live like monks during this period: the nerves are quite sensitive enough in the pre-mission phase and we don't want to risk being hauled out of bed by the telephone right in the middle of everything. The girls wouldn't like it either.

Perkins hadn't been on immediate call but they'd still got on to his known girl friends because it was urgent.

I lugged the suitcase out of the boot and slammed it shut and went up the steps and opened the front door. The obvious choice was a full *yoharka* and I did it very fast and one of his shoes came off and smashed into the mirror on the wall as he went down with the breath grunting out of his lungs. Part of the butt was showing through the gap of his jacket and I pulled the thing free of the holster and took the magazine out and put it in my pocket and kicked the gun across the floor where he couldn't reach it. Then I checked his eyelids and saw he was still well under. The trouble with the *yoharka* is that you tend to use it only when there's no time to prepare anything more subtle, so you can't always place it correctly or work out how much force the situation requires: it's a very fast nerve blow and strictly for killing unless you pull the momentum a little, and I'd used it about halfway between because I didn't know whether he was armed.

I felt for the heart and it was all right so I went into the kitchen and got an ice tray and came back and propped him

46

up and stuffed some cubes inside his jacket in line with the spine. He took three or four minutes to surface.

'How do you feel?'

His eyes rolled a bit and his hand went at once to the holster. He was a middle-aged Slav with a gold tooth and slight stubble and garlic on his breath. He was focussing at last and trying to move so I used a pressure point progressively to stop him from fidgeting. There hadn't been time to shut the front door after me and I could hear the rain starting again, pattering on the roof of the porch.

'Who do you work for?' I asked him.

He didn't say anything and I realized he wasn't feeling too happy about this because he shouldn't have let it happen. He'd got into the place from the kitchen window – there was mud on the floor by the fridge – and the first thing he'd done was to prepare an exit on the other side of the house and he'd been too close to the front door to get the gun out in time when I'd opened it.

This was the third since last July: it's almost routine and we just phone the Bureau for someone to come round and clean the place up. Accounts get terribly fussed because we always insist on reasonably decent furniture and of course they have to replace it, but it's mostly drawers and in my case the Chinese lacquered cabinet in the study because it looks as if it ought to have a lot of secret panels so they always rip it to bits, and the best of luck.

'Who do you work for?'

I put some pressure on and he began going white.

They're going to get in, whatever we do, and we're damned if we're going to have two-inch-diameter steel bars at all the windows and electronic alarms everywhere because in between missions we like living in a fairly civilized way. Of course we never keep anything useful in our flats or wherever we live, but they can never be certain about that and I suppose it's tempting.

'Who do you work for?' I said it in Russian and Yugoslavian as well, just in case there was any connection with Zarkovic. He still didn't say anything and it annoyed me and I used quite a lot of pressure and he gave a reflex jerk

47

and passed out for sixty seconds.

We don't often bother the Bureau, except to clean up and take the broken stuff away for replacement. The Bureau has been established ten years or so and in the early days we used to report a break-in by phone right away and they'd send a whole team along and if we'd caught anyone they'd take him back for interrogation because we were very keen to build up files on anything we could get our hands on; but these types never turned out to be interesting: they're mostly second assistant economic attachés or local characters making a bit on the side while they're out on parole. At this level the major international networks leave each other alone and it works perfectly well: otherwise we'd never get any work done. We know all the restaurants and girl friends' flats where we can drop on any number of lower-rankers in the opposition field but there wouldn't be any point; they don't know enough to warrant the trouble and they'd only start tagging us everywhere and trying to get us into a corner and the whole thing would grind to a halt.

On an active mission it's totally different.

Some of his colour was coming back.

I lifted his eyelids. He wasn't ready yet.

Give him five minutes, then I'd have to get someone to take him away and leave him outside a police station because I wanted to put most of the stuff in my suitcase into a laundry bag for picking up, and find some clean shirts. If Egerton was sitting in at Signals it was because he was expecting something to break and he hadn't put me on immediate call just for a laugh.

'Right, I want some answers now.'

We're all of us sensitive to our own peculiar points and I shifted about and got him interested at last, giving him slow periodic stimulation just this side of syncope.

'Who are you working for?'

'I don't know.'

A certain amount of writhing about, but it looked like transfer: I was offering physiological fear rather than actual pain and he was worried about what I was going to do next.

'Who pays you?'

48

'Nobody. I come to steal.'

Slav accent.

I thought the quickest way would be to take him into a steady pressure-reaction rhythm, and within fifteen seconds he couldn't stand it any more because his nerves were having to deal with repetition, the equivalent of the aural situation where a loud and monotonous noise begins driving you up the wall.

'Tony.'

'What?'

'Tony pays me.'

'When?'

He didn't say anything so I tried again and succeeded.

'Monday,' he said on his breath.

'Monday nights?'

'Yes.'

'Where?'

'In pub.'

'Which pub?'

'Beefeater Arms, the one – '

'All right.' I knew which one.

He was losing colour again so I gave him a rest.

'Is that where you give your information?'

'No.'

'Where do you give your information?'

'I leave in library.'

'Come on then, I want the details. Don't keep stopping.'

'In library, between page ninety and ninety-one of Economic Lexington.' He began sweating a little.

'Lexicon?'

'Yes, is – '

'What time?'

'Five minutes till hour, when I have information.'

That meant they must have someone in place: one of those earnest little librarians with ginger hair and rimless glasses and a portrait of Lenin pasted behind the Landseer in their room at the boarding-house.

'What do you do if you have some urgent information?'

'I already tell you that.'

'*Come on.*'

His leg jerked and he took a few seconds to get his breath.

'When urgent information, I telephone number in Kensington and wait under tree in Park, where – '

'All right, that's all I want.'

I'd found a packet of Gauloises when I'd searched him for spare ammunition, and I got it out and put a cigarette between his lips and lit it for him. 'Just sit still for a minute or two and you'll be all right.'

I went into the sitting-room and my study: there was nothing out of place and this agreed with my theory that he'd come straight from the kitchen to prepare an emergency exit in the hall when I'd opened the door. But I checked the upper floor just in case and found it in order. When I came down the stairs he was standing in a shadowed corner of the hall with his gun trained on me.

'Come on,' I said, 'I'm going to drop you home.'

'Where is safe?'

'What?'

'Where is safe?' He jerked the gun.

It's all spelt out laboriously for these local domestics in the little maroon booklet they issue at the Embassy: *Al-ways look for the wall-safe be-fore any-thing else*, and that sort of thing. There's a translation into their idea of English and we keep a copy in the Caff to read to each other when we feel like a giggle.

'Don't muck about,' I said, but he kept on his Al Capone expression and wouldn't budge so I went right up to him and panicked him into pulling the trigger and he heard the click and his face went blank, like a baby's when you take away the bottle. 'Now you've got the message,' I said. 'Listen, I'm going to take you home – you can't walk there in all that rain.' It was pouring again, with big drops coming through the half-open door.

He was all right after that, and followed me down the steps and into the car and sat there in a despondent hump. I started up and got the wipers going and unclipped the mike.

Fox mobile.

They said okay and I put the mike back and got past a bus that was sending up a filthy stern-wave. It wasn't far, but before we got there he keeled over and came to rest with his head against the door. I don't know exactly what happened: probably delayed reaction to the whole thing. I left him like that till we pulled up outside No. 13 Kensington Palace Gardens. There were a couple of men at the doors but they didn't come out and I didn't blame them in this downpour. I got him in a fireman's lift and took him up the steps and propped him there and went back to the car already half soaked. They were coming out to take a look at him as I drove away.

We don't normally deliver Ruskies back to their Embassy but I suppose I was sorry for this one and felt a bit guilty. But until he'd given me the typical pattern of operation (pubs and libraries and trees in the Park) I hadn't been sure he wasn't a Yugoslav with some conceivable connection with Milos Zarkovic and I couldn't just let it go.

Halfway back to Knightsbridge they called me up.

Base to Fox.

Read you.

Communicate 4 soonest.

Five minutes.

Roger. Over and out.

There was time to spare because they'd accepted my five minutes instead of switching to speech-code and giving me a directive but I put my foot down slightly and took the short cut through the mews because Extension 4 was Travel and it looked as if Egerton had made up his mind to set me running.

Within three and a half minutes I had the Jensen standing outside the flat and got the ammunition clip out of my pocket and dropped it down the drain and went in and picked up the phone in my study, checking for bugs. Negative.

'I think we're clear, aren't we?'

It was Jeffries, in Travel.

'Yes,' I said.

'All right, you're booked out on Flight AZ279 by Alitalia, Terminal 2 Heathrow, depart 19:15 today, minimum check-in time thirty-five minutes. Your flight is non-stop to

Fiumicino Airport, Rome, arriving 22:30 hours and the aircraft is a Douglas DC9. Your ticket is waiting for you at the check-in counter and we have a dark blue Fiat 1100 for you at Fiumicino. Any queries so far?'

'No.'

Rome was somewhere new, unless it was Brockley doing that one. According to Macklin, Smythe had last reported from Cairo and Hunter was doing Geneva and Fitzalan was keeping tabs on Fogel in Tangier.

'All right, are we still clear?'

'Yes.'

'Your contact in Rome will be Fitzalan. You will – '

'Say again?'

'Your contact in Rome will be Fitzalan. Any queries?'

'No.' We don't keep the office on the line arguing the toss: if Travel said my contact was to be Fitzalan they weren't making any mistake. But the last I'd heard of him was in Tangier and he must have been getting on a plane while they were playing his report on the monitor tape in Signals: he'd said that Fogel had gone to ground but he must have come into the open again very fast and he'd broken for Rome.

Jeffries was talking.

'The rdv is to be outside the Cielalto office on the ground floor and at this time we don't know who will arrive there first. No code-intro necessary. Now I'll give you the routine checks.'

He began going through them and I half-listened: they were just fail-safe reminders to leave private keys behind or in a deposit box at the airport, look for a message at Heathrow and Fiumicino, so forth. What interested me was that Fitzalan and Fogel must be arriving in Rome on the same flight from Tangier and since they were in a surveillance situation Fitzalan was going to have his work cut out to make a rendezvous with me and keep the peep on the objective at the same time. Not that I was worried: you learn to have faith in people like Parkis and Mildmay and Egerton when they've controlled you through half a dozen missions. If they said that Fitzalan would make contact with me and keep surveillance on his objective at the same time then that was precisely what was going to happen.

Jeffries finished the routine checks and asked for queries.

'Any backups?'

'We don't know at this stage.'

'Who's his local control?'

'There hasn't been time.'

I should have known. Egerton had been expecting *some-thing* to break because he'd been sitting in at Signals but he couldn't have known *what* was going to break or he would have sent out a director to local-control Fitzalan before he got there. That man Fogel had broken ground with the speed of a ricochet and nobody in the Bureau had been given time to set up the necessary machinery to contain his travel pattern: at this stage they were relying totally on Fitzalan.

'No more questions?'

'No,' I said. 'But tell Egerton there was a Ruskie in here, and get someone to put the kitchen window right when they come to shut the place up.'

'Is that the only damage?'

'I got him in time.'

'Noted. All right, we want you to keep in continuous contact between 15 and Heathrow, and we'll have your car picked up and put in the garage, so leave the key in the usual place.'

'Will do.'

I hung up and got some clean shirts and things and dropped them into the suitcase, stopping once to listen to the small sounds in the house: the spitting of rain on a window, the creak of a swelling timber, the drip of a tap. The place seemed already abandoned, and in the morning they'd send someone to see to the kitchen window and turn off the electricity and take the laundry bag; and afterwards there'd only be these sounds here, and sometimes the ring of the telephone that no one would answer.

Normal introspection at this stage: ignore. It was just that we never know, for certain, whether we'll be back.

I took the suitcase downstairs and passed the puddle

where the ice cubes had melted and shut the front door, dropping the case into the boot of the car and starting up, reporting mobility to base.

There was a delay going through Richmond because some bloody fool had lost traction on the wet road and wrapped his Vauxhall round a traffic-light standard and someone else had gone into him: glass all over the place and bobbies' capes and flashing lamps while the time ticked away and I sat listening to Signals telling one of the executives to cancel niner-niner and freeze all movement: I suppose he'd blown a fuse somewhere and they'd got a flap on.

There'd be another one on if they couldn't get this road cleared in the next ten minutes and I started tinkering with the idea of going across to one of the police cars and asking them to get me to the airport without touching the ground anywhere, but the breakdown crew had swept most of the glass into the gutter and the ambulance had made a U-turn and gone off into a No Entry street with its headlights on and five minutes later the nearside line of traffic began moving and we did a slow crawl for the next half mile until the whole situation was back to normal except that some of us were doing well over the limit to make up for lost time.

Terminal 2, Heathrow, 19:07.

No problem at the check-in counter.

No message on the board.

But I noticed a headline on the news stand and bought a copy on my way to the departure gate and didn't like it much. Innocent bystander shot dead in Geneva. He was a British tourist and his name was Hunter.

Things were getting rough out there.

54

5
Flame

'Would you like anything to drink?'

A brilliant smile, the eyes by Michelangelo.

'No thank you.'

London is tilting away below, its lights hazy with rain.

'Something to read?'

'No.'

Thank you very much, I've read all I want to. He'd been coming out of a bar along the Rue du Lac: there was some kind of disturbance and an 'inebriated patron' had fired a gun and the unfortunate British tourist had been hit by accident. Owing to the confusion the police had been unable to make an arrest.

You can bet on that. There's a strict routine and we all use it when we're hot-operating in a red sector. They'd gone for Hunter with the whole thing worked out: timing, topography, escape lanes and mobile pickups and finally a fake brawl to provide the confusion. And Francisco Ventura had vanished into the thin mountain air and left the Bureau's signals network quivering. Quite possibly the man with the niner-niner directive had been ordered to freeze his movements as a preliminary to switching him to Geneva and if that were the case they'd have to get him out there in an R.A.F. interceptor with automatic overflying rights under the N.A.T.O. umbrella. They'd do that, if this operation was big enough.

By the way things were shaping, I thought it was.

Gjesk lqoilz piu oma kelasx.

May Hunter rest in peace.

I did some inversions and threw in five alert numerals and transposed them, cupping the thing in my hand and taking a look when I felt a need for reinforcement. The radicals were tricky considering I'd chosen a short flexible pattern, and it took me fifteen minutes before I was confident.

The girl brought me scampi and I put the plastic card into an emptied compartment of the dish and squeezed the lemon over it and watched it destruct; then I got the paper and went through it to see if I could get some kind of a clue as to what operation the opposition was mounting out there. The P.L.A. was active again on the Palestinian border but that happened every week and they didn't seem to be getting anywhere; the Arab People's Delegation was still pressing the U.S. Secretary of State for a voice at Geneva and the U.S. Secretary of State was still turning a deaf ear; and the fourth riot in three weeks in Lisbon had left the Soviet Embassy in flames. None of these events had much interest for the Bureau, but I suppose that loopy Swede in Room 6 was going to use the Lisbon thing for exercising his scout troop along the sidelines, with communication through open channels and all that balls.

I was getting annoyed because Egerton was playing it so close to the chest: he was pushing me out on a pre-mission directive and into a field where Zarkovic and Harrison and Hunter were already eliminated and where he was throwing in reinforcements – Perkins, Whitaker – as if the entire executive staff were expendable: and Egerton was a man who would go farther than any other controller to bring them home alive. With a thing this size breaking out there must be a political motivation somewhere big enough to make the headlines and in this paper the headlines were about the dustmen's strike in Norwich.

I didn't like this one.

It was too big, and going too fast.

I think we ought to go back.

Bloody little organism rearing its head: all it could think about was survival.

Shuddup.

'Will you please fasten your seat belt? We are landing soon.'

'What?'

'Please fasten seat belt now, sir.'

'Oh. Yes.'

I think we ought to go straight back to London when –

Oh for Christ's sake you've got a seat belt on now, what

56

more do you want? Shuddup.

Captain Lorenzo hopes you have enjoyed your trip with us.

Not terribly.

'*Non ho nulla da dichiarare.*'

They were very slow.

'*Sono tutti effetti personali.*'

For some reason they were going through everything, looking specially at any books and pamphlets. The new Communist regime on the lookout for subversive literature, perhaps.

'*Qui c'é solo vestiario, signore.*'

But I wouldn't advise looking inside the razor barrel, *signore*, because it's meant for blowing locks.

'*Ha finito?*'

'*Si, signore. Grazie.*'

'*Prego.*'

The slightest tactile sensation, right buttock.

I waited till his fingers were well inside the hip pocket and then went for his wrist without any fuss, turning round and checking his face because it could be someone I knew: someone in the opposition. After fifteen missions I've come to know a lot of faces.

I didn't know this one.

He wasn't trying to get away: I think he could feel I wasn't going to let him. His quick dark eyes flicked from my face to the customs officer and back. He looked about fourteen years old.

Get your unworthy person the hell out of here, I told him in gutter Roman, before I pull out your gizzard and tie it in knots.

He slipped through the crowd, rubbing his wrist, and before he was halfway to the barrier I saw him begin on someone else.

I snapped the case shut and took it out to the main hall and looked for Hertz.

Dark blue Fiat 1100. I told them to leave it where it was: I was meeting some journalists on a later flight. Then I told a porter to put the case into the car and bring me the keys. He found me along at the check-in area: I didn't know which airline Fitzalan and Fogel were on, so I memorized the arrival boards from one end of the counter to the other, Moroccan, Iberian, Alitalia, Air France and the transit companies operating across the Mediterranean. The time intervals were close in some instances but there were two fifteen-minute breaks before midnight when I'd be able to slide off for some milk and orange juice at the all-night trattoria.

There was a message for Mr Paul Wexford at Alitalia.

I didn't ask for it right away because he'd been standing by the big Cinzano poster doing nothing ever since I'd come through the arrival gate, so I went along to have a look at him. He was a young Italian and didn't belong to any kind of outfit where they'd heard of training people, because the main background colouration of the poster was white and he was wearing a dark nylon zipped jacket and if he'd had even basic training he would have been standing over there against the black futurist sculpting.

He hadn't looked at me directly and the only reflecting surface was twenty yards away and had a lot of glare across it from the overhead lights because it was set at an angle through the vertical so he'd have to be pretty good on the peep and I didn't think he was, because of the background thing. I was going across to ask him were I could find the telephones when a plump girl in black satin ran up to him. He threw away his cigarette and kissed her and said something that made her give a shrill little laugh as they turned away arm in arm. I tagged them as far as the bus terminal and saw them get into one of the airport coaches. He hadn't looked once in my direction.

He'd been the only suspect: I'd double-checked and made two feints since leaving the exit gate and the whole area was clear. I went back to the check-in counter.

'Paul Wexford.'

I showed him my passport.

'*Ecco, signore.*'

'*Grazie.*'

I took the message slip across to the Cielalto office, reading it on the way. *Please notify Alitalia if press conference is delayed. Frank Wainwright.*

It's the simplest form of code and impossible to read without the key, and we carry the key in our heads. The pattern is very flexible and you can throw in anything you like without affecting the sense. This one could have read: *Weather expected to worsen so please number all itineraries according to severity of local conditions*, and the message would have been precisely the same. The theme is varied to suit the cover: *press conference* for Paul Wexford of Europress. (The example with the weather theme would be used for someone ostensibly following the Monte Carlo Rally, so forth.) The trigger word is *please* and you ignore everything preceding it. The message is contained in the initial letters of the three words following: *notify Alitalia if=n-a-i*. Everything that appears after the three significant words is also ignored; thus the entire message is contained in the three letters *n-a-i*. The key comprises a list of twenty-six directives, each of three words: *Report on arrival, Liaise with agent-in-place, Abort mission immediately*, so forth. These directives are encoded into any number of varied phrases and London could have sent *Number all itineraries* or *nullify any instances* or *nominate appropriate inspectors*, according to the cover-theme.

The key directive for *n-a-i* is *No active involvement*.

I was ordered to keep off.

If Fitzalan didn't arrive, I wasn't to make any enquiries. If Heinrich Fogel arrived alone, I wasn't to tag him anywhere. If they both arrived and Fogel was able to raise a cadre of hit-men and capture, interrogate or kill Fitzalan, I wasn't to help him.

I was to keep off.

Blast your eyes, Egerton, what did you send me here for?

There could be a dozen reasons and I didn't think I'd like any one of them and I stood in front of the Cielalto office wondering why I had been such a monumental bloody fool in letting that poor-man's priest con me into an operation that was already running wild and counting its dead while I stood here without a hope in hell of taking the initiative.

Keep off.

Blast your eyes.

Speeding down the sunlit slopes with the blue sky above your head, you feel as if you are flying, free as a bird! At night you will look

59

down over the lights of the town, nestled at the foot of the giant Matterhorn.

Rough translation. There wasn't a lot of light on the posters and the reflective power of the window was adequate. Blown-up colour photograph: blinding white snow, dazzling blue sky, the skier in black with dark goggles, poles whirling through a slalom, his smile exhilarated.

I checked my watch.

22:44.

The next Moroccan flight was due in at 22:50.

There weren't many people in the main hall: perhaps thirty. A man in a round-brimmed hat approached in reflection and stopped, eyeing the smiling skier for ninety seconds, their figures appearing on the same scale. I moved fractionally to sharpen the image and get the angle into perspective: he was watching one of the closed-circuit television screens at this end of the check-in counter. In another thirty seconds he turned away and walked down the slope of blinding snow, leaving the skier behind. When I turned round I saw him going into the trattoria on the other side of the hall.

22:59.

The first of the passengers off the Moroccan flight was just reaching the exit gate and I stood facing in that direction as the rest of them began coming through, spreading out into groups and individuals, many of them in robes, the fez much in evidence.

I would recognize Fitzalan because we saw each other sometimes along the corridors of that mildewed mausoleum in London, and a month ago we'd shared a table in the Caff for a salt beef sandwich because I needed information on the Helsinki airport explosion and he'd been there.

I would recognize Fogel because I'd questioned him for three hours in Budapest while they were getting the bullet out by the light of one 40-watt bulb and with no anaesthetic, studying the hawklike face as the scream of the sirens rose and fell among the distant streets.

He wasn't on the Moroccan flight.

Nor was Fitzalan.

23:12. Iberian.

60

Blank.
23:25. Alitalia.
Blank.

Then there was a longer interval and I went across to the trattoria for some milk, suggest supplementary intake of 100 mg Calcium, so forth. An Air France transit flight was due to land at midnight and I went back to the Cielalto office and checked the new arrivals in the main hall. There were only three or four and none looked suspect. A few Greeks left over from the last Alitalia flight were still hanging around Hertz and Avis and a dozen or so people were now coming in to meet the Air France plane. A group of porters moved slowly back to the baggage claim area, one of them singing quietly. A huge woman in black heaved past me, her face streaming with tears, and a small boy was throwing an aerodynamic disc high across the porters' heads.

I went over to check for a message and came back, doing a systematic sweep of the hall and noting people's movements. If one contact in any given rendezvous is blown, the other is left totally ignorant of the fact that he is moving straight into a trap. It happened on a dockside in Reykjavik two years ago when I had a rendezvous with Tremayne and they caught up with him and trod on his face and put a few questions and when I walked into the shadow of the crane they were there with icepicks, three of them. I got out fast but they began using some kind of repeater rifle and it was only the moonlight that saved me but oh God that water was cold.

That is why my index finger, left hand, is missing: I caught it between two planks at the edge of the dockside as I went over. And that is why I watched the two men coming across from the main doors, and the group of students waiting at the far end of the check-in counter, and others. By moving around I altered their lines of sight and they didn't respond; but the two men in dark suits were also moving, their eyes covertly observing as mine were.

They had checked me twice but made no follow-up: no movement away, no sign to a distant contact. Within the next three minutes they hadn't looked at me again and there was no reflective surface where they could watch me. I put them down provisionally as Italian police, detective branch, because of their shoes, their suits, their hats, the way they stood. They weren't out of an intelligence cell: I've seen hundreds of intelligence men and I've seen hundreds of policemen, detective branch, and on one point alone I was willing to lay my bet: you are as liable to see an intelligence man wearing those neat, cheap tailor's-dummy clothes as you are liable to see him wearing a Guy Fawkes mask and a piss pot on his head.

In one minute I checked Alitalia again for any message for Paul Wexford. Negative. If Fitzalan had come unstuck in Tangier at any time up to the departure of the plane Fogel had taken, the Bureau's man-in-place would have flashed London and London would have flashed me in Rome and that was why I had to make regular visits to Alitalia. If Fitzalan had in fact boarded Fogel's plane and been recognized as a surveillance hazard there was nothing Fogel could do about it unless by a thousand-to-one chance he was able to have the pilot radio the tower here with a message in code for a specific contact, in which case I was blown wide open as I stood here but I went on standing here because the odds of a thousand to one are acceptable.

Fogel was a wildcat operator without any kind of network behind him and I was virtually certain that even if he could call upon active support in Rome he couldn't do it before his plane was on the ground and he could reach a telephone.

From here I could see the telephones.

I could also see why Egerton had been so sure that Fitzalan would be able to keep his rdv with me and maintain surveillance on Fogel at the same time: the Cielalto office had been chosen because it was within sight of the exit gates where Fogel must arrive.

The faint whine of jets came through the walls of the building, then the roaring of reversed thrust. Eight minutes overdue at 00:08. Possibly slight headwinds, or traffic congestion.

For the last time I went to check Alitalia for a message and there wasn't one.

00:21.

The porters began moving across to the customs area.

The two plain-clothes men had now taken up overt station. They were interested in the Air France flight but only in general terms: if they were here to pick anyone up they would either have gone out to the plane or moved across to the exit gates. They had forgotten my existence.

'He'll be coming through in a few minutes.'

'All right,' I said.

We stood close together, watching the smiling skier.

'So far, I've got him cold.'

Fitzalan sounded rather pleased with himself and I suppose it was understandable because a surveillance situation gets very sensitive in confined spaces.

He was still breathing a little fast: he'd obviously shown his Interpol facilities pass to the chief stewardess and the immigration officer and got through the tube before the rest of them had been released and from then on he'd hurried. I'd seen him coming across from the exit gates and the two plain-clothes men had checked him and lost interest. Fitzalan himself had given me no signal as he'd approached the rendezvous and it couldn't have been because it's a difficult thing to do: you can look up at the ceiling for an instant or turn your head or drop something or make any one of a dozen signals. The one we use as a routine in the absence of a specific change by directive is the slight trip. He hadn't tripped.

But he would have done it if he'd been blown in Tangier or on board the aircraft, because if you go down and the opposition starts running you and you can't help yourself until there's been time to get out from under, you can at least let your contact know in the final half-minute that the rendezvous has become a death-trap, and if he's quick he can save himself.

There'd been no signal. At this precise moment the situation was contained and even encouraging: Heinrich Fogel and two of the Bureau's executives were now together in Fiumicino Airport, Rome, their formation as orderly as if Control in London had moved three pieces across an operations board.

I watched the exit gates.

'Is he alone?'

'Yes.' There was still a note of slight elation in Fitzalan's voice: the Bureau had only been running him for eighteen months and he'd blown a minor radio-snatch assignment in Brussels and was immediately pushed through Norfolk again for a refresher course, and this time he was out to prove his colours and so far he was getting it right. A surveillance operation is low key but in this case the objective was Fogel and the overall situation was massive in terms of deployment in the field.

'You know what you're here for,' he said quietly. It was a statement.

'No.'

He swung his head and looked at me and I noticed the black dye was running slightly at his temples. Fitzalan has bright red hair and is obliged to keep it permanently dyed.

'My God,' he said, 'things are going so *fast*.' He turned back to watch the gates with his faded blue eyes. 'You're here to identify Fogel.'

I waited five seconds but he wasn't going to add anything.

'Is that all?'

'Apparently it's very important.'

I suppose Macklin had started this: our people in Tangier had only *thought* it was Fogel they'd got hold of, and London wanted him identified with certainty as soon as he left cover.

'You were on opposite sides, weren't you,' Fitzalan asked without turning his head, 'on some job or other?'

I watched the two plain-clothes men.

'Yes.'

They hadn't actually moved but their heads were now angled back half an inch as they stared towards the exit gates. A man and two women were now coming through, and there were people behind them.

'You think you'll be able to identify him?' Fitzalan asked me.

He was rather full of questions. Eighteen months isn't long.

'Yes.'

An Air France stewardess came past us, hurrying a little with her high heels on the point of buckling. She was making

64

for the check-in counter.

A hint of *Madame Rochas* on the air.

'Any minute,' Fitzalan said.

He was getting worried.

Three Moroccans came by in flowing robes, their hands gesturing gracefully as if in some kind of prayer as they talked. A party of Europeans broke from the main stream of passengers and headed for the trattoria, and one of the air-crew, a two-ringer, was making for a door on the far side, marked *Private*.

'Any minute now,' Fitzalan said.

Poor little bastard: if he dropped this one he'd be out on his neck. We're only allowed two mistakes running, during the probation phase.

'Where was he sitting?'

He turned his dyed head slightly towards me but didn't take his eyes off the gates.

'Fifth row back, port side, first class.'

He was trying to sound confident.

'He'll be through,' I said.

'Oh sure. Any minute.'

It wasn't of course certain. Fogel could have turned off at a dozen points after leaving Immigration and Customs, or they could be holding him up in there. I gave it another two minutes and said:

'What do you want to do?'

It was up to him, not me.

No active involvement.

Fitzalan looked at me now.

'You think we ought to go in there?'

After a bit I said: 'He's your pigeon.'

Theoretically I should be local-controlling the man because I was his senior within the executive echelon and it was my responsibility to see that he didn't lose his objective but I wasn't interested in theory: the Bureau is a secret operations service and not the bloody Army and I only ever use my rank if it's to save my neck. I wasn't out here in the field to baby-sit for Fitzalan or anyone else: he'd sewn up his objective and if he'd done it the wrong way he'd be slung out and the rest of us would go on working in more safety.

More people came through: Customs were getting them cleared a damned sight faster than when the London flight had come in.

'I'm going to give him another couple of minutes,' Fitzalan said.

His tone was shaky now.

'Fair enough.'

'Of course,' he said, 'I'm absolutely certain he was on the aircraft when I – '

'Hold on,' I said.

A square of faint light had swung across the black surrealist sculpting: a glass door had opened somewhere behind us and I looked first at the two plain-clothes men but they didn't react. They were watching the exit gates, their heads perfectly still. It wasn't just the swinging light that had alerted me: there'd been the thump of the doors too, and a slight increase in the noise of the traffic outside. There was also a change in the actual character of the noise and when I looked round the first thing I saw was the flashing of an emergency light on top of the police van that was now standing opposite the main doors with its engine running and the driver still at the wheel.

The party of six *carabinieri* were coming at a steady pace and looking straight in front of them: two officers, a sergeant and two rankers led by a captain. They weren't actually in step but they seemed to be, because they walked so steadily.

'Watch the gates,' I told Fitzalan. 'Don't look at anything else.'

He didn't answer.

The two plain-clothes men had heard the *carabinieri* coming but didn't give them more than a glance because there were a lot of passengers spreading out from the exit gates now and they didn't want to miss anyone. I was watching the *carabinieri* most of the time and relying on Fitzalan to alert me if he saw Fogel coming through. I had quite a few questions in my mind because the data was beginning to form logical patterns for analysis, but there were too many gaps: the plain-clothes police could be here for their own reasons and those reasons could have nothing to do with the *carabinieri*; the *carabinieri* looked as though they were in a hurry and trying not to show it, but they were obviously hoping to meet someone off the Air France flight from Morocco and they looked quite serious about it but I didn't know why they hadn't come a bit earlier and driven their transport up to the aircraft and made sure of a contact.

It would be dangerous to assume that either they or the plain-clothes men were here to intercept Heinrich Fogel. It is dangerous to assume anything at all during this kind of active situation because if the action speeds up you can find yourself making a wrong move precipitately and a wrong move can be fatal.

Of course the one answer to every question in my head could be that the situation was precisely as it appeared to be: the plain-clothes men had been sent here to watch for a certain passenger or certain passengers coming off the Air France plane, and the *carabinieri* had been sent here in response to information received so late that they hadn't had time to intercept the passengers at an earlier stage.

They walked steadily past us.

'He's here,' Fitzalan said.

'Fogel?'

'Yes.'

It took me a couple of seconds.

He was the lean man with the sunken cheeks and the thinning hair. I thought I could see the pink crescent-shaped scar on his right temple even at this distance but the brain tends to present visual data that the eye doesn't see: I knew there was a scar there, because I'd watched them pull the bullet out in Budapest.

'How close do you want him?' Fitzalan murmured.

'That's not your problem.'

I would need to see Fogel from a distance of a few yards and I would need to see him in circumstances where he couldn't see me and that wouldn't be easy and it could take till morning. I wasn't going to hurry it because I hadn't needed a specific directive to tell me that if Fogel saw me, just for a second, the Rome phase would be blown.

Egerton hadn't sent me here to blow anything.

Fitzalan was standing perfectly still.

The plain-clothes men had seen Fogel and were immediately interested in him but were not approaching him. The captain of the *carabinieri* had seen him and was leading his unit steadily on.

'Fitzalan.'

'Yes?'

'We use the window now.'

He turned round and we looked at the skier.

'You know the form,' I said.

'Yes.'

'Let's recap.'

I didn't know what briefing he'd received.

'You'll stay with him till you've got close enough to identify him. I'll follow up. If you lose him, I'll keep him.'

'All right.'

The rest of the situation was covered by routine procedures: from the moment we left this rendezvous we wouldn't acknowledge each other; there would be no obligation to make any signal at any given phase; if we felt the need for a further rdv it would be made in the house of the Bureau's agent-in-place, Rome: the Villa Marco Polo in the Piazza Piccola. Finally, Fitzalan was aware that he could expect no support from me if he got into any kind of trouble because each of us was in effect operating solo with a common objective: Fogel.

The figures moved against the slope of dazzling snow: Fogel coming alone from the exit gates, the *carabinieri* walking steadily towards him. The plain-clothes men stood perfectly still. A few of the other passengers were looking at the *carabinieri*, wondering what they were doing here.

The captain halted his men.

It was then that I decided to turn round because it looked as if Fogel was the passenger they had come for and he wouldn't have time to check for surveillance before they met him. He wouldn't see me, and he wouldn't see Fitzalan. He would see only the officers.

At this instant he was isolated, with the nearest passenger ten or twelve feet away. They were spreading out and he was one of the few people without a companion. He had seen the *carabinieri* but was not reacting.

The captain took a sidestep to block his path, and his white-gloved hand came up in a salute.

Fogel stopped.

The captain was saying something to him.

Fogel listened. His expression and attitude were those of a law-abiding passenger arriving in Rome by air. The captain appeared to be asking for his passport.

Fogel used his right hand to double the officer, pushing the blow upwards into the diaphragm while his left hand went for the captain's holster and wrenched the gun out. He worked very fast and he was armed and ready to fire before any of the party could reach for their own weapons.

The first shot smashed the glass of a show-case a few feet from where Fitzalan and I were standing and I couldn't tell if Fogel had aimed at the *carabinieri* and the shell had passed between them, or if it had been meant as a warning shot. They were diverted for a second or two and the captain was still doubled up on the ground as Fogel broke away and began running, colliding with a group of passengers and leaving one of them sprawling as the *carabinieri* began shouting for him to stop. He saw the flash of the emergency light through the glass doors and swerved to his left, running fast and steadily and thinking his way out of the building and past the obstacles that threatened him: mostly the groups of people in the check-in area.

At this moment the *carabinieri* began firing as they ran: their officer had given the order. I saw plaster chipping away from the wall beyond where Fogel ran, at a height of some ten feet: there were too many people about for them to try hitting the fugitive and I assumed the purpose was to warn him to stop and at the same time to alert the driver of the emergency vehicle outside.

As Fogel reached the glass doors at the end of the check-in area I was a dozen yards behind him, running at the same speed and ready to swerve the instant he began turning round to fire into his pursuers. I could hear Fitzalan's shoes thudding behind me and slightly to the left. The situation worried me because I believed Fogel would fire back into the *carabinieri* before he went through the doors: it would be logical and of course feasible, costing him something less than two seconds and gaining him anything up to five or six as the soldiers scattered. The thing that worried me was that there was no close cover for me or Fitzalan: the people in this area were now frozen into immobility and there were no central stands or pillars and I would have to rely mostly on speed as I hurled myself obliquely at the row of glass doors and smashed one open before his gun fired.

The whole set-up was impromptu and I didn't like that either: a penetration agent gets into comfortable habits and he likes premeditated action, preferring to set a trap rather than run a man down, preferring the dark to the light. It's rather like assembling a small but intricate bomb, step by step, dovetailing the components until they become potent, then setting it ticking. This was a totally undisciplined situation where anything could happen and I was uneasy because Fogel would see me as his most immediate threat and would possibly fire at me instead of into the soldiers. I believed I could be quick enough to get out of the way but a certain amount was going to depend on chance and that made the situation dangerous and untidy.

Fogel reached the doors.

I was watching him the whole time.

Fitzalan had dropped back or was taking cover across the check-in counter: I couldn't hear him any more. The check-in counter was no use to me because it would waste a lot of time: Fogel was getting clear of the building and I had to be out there with him to see where he went. *No active involvement* wasn't a finite directive: it had been in part countermanded by the last order, which was to identify Heinrich Fogel. Ideally I would stay with him, get close enough to identify, and withdraw. It could be done, even now, but I was going to need luck and that was the thing I didn't like, because my job is to arrange for certainties.

Fogel's weight hit the glass door and I saw his right shoulder begin turning and that was all I waited for because this was the time when he was most likely to fire.

There were two shots with almost no interval and I heard one of the shells ricochet, whining to silence as I smashed into the nearest door and pitched through the gap as it swung open while part of the forebrain registered an item of data: *Three shells fired, three left.*

The situation now became dangerous: he would have seen me and taken me to be a passenger trying to help the forces of law and order and he would drop me without a thought if I looked like stopping him. We were both on the pavement now and the driver of the emergency vehicle was liable to open fire on Fogel and hit me instead if I began running again. This kind of thing had happened to Harrison in Milan and to Hunter in Geneva and the action was now in Rome and it didn't look any more promising, so I went down headlong and rolled over with the soles of my shoes towards Fogel and lay without moving.

Three shots banged out of a repeater rifle from the opposite direction and I assumed it was the driver. I could hear Fogel running again.

Someone screamed.

I had a key in my hand.

In very fast action a lot of the work is done on the sub-conscious level, with a certain amount of reasoning responsible for decision-making: Fogel had knocked into a group of people and a woman among them had screamed as he dragged at the door of their car; they saw his gun and held back. He was still working fast and very efficiently but any physical action is slower than thought and the key in my hand was the one they'd given me at Hertz. I knew where the dark blue Fiat 1100 was: they'd shown me.

The Alfa-Romeo had drawn in to the kerb half a minute ago and the people had got out and were standing in a group on the pavement when Fogel had knocked into them and pulled the door open. Part of his thinking must have been that he would find the ignition-key in place, because this was a no-waiting area and the driver would have to stay near the car and wouldn't remove the key. Fogel had been very good in Budapest, stalking me with his telescopic rifle and placing three shots in two days, all of them beautifully worked out and unsuccessful only because I'd operated with cat's nerves and used every defensive trick in the business to stay alive. Now on the defensive himself he was still very good, working steadily and fast and relying to a certain extent on surprise manœuvres.

A heavy thudding began as the party of *carabinieri* came through the glass doors and I waited for the first shot and then got on to my feet and made for the Fiat on the other side of the road. There was only a medium volley because they hadn't seen him get into the Alfa-Romeo but it gave me cover and I reached the Fiat with all the momentum necessary: I needed the key for the ignition but not for the door because that way would take too much time. My heel struck the glass edge-on and the stuff was still falling away as I reached inside and opened the door and got in and used the key and gunned up.

Fogel was turning across my bows and I didn't think he had any particular route in his mind: if he drove straight off alongside the pavement he would run through a curtain of bullets because the *carabinieri* were strung out and already taking deliberate aim instead of firing wild and his only chance was to make a fast U-turn and try for distance. He was doing that and at the same time I was forced to make a decision because the situation was now mobile and I didn't stand a chance of tagging him without his knowing. The thing was beginning to look shut-ended because my orders were to identify without being recognized and I couldn't do that without tagging him and I couldn't tag him without being seen. Unless I could run him to ground and put the whole thing into a long-term surveillance phase I couldn't hope to get close enough to identify.

During a mission a lot of your thinking is done for you by Control and the moves are sketched out for you through signals, but sometimes the executive has to get into his controller's mind and make his decision accordingly and in this case the controller was Egerton and I didn't think he'd want me to abort the Rome assignment. There was also of course the other consideration: if I wanted him to give me the Kobra mission I'd have to give him a bit of an incentive and the best way of doing that was to tie up this Rome phase the way he wanted it.

So I wouldn't abort.

The Fiat was slithering a little because of wheelspin and I eased off and got the tyres biting and then gunned up again, closing the gap on the Alfa-Romeo and holding it as another volley of shots came from behind us and picked some paint off Fogel's car and smashed the rear window. The siren of the emergency vehicle had started howling and I could see its red flashing light in the mirror. There was some traffic coming the other way because a Pan American Jumbo was due in at 00:55 and the line of cars began slowing when they saw the emergency vehicle coming up behind us. A stray shot came from somewhere but it didn't seem to hit anything.

Fogel was trying for the main exit gate but his brake lights came on and the tyres began smoking because a police car had appeared from the other direction to cut him off: with that siren howling it wouldn't be long before every patrol on the airport zeroed in on the Alfa and at this point I began thinking he wasn't going to make it because they were taking him very seriously: I still didn't know what the two plain-clothes men had been waiting for but they could have been non-combatant surveillance men scouting for the *carabinieri* but even if I was wrong on that point the fact remained that the *carabinieri* had been sent specifically to meet Fogel so they wanted him pretty badly.

A single shot and my windscreen shattered and I hit the snow away with the flat of my left hand: I think it was Fogel himself, holding the gun across his shoulder and letting fly at random to cool off the pursuit.

Two shells left.

The Alfa-Romeo was now in a long curving slide as he took evasive action against the police car and I clouted the right offside wing of the Fiat as I went through the gap between the police car and a traffic island, driving into a blaze of light and out again and seeing the Alfa straightening up ahead of me. The only way he could go now was through the open gates to the tarmac and I followed him and saw the guard drawing his gun as I passed him. He fired three steady shots and two of them went into the Alfa, smashing a rear light and picking some bits of glass off the broken rear window. The car swerved and corrected and swerved again and I hit the brakes and pulled out a bit towards the airport building to give him room if he was going to turn over.

I couldn't see what was happening but it looked as if the guard's second shot had hit Fogel but hadn't quite knocked him out. He'd got control again but was veering towards the Air France plane that was now being checked and refuelled in the parking bay. This could either be typical thinking on his part or pure chance and I couldn't make out which: if he kept on his present course he could drive under the tail of the aircraft with a few inches to spare and give himself some excellent visual and tactical cover and force anyone behind him to hold their fire.

I swung the wheel and brought the Fiat into a wide curve that would take me past the tail of the aircraft and keep the Alfa in sight. The sirens were now a permanent background and I could see some lights flashing somewhere beyond the Air France plane and to the right. Fogel was still on course but there was something wrong with him because the Alfa swerved again and tried to correct and couldn't make it: on this course he wouldn't clear the tail of the plane with anything like the room he needed. Some of the maintenance crew had stopped work and I thought I saw one of them running for cover behind the fuel tanker.

Headlights blinded me for a moment and I hit the mirror. Either the police car or the emergency vehicle had been gaining on us and I pulled over slightly to the left again to give them a clear run if they wanted to go past: the Fiat was flat out and smelling hot and I wasn't certain I could keep up with the Alfa-Romeo if Fogel decided to head for the open runways; but this thought was academic because he swerved again and couldn't correct this time and hit the fuel tanker head-on and I was already putting the Fiat into a controlled slide when the whole thing went up and I was driving into a wall of flame.

6
Target

She was practising arpeggios.

The heavy lace curtains were half drawn and the light in the room was muted, softening the reflections in the lid of the piano.

I watched her hands. She was only a child, and having trouble with her right thumb, passing it under with a little jerk and using her arm to support the movement. Several times she gave up and sat perfectly still, gazing in front of her with her pale ivory face composed and her eyes quiet. A painter would have run for his brushes, though I could believe that if I hadn't been in the room she would have sworn aloud each time she stopped playing.

I was putting her off, I said.

No, not at all.

We spoke Italian.

I was only here for a moment, I told her.

She didn't blame me, she said with a wistful smile.

Then she began again, trying to get her thumb ready so that it didn't jerk. I sat listening until Rumori came in.

He was dark and thin with eyes that moved restlessly in the shadows of his brows, as if he were all the time half-listening to some distant drummer.

'Mr Wexford,' he said.

We spoke in English.

'Europress.'

He nodded absently, taking me into the hall, where an immense lantern hung from the ceiling, its coloured-glass pendants smouldering under a film of dust. The silk walls were torn here and there, and the plaster showed through: the Piazza Piccola was an area of crumbling villas where people tended to move in and out a lot as the rents went up; and the moving men were indifferent.

'She's making progress,' I said.

'You think so?'

He stooped towards the door of the music room, listening.

'Perhaps not,' he said, and turned away. There was an appointment book on the gilt console and he ran a long delicate finger down the page.

'You were to come for a lesson,' he said, 'on the Ninth.'

'The Seventh, surely.' I went to look at the book.

'In a series of twelve lessons,' he said reluctantly, 'I shall need you here at least twice a week.' He turned again and led me to the stairs and I followed him up.

Code introduction for the period Eighth to Fourteenth was any number at random, with an answering sequence of two below and three above, in this case 9–7–12. I'd only seen him once before, nearly four years ago, and remembered him as a larger man. I suppose you can't feel as mournful as that without losing weight.

The bandage was too bloody tight round my arm, and my hand felt numb. I decided to ask him to help me re-tie the thing before I left here. They'd done a reasonable job at the clinic but the nurse had been a real bitch and I'd finally got out of the place at dawn this morning, down the fire escape: they'd kept me for more than five hours and wanted to make a lot of tests because there'd been a head injury and they weren't satisfied with the reflex response. Good at their job, I'm not saying they weren't: it was just that I was so bloody annoyed about the Fogel thing that I wanted some action to drain off some of the adrenalin.

At the first landing Rumori looked at me attentively for a moment.

'You are feeling well?'

'Fantastic,' I said.

He'd been ahead of me on the stairs but he'd noticed me stop, halfway up: his thoughts weren't so far away as he liked people to think. It was the result of long habit: he'd been our agent-in-place for seven years and Macklin said this was the safest house in southern Europe.

'If you need anything . . .' he murmured, and we began on the next staircase.

He'd almost certainly seen the report in the press: they'd

held over some space for this one because it wasn't often they lost a 747 on the ground because some maniac blew it up with a fuel tanker. The Italian police were playing it close to the chest: a person whose identity had not yet been revealed had caused an accident on the tarmac, killing four members of the maintenance crew and a freight loader. The 747 was totally gutted. A British journalist, as yet unnamed, had driven his automobile through the flames and hit a maintenance trolley a hundred yards away on the far side without having caught fire. He had been dragged to safety by the emergency crews. Unfortunately it was impossible to reach the occupant of the other car, since it was in the heart of the conflagration.

No mention of the *carabinieri*, or the chase, or the exchange of shots.

Rome, like Marseille and other focal points, is a centre for every major intelligence network including Africa, South America and Japan. The Italian police knew who the occupant of the burned-out Alfa-Romeo had been, and so did the monitoring sections of every major intelligence network. The Italian police were very interested in the British journalist but I'd given them the Interpol routine and they'd called Paris and then asked me a lot of questions and got a lot of answers that didn't tell them very much and finally called off the two men they'd stationed outside the door of my ward. The third one had tagged me from the hospital as far as the nearest intersection, where I'd got rid of him for the sake of practice.

The thing was that the intelligence networks would also be very interested in the British journalist. They hadn't asked any questions yet but if they could get hold of me they certainly would. London would have got the story through Fitzalan right away, and the Bureau's sleeper agents in Rome would have been alerted. Emilio Rumori had got it direct on the air from London or from Fitzalan, long before he saw the newspapers. Fitzalan had rung me at the hospital twice in the name of Jones, asking for news of my progress. He'd been hanging around the out-patients department when I'd gone down there to see if I could get away, so he knew I was back on my feet and presumably he'd cleared the area because I was hot and if anything happened to me he wouldn't be involved.

That nurse had been such a bitch that I finally had to bribe one of the cleaners to get my clothes back for me so that I could do the fire-escape thing. They were in a pretty bad condition because I'd been dragged out of the Fiat and there'd been a lot of fire-foam about, and I had to re-kit in a man's shop and pick up another suitcase, real pigskin because I liked the look of it and because I was so bloody upset about blowing the Fogel assignment that I thought I'd pass on some of the angst to those withered old crones in Accounts.

All I hadn't replaced was the razor with the fancy modifications and I didn't imagine Rumori kept things like that around. If I came across any locks that needed blowing I'd have to do it the hard way and go in shoulder-first.

I stopped again, near the top of the second flight of stairs. The whole thing was reeling and I held on to the banister and waited, you should take it easy for a couple of weeks, the specialist had told me, the banister rail tilting up and down under my hand, Rumori's pale ivory face looking at me from above, his deep eyes lost in shadow, take it easy, the roar of the flames again and the wail of the sirens.

' – Right?' His voice coming and going.

'Perfectly,' I said, and began climbing again, one ankle weak and the shoe slipping a bit on the edge of the stair, *come on for Christ's sake, put some bloody effort into it*, watching me carefully with his pale ivory face.

'You can rest here, of course. Nobody would disturb you.'

'Some other time.'

He watched me for a bit longer and then took me across the high-ceilinged landing to the small room at the end, where there were two ceramic cherubs above the door, one of them with an arm broken off. A fly buzzed against the coloured-glass skylight. He stood perfectly still for a moment with his head inclined and his eyes half-closed, listening to the uncertain run of notes from the music-room below.

78

Then he straightened up with a slight sigh and unlocked the door of the room with a large iron key and led me inside.

This was the lumber room, full of Florentine stools and chipped porcelain lamps with their shades at all angles and the parchment torn away. A huge bronze lion on a marble base was wedged between a console and a hand-painted urn, and they were obviously on some kind of base because he twisted the lion's head and swung the whole thing round, sitting on the stool that was part of the base and flicking a switch.

'Q-15,' I told him.

'Yes,' he said, 'I know.' He began fiddling with the set until he got the station identification bleep sorted out from the squelch. After a minute he got a successful series of nines in three blocks and told them I was waiting. It was now close on 10:00 hours in London and it was just conceivable that Egerton was sitting in at Signals: his standard practice when there was something big breaking was to stay with it until three or four in the morning and then come in again about noon, but the Rome objective was dead and standard practice might no longer apply.

999–999–999.

Rumori leaned over the set, shifting the band-spread and watching the carrier needle to get the signal as pure as he could. All they were doing at the moment was keeping us open with the mission identity sequence: 9 was for Kobra.

Egerton had possibly told them to call him in if they got anything from Rome, but they wouldn't wait until he'd driven all the way to Whitehall from his place in Richmond: they'd only keep us hanging around if he were already in his office.

The arpeggios came faintly from below, both hands now.

999–000–000.

Control at console.

Perched on the packing case with his long legs dangling and his eyes wandering vaguely around the room. He is one of the few directors who sit in at Signals and respond at only one remove: through the scramble encoder. The others use their yellow telephones and demand memoranda in duplicate, according to the rules. Egerton doesn't do it for the benefit of his executives in the field: it's just that underneath his remote and donnish appearance he runs at very high voltage and likes to be close to the action. As a spin-off advantage his executives feel more comfortable because the exchange is a lot faster and we know there won't be any confusion, send three and fourpence, we're going to a dance, so forth.

2829–7476–0198 . . .

Rumori cleared his throat and glanced round at me to see if I looked all right. I nodded and we began reading the signals as they came off the integral unscrambler. The voice we were listening to wasn't Egerton's because he didn't have the skill or experience to choose fast abbreviations and pick out routine phrase patterns to suit the messages, but some of Egerton's personal signature was coming through and I could tell he was worried.

There was another thing I noticed.

8387–9817–9166.

An encapsulated summary of the info they'd received from Fitzalan. Then they asked me to talk and it didn't take me long: I hadn't been able to identify Heinrich Fogel with absolute certainty in visual terms but yes it was his face as I remembered it and yes the cranial scar was there. From the way he had got clear of the airport I had recognized his thought patterns and I would go further towards identification on that score. Message ends.

Wanted to know if I required further medical treatment, whether I would ask to withdraw on physical grounds, whether I felt the Rome phase was terminally abortive, so forth.

No, no and no.

Then Egerton began talking again through his signaller and I began listening a little harder because the other thing I'd noticed was the tone of his phrases: he was diffident ('would the executive feel prepared'), persuasive ('assuming a developing potential for the mission') and specious ('the Direction would fully understand if the executive opted for replacement in the field with all immediacy').

These windy phrases had been designed by their lord-ships in Admin. but most of them had been chosen so that their initial letters could be transferred straight into numerals and shot through the scrambler at high speed. At the receiving end we habitually decode into the original phrases but what Egerton was telling me now was that he was desperate for me to remain in action because he was lining up something very big for me.

The specious bit was typical of Egerton. At this stage I could honourably tell London that there was nothing else to do out here and they hadn't got a mission assembled for me yet so I wanted to come in and do something more interesting. But the brief signal *7372 – the Direction would fully understand if the executive opted for replacement in the field with all immediacy –* is normally used when there's a wheel coming off in a shut-ended situation and the poor bastard can either get out or get killed. Egerton had thrown me the *7372* as a sly attempt to persuade me by an obvious association of ideas: if I'd got cold feet at this stage he was willing to re-place me.

For a brilliant man he can be sometimes naïve: he knew damned well I could see through that signal. But naïveté is emotional, gut-think and not brain-think, and the thing that came through so clearly was that he was desperate to keep me running. Desperation, too, is emotional.

'Oh Christ,' I said softly, 'that bloody Egg.'

Emilio Rumori half-turned his head.

'Excuse me?'

'Don't send that,' I said.

But you can come full circle, you know.

Listen: if I *did* come in because there was nothing to do in Rome and there wasn't a mission lined up for me, I could never be *certain* that London believed those were my reasons. They'd be justified in believing that when you've been shot at and gone through a tanker explosion and come out with head injuries you're liable to get cold feet.

My feet can get as cold as the next man's. I'm in this trade to prove myself. I'm frightened of pushing things to the point where they might blow up, so I push things to the point where they might blow up, to prove I'm not frightened.

Egerton knows this and this was what he was working on and the whole thing was coming full circle: maybe he wasn't so naïve. Maybe this was pure brain-think: he knew the *one* thing that could persuade me to stay in the field – an implication of cold feet. And to a certain degree it could even have some truth in it because that craven little organism was still making its voice heard in the dark roaring of the after-shock that was keeping one hand on the banisters: it didn't want any more tankers on fire; it wanted to go home now.

I said to Rumori:

'Tell them I'll stay in the field.'

'Yes.'

'Ask for directives.'

'Yes.'

He selected 938 and 635: *Executive prepared to continue mission. Please brief as fully as possible.* It wasn't accurate because we hadn't got a mission yet and a full briefing is only possible with a director in the field, but Rumori had picked the two phrases with almost no hesitation and got them through, and the saving of time was vital. The whole idea of this method of sending is that you can put through quite a lot of information before the opposition starts getting on to you with a mobile D/Fing unit. There might not be a unit within miles but we always assume it's next door and for this reason the communication between two first-class signallers resembles championship table tennis: the ball seems to vanish because it's going so fast.

276–412–398.

Routine stuff: *Proceed solo – prepare to rdv – report arrival.*

Then they said where.

Cambodia.

'Get it again,' I said.

He asked for a repeat. You can't make a phrase out of a name-place, so they'd sent *Kmbdia*. Now they put it in full: *26358193.*

'Are you reading?' Rumori asked me. His narrow dark head had been turned to look at me because I was sitting on the floor now with my eyes half closed.

'Yes.'

They stayed on the air for another six or seven seconds and he only asked for two repeats. Contact was to be made at the British Embassy with the second cultural attaché and I was to retain my cover: I would be in Phnom Penh to liaise with a Berlin correspondent of Europress in an attempt to get the final stories from wealthy merchants fleeing the capital. By the phrasing I suspected that the Berlin correspondent of Europress was probably a replacement for Heinrich Fogel, because Europress doesn't actually exist and this presented the man as a shadow figure and the only shadow figure around would be in the opposition: I was proceeding solo and wouldn't have a local director. But reading between the lines of a signal exchange that's taking place in one-second flashes can be difficult and I shut my eyes and let it go.

Of course there was a lot of data that didn't appear in the stream of coded digits: it looked as if Heinrich Fogel were being replaced within hours of his death and it looked as if he'd been feinting his travel pattern by landing in Rome because the two places were a hell of a distance apart, considering the Kobra people were assumed to be zeroing in for a rendezvous. Further indications: Kobra now realized their operation was being surveyed (by the unnamed journalist in the Italian press) and might even be penetrated, but they weren't intending to call the whole thing off and go to ground and come up somewhere else. London wouldn't send me to Cambodia unless they had a strong lead, because Egerton was running this one and he didn't like shifting his executives around like pawns. He was sitting there in Signals with the pattern spread out on the board as far as it was known: he was pouncing and missing and he'd pounced on Rome and missed Fogel and now he was pouncing on Phnom Penh and with luck I'd make a hit.

'Shut down?' Rumori asked me.

'Yes.'

Q–15–000.

He cut the switch and swung the tableau of bric-à-brac into place and got off the stool and stood looking down at me with his head on one side.

'You need medical attention,' he said reflectively. 'We have the services of a highly – '

'It's delayed shock, that's all. But you can get me some air tickets.' Phnom Penh would be like a beehive someone had kicked over and the last scheduled airliners had stopped operating five days ago. 'Get me as close as you can, all right? Then I'll try cadging a lift on a U.S. Air Force chopper or whatever's available.'

'It will be very difficult,' Rumori shrugged.

'It'll be close to bloody impossible, but I've got to get in there. You heard what London said.'

A storm of dust whirled up, blotting out most of the airport buildings at Pochentong, and the pilot left the rotor spinning as the doors were thrown open.

'Whadd'ya want to come back here for, buddy?'

He sat loosely at the controls, a cigar jutting out of his stubbled face and his eyes red from fatigue as the armed escorts began dropping through the doorways.

'I'm here to get a story,' I called back above the noise.

'That right? Listen – ' he poked a thick gloved finger at me – 'there's only one story about this goddam place. We're gettin' out, and we should'a stayed, okay? Tell 'em that from me!'

I nodded and someone gave a yell and we all crouched, waiting. Dirt flew up fifty yards away and the debris pattered across the windscreen of the helicopter. They said the airport had been under mortar fire for the past five days, and as I dropped through one of the doorways I saw a big 3-130 standing keeled over near the end of the runway with its tail blown off. The Communists had pushed a unit within a mile and a half of Pochentong and I could feel a series of thumps under my feet as the mortars kept up their fire.

'Okay, let's get goin'!' a man yelled and we spread out as we ran through the dust, half-blinded. Dirt fountained again on our left as the transport vehicles started from the main building towards the helicopter, packed with refugees. A line of U.S. Marines were strung out towards the road, holding back a crowd of Vietnamese civilians; and blobs

84

began darkening in the sky as the next wave of choppers came in from the carriers lying off the coast. Somewhere a siren was screaming an alert, as if no one could hear the mortars or see the earth flying up.

A military jeep was making a close turn on the tarmac with a bunch of Europeans clinging on, so I grabbed one of the hand-grips and got some kind of a purchase as it gunned up and headed for the roadway past the line of Marines.

'Where's this thing going?'

'The U.S. Embassy!' someone shouted back.

I got a better grip and hooked one leg inside and relaxed and felt the throbbing in my head take on a slower rhythm. Maybe there'd be time to get a rest, somewhere along the line: at the moment I wasn't physically mission-ready and if London threw me anything serious to do I didn't know how I was going to do it.

The British Embassy wasn't far from where the jeep dropped me off, and I walked there in the hot sun with my jacket sticking to my back and the glare of the sky in my eyes, trying to think of even one good reason for an international terrorist being holed up in this place on his way to the Kobra rendezvous. One possible answer could be that he wasn't in fact an international terrorist: he could be any kind of contact with connections London wanted me to use. His cover was Europress but he wasn't on the Bureau staff because they would have told me, and if he were in fact a Berlin correspondent for anyone there were possible links with Heinrich Fogel and Baader-Meinhof.

I went through the doors of the embassy.

'Are you looking for H.E.?'

'No,' I said.

The thin youth turned away and said to the girl at the reception desk: 'Then who *was* looking for H.E.?'

'Pretty well everyone,' she said, tucking a curl in. 'He's at lunch anyway, so you won't get near him.' She turned to me with a direct stare and said: 'Can I help you?'

'I'd like to see the second cultural attaché.' I dropped my Europress card on her desk but she didn't look at it.

'Have you been hit?'

'No. I always look like this.' I was getting fed up.

She gave a sudden bright laugh and ducked and waited, looking away from me. Something like a wall went down, not far away, with a long rumbling of masonry, and the siren began again from near the airport.

'Dick,' she called to the thin youth, 'is Brian in?'

'Far as I know.' He went and stood at a window, shading his eyes. 'You know, we haven't got a single tin hat in the place – don't you think that's a bit much?'

'First floor,' she said to me, 'third door along. His name's Brian Chepstow.' She tugged her thin sweater down, outlining her sharp breasts. 'Anything else I can help you with, it'd be a pleasure.'

'Not even a blinking first aid kit!' the thin boy said, 'it's an absolute disgrace!'

Halfway up the stairs I heard another series of crumps from the direction of Pochentong, and some plaster drifted down from the ceiling as I reached the top. The third door along was wide open and I looked in.

'Chepstow?'

He swung round quite fast and I wondered why he'd left the door wide open when he was so uneasy.

'Who are you?'

'Are you the second cultural attaché?'

'Yes.' He said it defensively. He was tall and disjointed-looking, quite young, with thin hair and colourless eyes. There was a suitcase on the desk and he was packing it with files.

'I'm Paul Wexford.' I put a Europress card on the desk and he looked at it straight away as if it might go off or something. There was no code-intro for this rendezvous because he wasn't Bureau.

'Oh yes.' He looked up again, less worried. 'Like to sit down while I finish packing?'

'Not really.' I looked around at the walls: portrait of the Queen, calendar from the Cambodian Packing Company, two scenic posters, one ornamental fan. And there was a photograph, framed, of a pretty girl in a twin-set with the sun in her eyes.

A lot of noise started again in the distance: the thump of explosions and people screaming with high thin voices, like birds.

'Oh God,' he said, and dumped another batch of files into the suitcase. A bell had begun clanging, possibly from one of the temples.

'I thought all the embassies were besieged,' I said, to take his mind off.

'The U.S. Embassy still is,' he said, 'obviously.' One of the files hit the floor and he picked it up, turning it the right way round. 'We got all our people out five days ago.'

The phone rang and he jumped slightly.

'No,' he said into it. 'I can't. Not now.' He put it down.

'Is your cypher room still manned?' I asked him.

He looked at me quickly. 'The Telex is open, if that's what you mean.'

'No,' I said, 'I don't.'

He considered this, half-listening to the mortars and perhaps wondering if there was going to be a plane left to take him out. I was getting a bit annoyed because this contact had been lined up for me by Control and he didn't seem to know what the situation was. The Telex was no use to me: I had to get into signals because one of the routine directives received in Rome was to report my arrival in Phnom Penh.

'You're the second cultural attaché, is that correct?'

'Yes.' He tried to concentrate. 'Have you got a passport I can see?'

I showed it to him and he gave it a quick glance and said: 'Fair enough. Sorry, but things have been a bit confusing here for the last few weeks. Mind telling me the name of your editor?'

'Frank Wainwright.'

He nodded, swinging the case off the desk and dumping it into a corner. 'I'll take you along.'

The cypher room was at the end of the passage on the floor at the top of the building, where all embassy cypher rooms are if they're located with an eye on security.

Chepstow introduced me to the man at the console and said he'd vouch for me, though he didn't sound too certain.

The man gave me a stuffy look and said he couldn't send anything for the press, and I told him the station and asked him to do it through Crowborough. He went rather shut-faced because the station I'd given him was number three in the secret log and I doubt if he'd ever made contact before.

'When you're ready,' he said.

The thing was an ordinary diplomatic wireless and hadn't got a scrambler so we used speech-code while the second cultural attaché stood listening near the window, sometimes turning round and then turning back.

As soon as London came in I reported arrival and asked for directives. There was an awful lot of static, partly because of aircraft movement; and someone was trying to jam us but not very successfully: Crowborough was seven-tenths audible and we didn't talk for long because London didn't have anything new for me. I was to survey and report on the objective until the situation was critical and I had to leave the city. The key contact was still the second cultural attaché. I thought of questioning this because Chepstow didn't seem as if he could help me much, but that was possibly because he wasn't sure of me yet, and the fact that I was in signals with the number three station on the secret log should give him a lot more confidence than a passport.

'Any repeats?' the man at the console asked me.

'No.'

'Addenda?'

'No.'

'Shut down?'

'Yes.'

Chepstow came away from the window, still stooping a little and with his hands dug into his pockets. Possibly he'd banged his head on some of the doorways here in the native quarter. I couldn't make out his attitude and it worried me: he seemed too abstracted to take more than a half interest in anything that was going on around him. He seemed to be waiting for something.

'Was that satisfactory?'

'Mustn't grumble,' I said.

'I'm going off duty now. Want to have a coffee with me?'
'All right.'

The mortars had stopped by the time we were out in the street, and he looked around him with a certain pleasure, as you do when you realize the rain has stopped.

'About time,' he said, and took me across to a battered little Hillman with some sticking plaster across the rear window and one front tyre almost flat. 'Can't get anyone to repair it,' he said in lost tones, 'so I have to keep putting more air in. Look at these blisters – ' he showed me his palm. 'One of those hand pumps, you know the kind? Spare's flat too, but I didn't know till I looked at it.'

We turned into a courtyard where a few other cars were parked at all angles, as if it didn't matter any more. 'This poor old thing's only got to last me a few more hours anyway, with a bit of luck. That goes for the whole city, as you can see for yourself – whole place is on its way out.'

There were some small bamboo tables under the fan-palms, with half a dozen people sitting there over coffee. Most of the conversation I could hear was in French. Chepstow nodded to a huge man with a tiny glass of cognac in front of him.

'Still here, François?'
'Not for long, *mon ami*!'

He raised the little glass to us.

'They've got Turkish,' Chepstow told me. 'You like it?'
I said I did.

'Black as sin,' he nodded with a wan smile, 'about the only good thing left in this bloody dump.'

He didn't talk again until the coffee was brought.

'All right – this chap Stern,' he said.
'Who?'

'Erich Stern.' His tall body drooped over the coffee cup. 'There's a "von" in it somewhere, big deal. Anyway, he's your man. That's what you came to me for, isn't it? I mean, to get all the information you can on him?'

I said it was.

'Right.' He looked around him again, at the balconies that vanished and reappeared among the palm trees. I was beginning to get a fix on his attitude: Phnom Penh was a place that meant something to him, and he was losing it. Worse still, he was having to watch it die before he left. This could explain my impression that he was waiting for something: he was waiting for this place to become nothing.

Three American ambulances went past the courtyard and left dust drifting across our table in the sunshine. Chepstow raised his head to watch them and then looked down again.

'I'm on a plane out,' he said conversationally, 'first thing in the morning. If there is one.' He sipped his coffee, but it was too hot. 'How are you getting out, Wexford?'

'I haven't made any arrangements.'

He gave a weak laugh and stared at me. 'Then you'd better make some, hadn't you?'

'Tell me about Stern,' I said.

He shrugged his thin shoulders. 'All right. You can find him at the Royal Cambodian Hotel. Just ask for him. He doesn't see people by appointment – you have to get in the queue.'

'What does he do?'

He looked up, surprised again. 'Don't you know? He's selling visas. Five thousand U.S. dollars a go, minimum. He got seven members of the government on to a plane when the panic first started, then he took on industrialists and the odd prince or two, anyone with enough cash.'

'Is he alone?'

He frowned. 'How d'you mean, alone?'

'Never mind.'

Another shrug. 'The best way in for you,' he said, 'is to tell him you want to get a girl out. A local girl, of course. You want me to go with you?'

'I don't know, yet.'

The leaves of the palms stirred to a breath of wind, and their shadows moved across the bamboo table.

'The best thing,' he said reflectively, 'is for me to point him out to you, from a distance. Don't you think?'

'I don't know.' I was getting fed up because he hadn't been trained to give information and he'd only got half his mind on it anyway. 'Listen, give me a few facts, will you?

When did Stern arrive in Phnom Penh? Was he alone when he arrived? Did he have any contacts here? Let me have everything you've got.'

'Do my best,' he said.

He lifted his cup to take another sip, and that was what I remember particularly: the way the cup stayed in the air for an instant as his skull shattered and he pitched back with his legs flying up and one foot kicking the table over.

7
Key

The ambassador was on the telephone when the girl took me in.

'That is not my concern, Colonel. One of my staff has been brutally murdered and I demand a full and immediate enquiry.'

The young man who'd been complaining about the lack of tin hats came in with a bundle of letters and stood listening.

'Full and immediate, regardless of other considerations.'

'Have you got any money left here?' I asked the girl.

'Money?' she asked vaguely. Her face was white.

'I want five thousand riels in cash, for traveller's cheques.'

'The best of luck,' she said.

'Thank you, Colonel.'

The ambassador dropped the receiver and looked up.

'What the devil can they do? One foreigner gets killed in the middle of a minor war. Who's this man?'

'Wexford,' I said, 'correspondent for Europress. For your – '

'Keep all journalists out of here,' the ambassador told the girl, 'until I change the instructions.'

'For your information,' I said, 'the bullet was fired from the block of apartments called *Les Palmiers*, at the rear of the restaurant.'

He began looking at me with more attention.

'How do you know?'

'I was there.'

He went on studying me, a short grey-haired man with crooked white teeth and slight blood-pressure. By the look of his eyes I could believe he'd been working twenty-four hours without a break.

'Is that blood on your clothes?' he asked me.

'Probably. I haven't had time to look. I came here to – '

'What do you mean, you were *there*?'

He got up from behind his desk and came close to me and stared at me with his eyes screwed up in fatigue and suspicion and frustration. 'What else do you know about this?'

'Nothing.'

'Is that *his* blood?'

'Probably. It's not mine.'

I heard the girl say oh God, very softly.

'If you have any more information, Welford, I shall ask – '

'Wexford, and listen. I've given you all I know. Now I want something from you: five thousand riels in cash, for t.c.'s, and a message for BL-565 Extension 9. You can add it on to the one you're sending on the subject of Chepstow.'

I tried to think of anything else I wanted from him but there were mental blocks forming because I'd got out of that courtyard very fast and gone to ground and surveyed the block of apartments corridor by corridor in the hope of locating the sniper before I'd drawn blank and got a lift from a street-cleaning lorry crammed with refugees on their way to the airport.

The mental blocks were forming because of other things too: mostly the need to reassess the situation in the light of what had happened. There were a lot of things I didn't know and would have to find out but the thing I knew for certain was that London had manœuvred me into the Kobra mission and set me running and it hadn't been done with a directive: it had been done with a bullet.

When they'd killed Harrison in Milan he'd been alone and when they'd killed Hunter in Geneva he'd been alone but when they'd killed Chepstow I'd been there and for the first time Control had a senior executive in the field to take over. Egerton had been pushing me into one phase after another, trying to connect me with the action before I got bored and took on a mission for Parkis or Mildmay or Sargent instead, and it hadn't worked in Istres and it hadn't worked in Rome but it had worked in Phnom Penh and I had an immediate objective: Erich Stern.

Kobra was mine now, exclusive.

'Who the hell *are* you?' the ambassador asked.

'It doesn't matter who I am,' I told him. 'All you need to know is why you should give me assistance. Tell your wireless operator to put through a special facilities request to BL-565 Extension 9, and you'll get the point.'

There was a distilled-water dispenser in the corner of the room and I went over and filled one of the waxed cups and drank, shutting my eyes for a moment and trying to forget. He'd looked surprised, in the instant before he was hit, but at the time I didn't understand. Conceivably he'd seen the bloody thing in the last few yards of its travel, the sun shining on it and its configuration growing larger with the passing of each microsecond. Just a look of surprise – not fear or anything. Perhaps he'd thought it was a bee.

I supposed they'd cable her: the pretty girl in the twin-set with the sun in her eyes.

'I imagine you know,' I said as I dumped the cup, 'what that particular station is?'

'I don't happen to work in the cypher room, Mr Wexford.'

He was still standing bolt upright in the middle of the office, perhaps wondering if he could get me arrested for anything.

'Good point,' I said. 'For your information it's the secret log designation for No. 10 Downing Street and the special facilities request I'm making will go direct to the Prime Minister's secretary. For Christ's sake,' I said reasonably, 'I'm not asking for troops or a destroyer or anything, so let's get it over with, shall we?'

He stood there for another five seconds and then went back to his desk.

'You intelligence people are a damned nuisance,' he said and picked up the intercom phone. 'Give me that number again – the signals number.'

So I gave it to him and he got on to the cypher room and I waited till he'd told the operator what was wanted, then I said: 'Tell them they can get a message through to Q-15, Asian theatre, till you shut this place up and go. With your permission, of course.'

He began talking into the phone again.

'Who was it?' the girl asked me.

94

'What?'

'Who shot Brian?'

'I don't know.'

She was staring at me, through me, with her eyes like ice.

'Jesus Christ,' she said, and her voice faltered, 'I'd give a lot to find out.' She turned away suddenly and went back into the hall and I heard her sobbing out all the four-letter words she could think of, as quietly as she could. Then I remembered that people can look a lot different in photographs, especially if the sun's in their eyes.

'As soon as you can,' the ambassador said, and put down the phone, pinching the bridge of his nose. 'I shouldn't think we've got five thousand,' he said, 'or anything like it. We'll need some for ourselves, to bribe our way through difficulties, if I know anything about it.' He got up and took the portrait of the Queen and Philip off the wall and began fiddling with the knobs on the safe. 'Poor little devil. If you know anything else about this terrible affair, I think it's your duty to tell me.'

'Nothing else. Nothing at all.'

He swung the door of the safe open and turned to look at me for a moment, his eyes weary.

'I suppose he was mixed up in some sort of intelligence work too, was he? That's why they – ' he shrugged with one hand, and didn't finish.

'It'll be easier all round,' I said, 'if he's remembered as the second cultural attaché. Full stop.'

The driver shook his head and said no good, no good, so I got in and gave him five hundred riels in denominations of fifty and told him he was my driver for the rest of the day and I wanted to go to the Royal Cambodian Hotel just as fast as he could do it. It was between the U.S. Embassy and the Presidential Palace and we had to make a detour round the evacuation zone near the Bassac River, where three or four hundred Marines were protecting the operation.

The ambassador had only been able to let me have a couple of thousand so I'd have to go easy with it. Most of the services were breaking down in the city and there didn't seem to be much of a future, so that hard cash was the only remaining key to a lot of things.

The hotel looked abandoned when we got there but I found a last-ditch skeleton staff in the foyer with a French-speaking Eurasian supervising at the desk.

'*J'ai un ami chez vous – Monsieur Erich Stern. Il n'est pas parti, j'espère?*'

He slid a perfectly-manicured finger down the page of the register, glancing up as the sound of light bombardment began vibrating in the air, then glancing down again.

'*Monsieur Stern est toujours là, m'sieur. Suite 9. Vous voulez lui téléphoner, ou –* '

'*Plus tard. D'abord, je voudrais une chambre pour moi-même.*'

He gave me Number 97, asked about luggage, and glanced a second time at my clothes without comment. My passport said 'press correspondent' and that explained a lot of things in a place like this, including the bloodspots and the bandage on my wrist they'd given me in Rome and the fact that I wanted a room at the best hotel in Phnom Penh when most people were getting out of the place in a hurry. I'd had to leave my suitcase behind when I'd got the lift in the helicopter because the pilot had been bringing troops in and the weight was critical.

He called for a boy to take me to my room.

A different vibration was in the air and I identified it as the throb of chopper blades as a new wave came across to the airport from one of the carriers.

'Please?'

I followed the boy. The lift wasn't working because some of the power lines had been hit last evening, which explained the candles everywhere in bowls and saucers. We took the stairs and the boy gave little bows on each landing and pointed upwards again. There was a suite on each floor and that was why I'd asked for a room on the ninth: Erich Stern was the immediate objective and I was going to stay as close to him as I could; but I didn't think there was any point in trying to see him about getting a girl out of the country until I'd got a few answers worked out in my head because this place had become a red sector for me when that bullet had

96

made a hit: the 'scope-sight must have passed across my image as the sniper had lined up his shot.

There was a certain degree of trauma still lingering, on that subject. The ideal mission is when London knows enough to brief you on the whole thing: objective, access, timing, so forth. The minute you leave Whitehall you know where you're going and you know what you've got to do and all you have to work out is how to do it. It doesn't often happen like that. Most of the time it breaks suddenly, and nearly always with a burst of signals from an agent-in-place or a Curtain embassy or just someone who's bust a code and exposed an operation the Bureau might want to penetrate: there isn't always time to London-brief an executive and work out his access before he's sent in. This was the kind of thing that was happening now: I was being pitched into the mission with London only one jump ahead of me at any given phase, and no director in the field. We don't mind that: it keeps us flexible; but it's dangerous because there hasn't been enough ground-work done and you can suddenly find yourself sitting in the cross-hairs of a telescopic rifle sight without even knowing it and that was why I'd hit the ground and bounced into a zig-zag run from cover to cover among the tables and the palm-trunks till I was inside the restaurant with nothing to show for it but grazed hands and the trauma that lingered in me now.

The bee could have come for me.

'One more please, yes?'

The boy pointed upwards.

'Yes.'

We climbed again.

One of the answers I had to work out concerned Chepstow. I didn't know who he was: I only knew what he'd been doing. He could have been in Liaison 9 like Steadman in Nice or he could have been nosing around for D.I.6 or any one of the overseas intelligence branches with or without the Bureau's knowledge. But somewhere along the line the Bureau had got a fix on him. It hadn't been done here in Phnom Penh while the forces of the Khmer Rouge were threatening the city: it had been done in London while the dustmen's strike was on. Egerton or one of the other directors had picked it up in a pub or a club or a Turkish bath: a word here, a word there, a raised eyebrow and a glance away, the talk becoming quieter and suddenly more disciplined. Erich Stern was in Phnom Penh and the second cultural attaché was surveying him: was this of any use? It was. Egerton had gone to a telephone and within two minutes the signal was filed on readiness for Q-15, Rome, to be received against the distant background of arpeggios.

I knew what Chepstow had been doing but I didn't know exactly how he'd been doing it. Not very well. He'd got in their way and they didn't like it and I needed a change of clothes.

'Please.'

'How good is your English?' I asked the boy.

'Pretty good.' He put the key in the door and opened it for me. 'Pretty good English, all time speak slow, yes?'

I tried him on French and got a blank look and went back to pretty good English. 'Listen. Here is money. I pay more if you work well, understand?'

He hesitated, I think because he'd never seen five hundred riels before, all in one wad. 'Yes. Work for you.'

'Right. A man named Mr Erich Stern is staying here in Suite 9.' I made him repeat. Then I gave him the rest: not to watch Mr Stern's room too closely but to warn me at once if the gentleman looked like leaving. If I weren't in the hotel, find out where Mr Stern was going and telephone the British Embassy and ask for me, so forth. And tell no one, repeat no one, repeat no one.

Then I sent him away and took a look round Room 91 and noted doors, windows, catches, locks, extreme angles of view from each window, hazardous aspects and areas, auditory factors (pile carpet in the corridor), ballistic vulnerability (the door panels were half-inch teak, judging by weight), escape patterns. No bugs under the telephone or behind the sandalwood plaque or in the television set or anywhere obvious. The chances of a permanent set-up in a random room of this hotel were acceptable and I ignored.

Within half an hour I'd checked the various closets, lift-shafts, and alcoves on the eighth, ninth and tenth floors and noted five people go into Suite 9 and four come out: two Europeans, the rest Asians. None of them saw me.

Then I went down the emergency stairs at the rear of the hotel and pushed open the door on the ground floor and waited, checking the environs and checking particularly the skyline where the tops of the buildings were broken here and there by the heads of the palm trees. A sniper works from ground level only when he is certain that no obstacle will cross his line of fire, and this courtyard had vehicles parked against the walls, one of them backing out and turning for the gates.

Two further checks: one halfway across, one at the gates to the street. Blank.

The three cars parked behind the cab I was using were all empty. So were the two in front. My driver was squatting on the pavement beside his battered Citroën, making a pair of porter-thong sandals.

'Remember me?'

He got up quickly and I watched his eyes. He hadn't been got at while I was away: I would have known. Only a poker player could have kept it hidden, or a trained spook. This boy was a cab driver.

I told him I wanted kitting out and he took me north towards Central Market and found one of the army surplus stores that had been springing up in the past few weeks and taking anything the refugees and troops couldn't carry out of the city. To change the image I chose a para-military bush jacket and slacks with outside pockets and a sheath on the belt.

'Have you got any sunglasses?'

'*Comment?*'

'*Lunettes fumées.*'

'*Par ici, m'sieur.*'

Through the narrow doorway I kept my driver in view. I had to watch everyone, everything. The 'scope-sight had passed across my image and settled on Chepstow before the finger had squeezed because Chepstow had been the target and not me. The marksman had been the paid employee of a private operator or the hit-man for an intelligence cell and there'd been nothing personal involved; but he would have reported that his target had been sitting with a companion who wasn't from the embassy and who hadn't been seen before, and it was conceivable that his report would be followed up, even though it didn't sound significant: Chepstow could have had a hundred friends and acquaintances. And if the report were followed up it could become, in the end, significant: my objective was Erich Stern and the closer I went to him the higher the risk of drawing his attention and the parallel became obvious – Chepstow had got in his way and they didn't like it, and the next time the 'scope-sight moved across my image it might well move back, and centralize.

Nothing personal but this was why I had to watch everything and everyone including the man squatting over there by his battered Citroën, making his sandals.

'*Combien je vous dois?*'

'*Allons voir, m'sieur.*'

He made the total and I paid him in cash and told him to wait for five minutes and then go across to the man with the Citroën and tell him I wanted him parked outside the Royal Cambodian Hotel, the side entrance opposite the jade emporium. Then I made my way between the rows of clothing and glass beads and sandalwood carvings and soup-kitchens and left the place by the rear entrance and walked three blocks to the cabstand I'd noted on the way up.

The sunglasses had a slight distortion in the frame and halfway to the hotel I took them off and bent one of the side-pieces, tilting them up a little and then down before I put them on again. The metalescent-grey Peugeot 404 turned off at the next intersection, taking its reflection with it. Discount.

The Citroën was already parked opposite the jade emporium when I went into the hotel by the side entrance. I passed close enough to the driver to make him look up from his leather-work but he didn't recognize me and I felt a bit more comfortable.

Another tremor came from the distant 81-mm mortars

and the people in the foyer froze for a moment in an impromptu tableau, and voices trailed off. I think they were listening for the actual volume of the sound, trying to tell whether the Khmer Rouge were closer now to the city. Apparently they weren't, because everyone began talking again and moving about as they'd done before: there was no particular mood of apprehension. Most of the voices were French, as they'd been at the restaurant: the man in the surplus store had told me that several hundred had decided to remain in Phnom Penh as the insurgents closed in.

The boy I'd engaged to survey Suite 9 was scraping the candle-grease from a brass tray near the stairs, looking up quickly at anyone who passed him. I kept clear of him and crossed the area in front of the desk at a fair distance, just close enough to make sure there was no message-slip in the niche for 91: with the lift out of service I didn't want to rely on a written message being sent to the ninth floor. It could come from only one person: the boy I'd engaged.

I went out through the front entrance and round to the courtyard, using the emergency stairs. The boy was watching everyone on the main staircase very efficiently and if he saw me I doubted if he'd recognized me, any more than my driver had done; but there was a risk and I didn't want to take it. This was normal procedure and right out of basic training: five hundred riels can buy you a friend but a thousand from someone else can buy you an enemy. I'd engaged the services of two mercenaries and then changed the image and from this point I would stay clear of them unless I needed the Citroën. The bell boy could contact me indirectly, by the room telephone or through the embassy, so at this precise point in the Phnom Penh phase of the Kobra mission the state of security was one hundred percent.

On the ninth floor I made another routine audio check at the door of Suite 9, noting the acrid scent of a Gauloise and the clink of a glass. There were voices but they were too low to penetrate a door this thick. A telephone rang once and was immediately answered; then the voices took up again. They were unintelligible but one was speaking in educated German: I'd heard it before, when I'd listened here on my way down the emergency stairs ninety minutes ago. I assumed it belonged to Erich Stern.

I turned away and went along to Room 91 near the end of the passage and put the key in the latch and stopped moving.

In most trades people develop a sixth sense appropriate to the work they do. In my trade we call it mission-feel. The instincts of man have become blunted and distorted by technology and habit: he will breathe carbon monoxide fumes for extensive periods in a traffic jam and accept them as normal, even though he knows they are lethally toxic in concentration; whereas a wild creature, scenting the first whiff of smoke, will run for safety. In the nervy business of active intelligence the instincts remain sharp in the almost constant presence of danger; and even in the early phases of a mission these instincts can approach the refinement found in the wild creature. The intention of the organism is to survive.

Incoming data was fairly banal as I stood at the door with the key in the lock and my fingers on the key. Visual and aural perception didn't give me anything of interest: the door was unmarked by any sign of a forced entry and the latch bore no scratches: there was no sound coming from the other side of the door. The subtler senses gave me nothing either: no vibration in the key or movement of air against my skin; no smell but the lingering scent of the Gauloise; nothing to taste.

There was only mission-feel.

Think.

Fact: if there were nothing of interest in the incoming data, it must be in the past, in the recent memory: because that was where the information existed now. In the memory. The eye had seen something; the ear had heard something; or my fingers, pushing the key into the lock, had felt something; and alarm arousal had taken place.

Remember.

Try to remember.

But it was difficult because the information had been presented so subtly that it had been barely on the conscious level.

There is an area of the eye that has no vision. But it detects movement, right at the periphery of the retina, and signals the motor nerves to turn the head and look in that direction. The ear is as sensitive, and even a microscopic shift of the eardrum will be recorded consciously: when the basilar membrane shifts through a distance of less than one hydrogen molecule a tonal sensation results. But other sights and other sounds, being grosser, overlay these refined experiences: the light in the window at the end of this corridor; the vibration of the mortars in the distance.

I turned my head slowly to the right, then to the left, remembering the flight of the bee. There was nothing, no one.

I left my fingers where they were: on the key.

Changes were taking place in the organism: the pituitary gland was being stimulated hypothalamically, promoting the release of adreno-corticotrophin; these and other sympathetic physiological changes were preparing to protect the organism against the effects of stressors.

The intention was to survive.

Consider possibility of psychological imbalance: I'd been with him when the thing had smashed his head open and it had been a shock and the shock still lingered and I might be standing here in front of this door in a dead funk because the nerves were still on edge and if that were the case then I'd better get a grip on myself and turn this bloody key and go in there.

Don't.

Wait.

Think.

Fact: shock doesn't induce hallucinations. I hadn't imagined anything. I hadn't seen anything or heard anything that wasn't there.

Touched anything?

The key.

My fingers were still on the key and I left them there because I didn't want to move. The organism was queasy, ready to start whining about all this, *I don't like it, there's something here I don't understand, I —*

103

Shuddup.

Bloody well concentrate.

The tactile area was a strong possibility because the visual and aural environs had no particular interest. It could be something to do with the key, the way it had felt when I'd pushed it into the lock. Or it could be something to do with the door. Some kind of movement or lack of movement: something unusual.

Think of *everything.*

Perhaps just the nerves. The aftermath of the Chepstow kill.

Listen for Christ's sake I know what I'm doing, I've taken on most things in this trade that'd kill a man if he didn't know how to operate and get away with it time after time, get away with his skin. There's nothing dramatic about it: you've just got to be cautious, that's all. Push your luck a bit now and then, but not right out of the window.

Faint voices.

Not from inside this room: they were coming from Suite 9. The city was in flight and this hotel would be deserted if it weren't for the few people staying on to the end: the brave, the stupid, the loyal, the ostrich-brained and the handful of international opportunists who were backing their chances of cleaning up by doing a deal with the Communists when they took over the place. But they weren't many, and most of the rooms in the Royal Cambodian Hotel were gathering dust; on the ninth floor only Suite 9 and Room 91 were taken, and none of the skeleton staff felt like climbing this high to turn down the beds.

For this reason the voices coming from Stern's quarters were audible to me, and a new hazard was presented. These voices had only just become loud enough for me to hear and the immediate explanation was the simple and obvious: in human congress the volume of sound during greeting and farewell is higher than during normal speech, since the parties concerned are at a greater distance from each other: they begin their speech when moving closer and continue their speech when drawing apart, raising their voices slightly.

Assume present visitor is taking his leave of Erich Stern.

Make a decision.

Not easy because vital factors unknown. I didn't want to go into this room: my whole instinct was against it. But I didn't want to be seen here in the corridor because Stern himself might emerge with the other man. When you are surveying an objective you will succeed only to the point when you are yourself seen: then you're blown because there's too big a hole in security and the *next* time the objective sees you he'll recognize you. *Finis.*

Once seen, you have to take so many precautions that the thing breaks down: you find yourself driving ten vehicles behind the objective instead of two, with ten chances of losing him instead of two; you get to the point when you have to go down a wall ledge by ledge over a sheer drop because if you take the stairs or the lift he'll see you for the second time and recognize you for what you are: an amateur. Some people do it – or try it. In a minor operation it doesn't add up to anything because the situation isn't loaded but if you're on a major kick and the phase is sensitive and you chance your luck on a thing like that you'll muck it up. Conway tried it, near the end-phase of the Bombay assignment when he was cut off from signals and directives and escape lines and had to keep on going or get out: and he kept on going and they saw him twice at the wrong time in the wrong place and some kid found his head on a rubbish heap when he was looking for cast-off shoes, Dusseldorf, 1973.

So I didn't want Stern to see me and I didn't want to go into this room so I made the decision because the time was short: I had no practical data concerning this key or this door and if Stern or another man came out of Suite 9 I would turn my key and go inside before they saw me. It was a one way situation because there wouldn't be time to reach the nearest alcove or the emergency stairs when their voices reached the pitch when it was certain one of them or both of them were coming out.

Control new hazard.

And concentrate on the immediate threat: the assumed danger of opening this door. Cover every aspect, analyse, and calculate the risk. Most of the necessary thinking had already been done and it had presented close to zero.

Make a guess but don't make it wild.

During my absence someone had conceivably raided Room 91 and searched it or bugged it. Unlikely because security stood at one hundred per cent.

Or: the lock had been tampered with and therefore the key had felt different when I'd inserted it. More likely because it would explain the sensory alarm-reaction when I'd done that.

Or: nerves. Not totally discountable because my arguments against this theory could be based on pride.

There were several other theories and I covered them and discounted them. The voices seemed progressively louder from the other end of the corridor but I waited because I could still use every available second for exploring the situation: once the door of Suite 9 opened I could get in here faster than they would be coming out.

The key was still under my fingers and I hadn't moved. Thought process is electronically quick and no more than nine or ten seconds had passed since I'd pushed the key into the lock.

Recapitulate.

But there wasn't time because the voices became suddenly clear and I heard the click of the latch along the passage and acted on the decision I'd made and turned the key and opened the door and the whole of the wall blew out and hurled me into the dark.

8

Foxtrot

'Cheers.'

'Cheers.'

He drank up.

'Which one are you down for, old boy?'

'Foxtrot,' I said.

'Same as me. Cheers.'

He gave a gusty laugh.

His group had been here since dawn, he'd told me.

There were thirty or forty of them in the breakfast-room
and they were making a lot of noise and my present thresh-
hold of stress was close to zero and in another minute the
whole place began swinging round and round and I shut
my eyes and leaned my head back against the banquette.

'You all right, old boy?'

'Yes.'

'Look a bit shot-up.'

'That's my affair.'

'No offence,' he said.

The thing was to keep still. Keep perfectly still.

And do something about the anger. Control it.

'Who are you with?'

'Agency,' I said. It was no good saying Europress: he
worked for Reuter and knew it didn't exist.

The anger was getting in the way of recovery and I
thought up a few excuses but they didn't really work because
there was *no* excuse for doing what I'd done: none whatsoever. I'd been warned by mission-feel and ignored it and
they'd put me into an ambulance and sent me to one of the
foreign-national casualty groups at the U.S. Embassy compound for early evacuation and I'd finished up at Pochentong Airport before I came to and found what was happening. That was an hour ago, at noon.

They'd wanted to ship me out in one of the helicopters

because I was down as a concussion case with possible complications but I said there was someone I'd left behind and I had to go and get them and they didn't argue: these were the last planes out of Phnom Penh and they could fill them ten times over.

A lot of the telephone lines were still intact and I rang the Royal Cambodian Hotel and asked for Mr Erich Stern and they said that Mr Erich Stern had checked out early this morning and that was why I had so much anger to control because I'd put myself out of commission for nearly eighteen hours and lost the objective.

'Weren't you in Warsaw, old boy? For the talks?'

'Not me,' I said, but that was where he'd seen me. I'd been using a second cover, journalist, working for *Dur Urheber*.

'Seeing doubles.' He laughed again.

I went on sitting still. Perfectly still.

Four zero Alpha. This is D Donald.

The head of each evacuation group had been issued with a walkie-talkie. Considering the proximity of the Khmer Rouge batteries the whole thing was incredibly well organized.

Assemble your group at my location please.

I opened my eyes. Fifteen or twenty of them were putting down their drinks and moving towards the hotel foyer, hitching their cameras and recorders.

'Christ,' said Burroughs, 'when's our turn going to be?'

He went to get another drink. He'd been on foreign assignments for years but I assumed this was the first time he'd got mixed up in a last-plane-out situation and it was getting on his nerves.

I finished my glass of pineapple juice and shut my eyes again and tried to put some of the pieces together. There were quite a lot of questions but the answers to a few of them were obvious.

The booby-trap had been set ineffectively: it should have been triggered to go off when I was going through the doorway and not when I opened the door. The work was probably done by a European because the Asians are subtle technicians: they invented explosives and know how to handle them.

Erich Stern hadn't known about the booby-trap: if he were running a cell or a hit-man and wanted me wiped out he would have ordered the work to be done in the open, as in the case of Chepstow. Stern wouldn't have wanted an explosion taking place so close to Suite 9: it could conceivably have damaged his own person and/or caused a fire that could have spread to Suite 9 before he'd had time to get out with his belongings. The kind of operator who sells freedom for great price when the buyer is desperate is a discreet man, working with one foot in the bank-vault and the other in the stirrup. He doesn't like loud noises or any kind of confusion to disturb his quiet activities.

The question of mission-feel was also answered in part: I still didn't know which precise sense had alerted me but that was now academic. The door of Room 91 was no longer a normal door: it had been tampered with and rigged with an alien device and this had produced subtle changes, one of which had been noted at the level where the conscious merges with the subliminal – the slight movement of the door as I had pushed the key in, or the faint scent of the explosive material, recalling associations with similar devices I'd handle in the past.

I couldn't find any obvious answers to the other questions: if Erich Stern hadn't ordered the killing, who had? If Stern had left Phnom Penh, where had he gone? Had he been the objective of a single phase in the Kobra mission like Heinrich Fogel or was he the objective for the whole mission? Put it another way: had I blown a local fuse or the whole assignment?

London was no help.

The ambassador had left the embassy when I'd got there and the wireless operator was on the point of destroying the set in accordance with instructions. The jamming by the Khmer Rouge had been pretty bad by that time but we put through a few words in formal code for the mission: objective no longer under survey, request directives. It had taken them nearly twenty minutes to make up their bloody minds and there was only one directive and it didn't tell me anything except a change of phase: reservation made Flt 373 Pan Am 21:00 today Taipei-Washington.

I didn't think they meant it.

'Get you another drinkie, old boy?'

I thought they meant it for a feint-jump in the travel pattern or some kind of rdv in transit. They wouldn't throw a complete change of phase at the executive's head without any local briefing. In any case I couldn't reach Taipei by 21:00 hours today.

'No,' I said, and opened my eyes.

'One for the road,' Burroughs grinned, his eyes still frightened. 'They say Foxtrot's coming up any time. Cheers.'

'Cheers.'

I suppose I should have told them about the bang but it had got stuck in my throat because it's bad enough losing the objective without letting yourself get into a terminal situation you could have easily avoided. I wouldn't have heard the last of it because this is the kind of fishwives' gossip that goes around the Caff while the tea's getting cold: what, *that* old bastard couldn't even sniff out a *booby*-trap? Jesus, what are things coming to?

All right, I should have told London anyway because they ought to know about any attempts by the opposition to knock out the executive: it helps Control to work out the next moves. But my answer to that was that if they imagined I could operate close to the objective in a place like Phnom Penh without getting the same attention that Harrison had got in Milan and Hunter had got in Geneva then they weren't thinking straight.

In this case Egerton was Control and Egerton always thinks straight and he would have realized that the minute I landed in this city I'd be in a red sector.

'Can't think why they're so bloody slow,' Burroughs said.

The windows began vibrating as another wave of helicopters passed overhead towards Pochentong. There'd been very little mortar fire today but we'd heard rockets in action while I was at the airport. The insurgents were reported to be at the outskirts of the city but it didn't seem to affect the evacuation programme: there were still several hundred U.S. Marines protecting the operation at the embassy. At the airport they'd checked my papers and said the foreign-national journalists were holed up in the breakfast-room of the Hotel Le Phnom with walkie-talkies, so I'd got a lift here on a fire-tender ferrying medical supplies from Pochentong to the downtown area where some mortar-bombs had hit a skyscraper.

Four zero Alpha. This is F Foxtrot.

'That's us, old boy!'

Please assemble your group at my location.

'In God we trust,' Burroughs said and drained his glass and hitched his tape-recorder and began lurching to the doors.

Then the whole thing began falling into place and I knew Control didn't mean it for a feint-jump in the travel pattern because as soon as the Foxtrot group was put down on the flying deck of the U.S.S. *Okinawa* I was sent for by the second-in-command and accorded an interview.

'I don't know who you are, Mr Wexford, and maybe that doesn't happen to be my business anyway.' He broke off and looked down across the flying deck as another wave of choppers began spiralling in. 'I'll just give you the instructions I've received through Washington, and you should be informed these instructions are classified. You will be flown from this ship by helicopter to one of our bases in Thailand, which presently will not be named. You are requested to report to the commander of that base immediately on arrival. You will then be out of my hands, but for your information you will be flown from there to Taipei, Taiwan, under classified cover of a one-flight military exercise. Is that understood?'

'I think so. Very good of you.'

It wasn't a feint-jump because with the deck cluttered with choppers they probably couldn't put a medium-range machine into the air. From Thailand to Taiwan there couldn't be any kind of rdv in transit because I'd be in a military plane, but there could possibly be some degree of local direction from Taipei across the Pacific or from the transit point across the North American continent.

Egerton had been thinking very fast: I *could* reach Taipei by 21:00 hours today providing there was no holdup at the U.S. base in Thailand. There were two other considerations and they were both major.

I'd only blown the phase in Phnom Penh, not the mission.

There was an American connection.

Add: Kobra was still running.

'Were these instructions duplicated, Captain?'

'Duplicated?'

'You've got more than one carrier standing off this coast.'

'Oh.' He folded his hands behind his back. 'No, we began checking on you in Phnom Penh. That's why you were assigned to the Foxtrot group: it was directed to this ship.' He studied me for three seconds. 'Do you need any food before you take off?'

'I don't think so.'

'Protein tablets, medical supplies or attention, any personal comforts?'

He was signing a form at his desk.

'Not a thing, thank you.'

'Okay. Your escort's waiting for you outside and I'll have him take you down to the flying deck. Just report to the senior officer of operations there and I'll alert him by phone so he'll expect you. It's been my pleasure to have you on board, Mr Wexford.'

'You've been most hospitable, Captain.'

He came to the door with me. 'What's it like over there?'

'In Phnom Penh?'

'Yes.'

'Bit of a shambles.'

'Uh-huh. How are those Marines making out?'

Inter-service rivalry is universal and I knew he wanted me to say they were making a balls-up.

'Bloody marvellous,' I told him and went out to join my escort.

Taipei Airport, Taiwan, 19:15 hours.

A hot damp wind blowing off the sea.

They cut up a bit rough in Customs: they didn't like a British journalist getting out of a U.S. Air Force plane without any luggage but I couldn't help that. When they finally let me out I spent thirty minutes going through the main hall and drew blank. It wasn't really necessary because the only place where anyone could have picked me up was the tarmac itself and the only people who knew I was arriving at Taipei Airport tonight were the U.S. Navy and Air Force and the operation was down as classified.

But I wanted to get it right this time. In Phnom Penh I'd assumed security was total and then I'd opened a door and got a wall in my face and it had sobered me up a little and I didn't want anything like that to happen again, because one of the most terrifying moments in the life of an active executive in the field is when you make a mistake twice in the course of a single mission and begin to wonder whether you've been in this trade too long, whether you're getting too old, whether you'll have the nerve to take on a new assignment if you get out of this one alive.

So this time I wanted to get it right.

Findings at the end of thirty minutes: it was a clear field, except for the man in the mackintosh.

Absolute certainty in this situation is of course impossible. If an opposition cell has set up surveillance for your arrival you can't assess their significance until they've seen you. There could be a dozen people here in the main hall on the peep for a given objective: but that objective didn't have to be me. Those two plain-clothes men at Fiumicino hadn't been looking for me: they'd been looking for Heinrich Fogel. Until they've seen you, it isn't possible to know who they're looking for; but once they've seen you they'll start giving themselves away because they can't help it: if they're going to keep you in their sights they'll have to look in your direction from time to time, especially if you move near a doorway or behind some kind of cover. So all you have to do is survey the field and look for someone watching you.

One exception. If they're surveying the field from cover it's not so cosy: in any given street there can be a hundred windows and there's nothing you can do about that except change the image radically or use a car and change that image too, as often as you can.

Tonight there was no problem. The field was clear except for the man in the mackintosh and he was watching the check-in counters most of the time, enough of the time to note every single person who entered the immediate area.

He hadn't seen me.

There weren't many people at the Pan Am counter because it was still more than forty-five minutes to the check-in limit so I went over there and asked for a non-smoker and picked up the ticket and turned to my left and kept on going, using the end door of the main hall and crossing the road to the nearest car park. He kept approximately twenty yards behind.

Then I stopped.

There was a pool of shadow here, thrown by one of the trees in a dead area between two of the lamps. The wind blew moisture against my face, and the heads of the tall palms glistened with it.

He walked with a loping stride, leaning slightly forward and looking at the ground, the mackintosh flapping and the wind ruffling the sandy fuzz of his hair.

I waited in the shadow.

A big one went up, tilting suddenly off the runway and sloping into the Pacific night, the fluting of the jets changing to a high thin whine as its lights winked smaller and then vanished into the cloud base. The stench of its burnt gases came into the air.

'I didn't think you'd make it,' he said as he came up.

I was checking behind him and to each side, in the distance. He was clean.

'Washington laid on a lot of transport for me,' I said.

He was studying my face, the plain lenses of his glasses glinting as they caught reflections, hiding his eyes. I looked away but it wouldn't do any good because Ferris is very sharp and he likes his executives to be in top form.

'Someone been treading on you, Quiller?'

'Oh for Christ's sake, what would you expect? Egerton

didn't send me into a place like that to pick the bloody daisies.'

He gave a short laugh.

Ferris always gets my back up because you can't ever put anything across him and he won't let anything go.

'Where did you come from?' I asked him.

'Bombay. What happened to Chepstow?'

He was particularly quick tonight and I didn't like it because Ferris is one of the really crack directors in the field and he doesn't normally show his nerves.

It made me think something had happened in London.

'Single shot, medium range, international class marksman.'

'Where were you?'

'Having a cup of coffee with him.'

He looked around him for a moment, his hands stuck into the pockets of his open mackintosh. He always wore that thing and he never buttoned it up: he'd been a schoolmaster once and I think this was his gown, really, in a different form.

'They take a pot at you too?' he asked me.

'No.'

'They didn't?' He swung to look at me, his yellowish eyes now visible behind the lenses.

I knew what he meant. He thought I looked like this because I'd had to get out from under a long gun and it had left my nerves all over the place and of course it was partly true: the long gun is one of the less funny toys they play with when they really want you off the perch – once you know it's there, you can't even walk down a street without knowing that every next second, every next step, you can lose the whole thing and send five thousand roses to Moira.

'They rigged a bang,' I told him.

He wouldn't pass it on: there wouldn't be any sniggering in the Caff. In any case I knew I'd have to tell someone, some time, because Control does a lot of his planning by positive and negative feedback and even an unsuccessful attempt to wipe out the executive in the field is very negative feedback and he can correct the pattern and take more care.

'What sort?' asked Ferris.

He meant what sort of bang.

In his deadpan way he was showing a lot of surprise, so I knew he'd been in very close signals with Control because the executive normally reports an attempted wipe and London would have told Ferris about this one and obviously London hadn't and he knew there was only one reason.

I wished he weren't being so particular tonight: I didn't feel like it. I felt like getting some sleep because every time I started any kind of thought process that bloody wall came at me again.

'They rigged something for me behind the door of my room at the Royal Cambodian Hotel,' I said carefully, because if I missed anything out he'd pounce and ask questions. 'I didn't know a lot about it once it'd gone off but there wasn't any retrograde amnesia. In any given five-star Asian hotel the doors are usually teak and quite thick and the lock's good quality, so you can normally count on something with a high-recoil slip-catch mechanism with a spear-type detonator and plenty of fudge, probably gelignite. For your information I walked into the bloody thing and now I'd like to start forgetting it if that's all right with you.'

He looked away.

'Happens in the best of families.' He paused two seconds. 'Why didn't you tell Control?'

'Didn't have the nerve.'

He looked at me quickly and gave another short laugh.

'The Egg wouldn't have said anything, old boy.'

'I know. If I could have relied on him to kick my arse I'd have told him. Listen, Ferris, are you going to be my director out here?'

'Yes. Out somewhere, anyway.'

'Well thank Christ for that. I haven't had one since Istres. You heard about Istres?'

'Yes.'

'I thought you were on the Tokyo thing.'

'They called me in.'

I took a bit of time to think about that. The Tokyo thing was one of the major assignments for this year and Parkis was handling it and if they'd called a top director like Ferris off a mission that big it either meant this one was bigger or something had come unstuck.

'What's gone wrong,' I asked him, 'in London?'

A pair of bright lights had come out of the cloud base towards the west and were lowering along the approach path, throwing fan-shaped beams through the haze. We stood watching them.

'Nothing's gone wrong,' he said in a moment. 'We've run out of objectives, that's all.'

He wasn't looking at me. He was looking at the lights of the plane.

The hot wind took on a chill and I didn't say anything till I was ready. I doubt if Egerton has ever run a priority mission into the ground because he takes an immense amount of care in setting the thing up and picking the right operatives and getting the signals network phase-perfect before he hits the tit and gets it under way, but this time he'd picked up the executive while he was abroad on vacation and sent him in without a director and in the third phase he'd had to call in a top man like Ferris from another mission and set up an in-transit rendezvous that could easily have been missed because of conditions in Cambodia.

To date he'd lost Harrison, Hunter, Chepstow, and every one of his objectives. All he'd got left were two men in a car park in Taiwan watching a China Airlines flight making its final approach to the runway, as if they'd got time on their hands.

'It's like that,' I said, 'is it?'

'It's like that,' he said.

'Should've hung on to Erich Stern, shouldn't I?'

He turned his head quickly, hearing the tone of my voice. 'Don't start that.'

'Listen for Christ's sake, why didn't Control tell me I was the last bloody hope you'd got of making any – '

'Quiller, there's no point in – '

'Lost every bloody objective right along the line and left me holed up in the wrong end of a war with signals breaking down and only that poor little bastard Chepstow to – '

'I'm not interested in – '

'Oh really?'

But it stopped me.

He knew how to stop me.

The wind blew against our faces.

The lights silvered the palm trees and the roofs of the hangars and then the landing-wheels hit and sent smoke out and hit again and the thing was down, vanishing behind the control tower with the thrust reversing and sending up muted thunder.

'Sorry.'

'Any time.'

Sweat all over me. Because if Egerton had run a priority mission into the ground for the first time it had been my fault: the one single objective remaining under surveillance had been Erich Stern and I'd been warned the opposition was operating because of what they'd done to Chepstow and I'd been warned they were on to me next because the door didn't look right or feel right or smell right and I'd been thrown out of commission for eighteen hours while Erich Stern had quietly got out of the area, taking his time.

My fault.

'We've all been up against it,' Ferris said. He was watching the plane emerging from the far side of the tower. 'You blew the phase over there but you could have had better directives and they could have told you the Phnom Penh objective was all they'd got left. It could have made all the difference. But we can't do anything about that now.' He went on talking, partly to steady me. 'We didn't think you could make this rendezvous with any certainty but we knew you'd have to get out of Cambodia with the Americans or risk being interned, so we called on Washington. I had to switch my flights – I was going Bombay-Hong Kong originally – because the U.S.A.F. said they'd prefer to drop you in Taiwan.' He turned to look at me. 'You've realized by now that there's a strong American connection.'

The China Airlines plane swung into the parking bay and cut its engines, their soft whine dying away to silence.

'Was the connection there from the beginning?'

I didn't think he'd tell me.

He told me.

'No. One of the objectives we lost was Satynovich Zade. Two days ago he was seen in New York.'

'Where was he lost?'

'Palestine.'

'What happened to Brockley?'

Ferris looked at his watch. 'No one has heard from him. We ought to be going, you know.'

We began walking out of the shadow.

'What's he down as,' I asked him, 'in the report?'

'Brockley? Missing. What else can they put?' He walked a little faster, and his mackintosh began flapping in the wind from the ocean. 'He might have gone to ground, of course: there wouldn't be much point in making signals once the objective was gone.'

'How did London know?'

'From his local director.'

So I shut up.

Harrison, Hunter, Chepstow, now Brockley.

And it was Egerton running this one: a director who prided himself on bringing his ferrets back alive. No wonder he'd pulled Ferris out of Tokyo: he needed the best men he could get.

We crossed the road and went through the main hall to the departure gate and I checked the environs at every yard because somewhere along the line this appalling sequence of casualties had to stop. The people in Kobra hadn't *had* to wipe out four men in a row: you can break out of a surveillance situation without doing that. They'd been spelling out a message for us, that was all.

Don't get in our way.

Ferris and I were standing a little apart from the other passengers but we kept our voices low.

'What do you know,' he asked me, 'about Satynovich Zade?'

'Only what I was given in Briefing. Undercover agent for Palestinian factions, once mixed up in the Fourth International, price on his head in Holland.'

'Who briefed you?'

'Macklin.'

'Fair enough.' He was studying me again. 'Going to ask you something. Are you fit for operations?'

I looked away.

'Nobody looks their best,' I said, 'under these bloody lights.'

He waited a bit and then said:

'Well?'

He really wanted to know. That was his job and he was good at it and he never let his people get away with anything.

'I could do with some sleep,' I said.

He went on watching me.

'I may put you through a medical in Washington. I want you to – '

'Look, I had a bit of concussion, that's all. It's a fourteen-hour flight so I've got some sleep coming to me. Then I'll be okay.'

He looked away from me, watching the people getting into line by the ropes, lowering his voice until it was lost in the background of the canned Chinese music.

'I want you to know something. London thinks this operation has got out of hand. Control himself suggested giving it to Sargent to run as a para-military number if the situation took that sort of direction. Then the people upstairs decided it's got to be done as a penetration exercise or not at all. Good logic?'

'Yes.'

Because we were still out in the open and jumping frontiers and the situation was too fluid for anything para-military: there were no targets, no bridges to blow up, no airfields to knock out. We had to zero in on the Kobra rendezvous, penetrate it and take whatever terminal action London ordered.

'The Egg has a lot of faith in you,' Ferris said softly. 'If this is a penetration job he thinks you can do it. He didn't want anyone else for this one – did he tell you that?'

'He was civil enough to mention it, yes.'

Ferris gave a wintry little smile.

'I don't know about his being civil. He's just backing the only horse who's got a hope in hell of coming in. The thing is, he's rather relying on you to do that for him.' He brought his eyes away from watching the line of passengers and looked at me steadily. 'He's had orders to stop the slaughter, you see. He thinks you can help him do that.'

'By staying alive?'

'That's right.'

I thought of the door and the wall and the shock of flame and the murderous blast of its thunder as my body was spun away at the fringe of the explosion.

'I could try a bit harder,' I said.

The trauma was still there and the light was too bright for my eyes and I wanted to lie down and sleep and go on sleeping.

'That's all we're asking,' Ferris said. 'The current situation is this: three of our people have got Satynovich Zade under surveillance in New York and they believe they can keep him in view till you reach there. Once you reach there and get Zade in your sights we're calling the others off.'

I like working solo and he knew that. And there was another reason: with three of them circulating in the immediate vicinity of the objective, someone was going to get killed. Again.

'Does Control think the Kobra rendezvous is going to happen in New York?'

'He doesn't know yet. We've got you lined up for a special interview in Washington first. Then he'll know.'

He was watching the departure gate again. The chief stewardess was there with her papers.

'This interview,' I said. 'Can you tell me a bit more about – '

'No.'

Strict hush.

Fair enough: he was here to direct me and he knew what was good for me and what wasn't good for me and I could rely on that because I'd been local-directed by Ferris before and he was first-rate.

I tried again.

'Zade. Is he the last hope?'

'Yes.'

'No one's trying to locate any of the objectives we've lost?'

'No. It's – ' he stopped, giving a slight shrug. 'It's Zade we're concentrating on now.'

That wasn't what he'd been going to say. He'd been going to say it was too dangerous. They were worried about the losses.

The line of passengers began moving.

'At this point,' Ferris said, 'Control has instructed me to say that if you're not fit for operations, or if you feel the demands are too high, he would perfectly understand your coming in.'

He pulled our tickets out of his mackintosh and checked them over.

I knew it wasn't a formality: he was waiting for a direct answer. I felt a bit annoyed about it but it wasn't his fault.

'I've told you, all I want is some sleep.'

'I'm sure you do.' He turned his head and watched me with his bland yellow eyes. 'But there's the other thing: the demands *are* rather high, and Egerton knows that.'

'For Christ's sake, I blew it in Cambodia didn't I? So now I want to give him Kobra. The complete works, and on a plate.'

'He doesn't expect that.'

'No, but I do.'

9
Siren

A series of soft thuds.

I woke.

The airframe was settling, and plastic creaked.

'Was that the undercarriage?'

'Yes,' Ferris said.

The sun was high in the windows opposite my berth.

'Los Angeles?'

'Yes.'

I checked my watch. 06:00.

Nine hours' sleep.

'What's the local time?'

'Fourteen hundred.'

We bounced twice.

'Do we change planes?'

'Yes.'

I went along to the lav.

A roaring began outside and there was a lot of deceleration.

'Have you altered your watch?' Ferris asked when I went back.

'Not yet.'

There'd be extensive jet lag to take up when we reached the East coast and I wanted to know my own metabolic time for a while in case there was a chance to adjust.

'They're having a bad day,' Ferris said.

'What?'

I still had some buzzing in the ears.

'Look at that lot.'

The smog was mud-brown, hazing out the tops of the buildings, and we caught the Euston Station smell of it as we left the aircraft.

'How long have we got?'

'Ninety minutes.'

'Call or take-off?'

'Take-off.'

We went along to the men's room and had a wash and then Ferris disappeared for a while and came back to our rdv in the coffee-shop and sat down on the next stool and ordered buttermilk.

'They've still got the road up,' he told me.

I suppose he meant in Whitehall.

'Taking their time.'

I didn't see why he'd decided to get into signals with London from Los Angeles when he hadn't done so in Taipei.

I certainly couldn't ask him now.

'How's Charlie?'

Not his correct name. Correct name was Diego.

'Trouble with his dentist. Suing him.'

He crouched over his buttermilk, using a straw.

Diego was our man in downtown Hollywood and that was the only way Ferris could have signalled London in the limited time he'd been away: by phoning Diego and getting him to crank up the short-wave radio. That was partly what he was for. I assumed Ferris had just been reporting our travel pattern but it seemed a bit superfluous.

'How the hell,' I asked him, 'did our chum over there manage to screw the price of first-class berths out of those poxy old tarts in Accounts?'

'He looks after people.'

His straw made a sudden sucking noise as he got to the bottom.

On our way back to the departure gate we had three or four minutes in an open space and he said:

'Your interview in Washington is arranged to take place in the White House. The contact's name is Robert W. Finberg and he's an adviser to the U.S. Secretary of Defense. You'll be put through a routine screening by the E.P.S. at the British Embassy some time before noon tomorrow, all going well. Questions?'

'E.P.S.?'

'Executive Protection Service. They provide security for the White House and the diplomatic missions in Washington.

The actual screening won't take long because there's only the question of identity to be taken care of: the purpose of your visit and the nature of the interview are both subject to very strict hush.'

He was watching the passengers coming across to the gate and so was I. So far, three of them had been on the Pacific flight with us, two of them in the coach class and one in the first.

'I'll brief you first thing in the morning but it might be as well to get one fact memorized straight away: at this point only one man in the whole of the United States has any knowledge of our mission to counter the Kobra operation, and only one man knows that you and I have arrived in the country. That man is of course Robert W. Finberg. Questions?'

There wasn't a lot of time: a Pan Am official was taking up his station at the departure gate. To be noted in passing was a man in a white shirt standing next to him and using a walkie-talkie and looking everywhere except at the passengers. He didn't look like a boarding inspector and I would put him down tentatively as F.B.I.

'Did Finberg come to us, or did we go to him?'

'I don't know that,' Ferris said.

'These people we've got surveying Satynovich Zade: do they know we're here?'

'No. They won't be told.'

'Not when I take over?'

'No. We're going to put out disinformation that they've lost their objective.'

'They don't know about the interview?'

'No. They won't be told. The minute you take over the surveillance on Zade they'll start for the airport. Anything you're unhappy about?'

'Not so far.'

'Fair enough.' He turned his sandy head and gazed at me for a moment like an owl. 'You look in good form.'

'The shave helped.'

'I told London you were fit for operations.'

'I should bloody well hope so.'

'And I told them you've no intention of coming in.'
'Not really.'

It was raining when we got into Dulles International Airport.

My watch read eleven in the morning Taiwan time and in Washington it was ten at night but I'd slept the whole way across the Pacific and some of the way across the States so the jet lag was minimal.

By the time we'd gone aboard in Los Angeles I'd noted a total of four people who were in transit from Taiwan and we stayed in the baggage claim area and saw them out of the building before we went over to Avis and picked up a dark grey Mustang. Ferris was touchy about checking the transit passengers: he said there was absolutely no chance of any kind of surveillance in this travel phase and I said there'd been absolutely no chance of the opposition getting on to me so early in Phnom Penh but they'd hit me with a wall just the same.

It rained all night.

Some of the time I slept again but Ferris used the phone in the next room at midnight and three a.m., initiating the first call and receiving the second: I could hear the bell.

I called him at eight o'clock and the line opened at once.
'Yes?'
'All in order?'
'Perfectly.'
'Thank Christ for that,' I said and hung up.

I'd been worrying more than I'd realized: three people were more than enough to hold down one objective but the opposition had been fighting all along the line and what had happened in Milan and Geneva and Phnom Penh could happen in New York. The three a.m. call to Ferris must have been from one of them, reporting progress, and they must have Zade still in their sights or Ferris would have got me out of bed for a crisis briefing.

But he'd picked up the phone so fast, just now.

Maybe he'd been close to it.

Discount.

The nerves always start jumping a bit at the start of a new

phase and this one was ultra sensitive because the mission now hung on a fine thread. If they lost Zade in New York it would finish us: Ferris had said this objective was the last hope. Despite this I was briefed to delay travel in Washington for an interview with the only man in the whole country who could help us.

The rain had stopped by half-past eight and when I went out at nine the sky was clearing for spring sunshine.

I took an hour, rekitting. The bush jacket I'd bought in Phnom Penh wasn't the right image for a White House meeting and in any case it was streaked with wall plaster and one shoulder was blackened. I was back in the hotel soon after ten and Ferris was waiting for me by the time I'd changed.

'Briefing,' he said.

'I'm ready.'

'You're due at the British Embassy at 11:00 hours and the screening will take some fifteen minutes. You'll use your present cover and if they try to shake you on it I want you to phone me at this hotel. All they need to know is who you are, not what you're doing in Washington. Finberg has told them he wants to interview you and that's enough for them. The Executive Protection Service does exactly what it says: it protects executives in the White House, and all they need to know is that you're not going to assassinate Finberg at the meeting – or anyone else. Questions?'

'Finberg knows I'm using a cover?'

'He knows you are operating for a London shadow agency under the aegis of the U.K. government; he therefore realizes you're not a *bona fide* journalist. In talking to him you don't have to protect the cover image unless someone else is present – *then* you protect it.'

I went across to the door of the room and stood there.

'What happens if the E.P.S. tries shaking me?'

'You phone me here and I'll ask Finberg to come to the British Embassy.' He paused.

I opened the door with a jerk.

Housemaids with a trolley of linen at the end of the passage.

I shut the door.

'At the Embassy,' Ferris went on, 'we'd open up what would amount to a hot line connection by radio, Finberg to Control. But that's last ditch. Don't let them shake you. More questions?'

'No.'

'Finally, you'll be met at the West Executive Entrance by a security escort and a man named George Ryan Jr. He'll take you to the meeting place, and by the way, he's in the Company.'

'What does he know?'

'Only that you're operating as a British agent. Nothing else.'

I went over to the window.

'How deep is the C.I.A. in this?'

'The C.I.A. isn't in it at all. He happens to be a member, but he knows absolutely nothing about Kobra or our mission. He's a courtesy escort, more or less – service to service.'

The trees were in early leaf below the window but there were still enough gaps between them to take in extreme angles and expose normal cover.

'Ferris,' I said, 'how important is this bloody meeting?'

He gave a soft laugh.

'Not your field, is it? Never mind.'

'I want to get to New York and take over Zade.'

'Don't worry,' he said. 'They'll hold him.'

The dark grey Mustang looked clean but total security wasn't possible because this was the third floor of the hotel and some of the downward extreme angles were critical or even useless: I wouldn't be able to see anyone sitting in a parked car within a thirty-degree vector from this viewpoint because the top overlapped the scuttle. But they could be checked when I went down there. The rest of the street looked secure.

'But since you asked,' Ferris said in rather precise tones, 'let me say that Robert Finberg *probably* knows the exact target of the Kobra operation.'

I swung round.

'Oh does he?'

'Probably.'

That could make quite a difference. Satynovich Zade could lead me all over New York for days and I could finish up blown or lost or dead but if Finberg could tell me what the target was I could drop Zade and go straight into the penetration phase with Ferris working out the access. I could be there at the Kobra rendezvous in time to set up support systems, audio surveillance, radio monitoring, the whole bazaar.

So at this moment the mission didn't depend exclusively on our holding down Zade: it depended also on what Finberg could tell me. I suppose I should have known. Egerton wouldn't keep me hanging around the White House if it wasn't fully urgent.

Ferris was checking his watch.

'How's the car?'

'It looks clean.'

'We'd better synchronize.'

'What's local?'

'Ten thirty-nine. Leave for the Embassy in six minutes.'

I turned the knob and reset.

'Ready when you are.'

He picked up his mackintosh.

'Want to recap anything?'

'No, I've got it.'

Ferris saw me through the clearance at the Embassy and then left for the hotel in a cab, leaving the Mustang outside. He didn't want to stay away from the base phone too long because New York could come through at any time.

The E.P.S. people didn't try to shake me on my cover but they were top professionals and some of their questions were throw-aways, casting for slips, and I couldn't relax.

There was a solid front at the West Executive Entrance to the White House and I cut the engine and got out and a man came forward and said he was George Ryan.

We shook hands.

'It won't take a moment, Mr Wexford.'

Medium height, crew cut, pleasant blue eyes and freckles,

the knife-edge of his right hand calloused by practice. He watched the pass being stamped and signed, a fixed half-smile on his face to let me know that this was all a ridiculous formality and that if it was up to him he'd usher me through this gate without any hesitation.

I didn't think he would.

'We've been wondering if it would ever end, Mr Wexford. Then the clouds rolled away this morning and now look at it. How was it in London?'

'Bright intervals.'

Another security agent signed his name on the pass and gave it to Ryan, who checked the stamping and signatures and handed it to me with a gesture of formality.

'Keep it to show your grandchildren, huh?'

I could hear the gate guard using the radio to the west lobby door as I went back to the Mustang and got in. Ryan came with me and talked most of the time as we took West Executive Avenue to the parking lot near the White House.

'I was in London a couple of months ago, took my wife along this time – she'd never been there before. First thing we took in was the Horse Guards' – er – '

'Parade?'

'Sure, parade. We really flipped over that, you know? Fantastic precision.'

'I think your majorettes are sexier.'

He gave a big laugh and we got out and began walking.

'What do you think about our security here, Mr Wexford?'

'It looks like a hundred per cent. Are these chaps all E.P.S.?'

'Some of them. The others are P.P.D.'

'I don't think I know that one.'

'Huh? Oh, that's the Presidential Protective Division.'

I counted sixteen agents within sight of the west lobby entrance.

'Are there normally this many?'

'Well yes.' He invited me inside. 'If you've read our history, you'll know the office is vulnerable.'

He asked me to show my pass to the sergeant at the door and took me deeper into the building, talking about London again and nodding sometimes to one of the agents posted in the cavernous hallways. There were footsteps behind us at every stage of the journey but he never looked round.

'In here,' he said and opened a plain white-panelled door.

Dark blue carpet, polished mahogany, framed and coloured photographs of various monuments. The acoustics were dead in here, in contrast with the high-ceilinged corridors and marble floors outside.

Assume bugs.

Ryan checked his watch.

'Mr Finberg should be along in just a few minutes, so why don't we sit down while we talk a little? The meeting will take place in the adjoining room: I'll show you in there and introduce you.' He took a chair and tugged at the creases in his slacks and sat down and crossed one knee over the other. 'It's a pleasure to meet somebody from – uh – a British agency.' He gave a sudden white smile. 'How's business?'

'Catch-as-catch-can. How's yours?'

Another big laugh.

'We keep busy, though we don't get much help, that's for sure. Guess you read the newspapers.'

'Not often.'

'You know what bugs me right now? These goddamn K.G.B. people crawling all over the Capitol! Guess you've read about that.'

'No.'

A very faint whining began and I couldn't place it.

The air-conditioning was going but the sound came from somewhere near the window. Or against the window.

'That place is a safe house for Moscow, no less,' said Ryan, not smiling any more. 'Hoover made a ukase in 1960 putting the Capitol off-limits for the F.B.I.'s counter-intelligence personnel, can you imagine that?'

It was a siren, that was all. Emergency vehicle.

'I suppose he had his reasons.'

He gave a brief snort. 'Who knows what goes on at the top, Mr Wexford? Who knows what reasons people have? Obviously I don't suggest Hoover wasn't a hundred per cent loyal to his office and his country – that'd be ridiculous. But frankly I can't think of any useful reason why Capitol Hill should be swarming with K.G.B. men at the express invitation of the F.B.I.' He turned his head as he heard the siren, then turned back. 'The thing is, it's created an invisible power bloc: a nucleus of thirty or forty K.G.B. officers who deal with the Congress staff on a daily footing. Now if you take this situation to its logical – '

He broke off.

The siren was close, howling past the front of the building. I didn't see the vehicle but a rectangular blob of white passed across the ceiling as the reflection came through the window. The siren was dying away but not into the distance: I thought the vehicle had pulled up near the West Wing.

It wouldn't be police. They had their own police here and they wouldn't use their sirens.

'Is that a fire engine?'

'Huh? No.'

Ryan got up and looked out of the window. In a moment he turned back with a slight shrug. 'Anyway, why should I bore you with my favourite *bête noire*? I lose a dozen friends a day!' His laugh seemed slightly forced. 'Have you met Bob Finberg before, Mr Wexford?'

'No.'

'You'll like him – he's a really great guy, I've known him for years. You'll find him a little reserved, maybe, if this is the first time you've met. Later on, you'll find he can relax with the best of us.'

There were voices outside the room and I could hear someone's footsteps across the marble, running. Somewhere a metal door slammed.

'Excuse me a minute,' said Ryan and went out, shutting the door.

He was absent for seventeen minutes. I think he'd forgotten me, and had then remembered. When he came into the room his face was white and he spoke haltingly.

'I regret to say your meeting with Robert Finberg is unavoidably cancelled.'

10

Silhouette

The street was quiet.

Four blacks were standing under the lamp at the nearest intersection, three men and a woman, talking. One swung a guitar case, laughing sometimes, stepping back a pace and half doubling over his laugh, stepping forward again, turning his head to look along the street, talking again.

21:15.

They stood there for another five minutes and then broke up, two of the men going north to the next intersection, the remaining man and the woman turning in this direction and passing the Mustang without glancing in. The man was the one who had been laughing; he swung the guitar case as he walked.

'Okay, he goes for the audition and they ask him who his agent is, an' he says I don't have no goddam agent, an' they throw him out on his ass!'

His laughter rang along the street.

The woman said something and the man laughed again.

There was nobody else in the street until the first car turned the corner and stopped outside the hotel. When five cars had dropped their passengers I got out of the Mustang and walked back to the traffic lights and bought a late edition of the *Post* from the box and opened it out as I walked back under the lamplit leaves, checking once, checking twice before I got into the Mustang and shut the door and reviewed the driving mirror for any change in the pattern.

At 21:40 a small police unit was dropped off by a van and took up station: two uniformed officers on each side of the hotel entrance.

Cars began arriving at regular intervals, dropping people off and driving away. Burdick was due to reach the hotel at 22:00 hours.

Ferris hadn't been specific on all points but I hadn't

pressed him because my report on Finberg had shaken him and he'd had to get into immediate signals with London via the Embassy radio. I was on what amounted to phase stand-off and feeling very worried because there'd been two fine threads keeping us in contact with Kobra and now one of them had snapped.

Post: Unconfirmed reports attribute Mr Finberg's death to cardiac arrest, and close relatives have spoken of the 'intense strain' he has been under for the past few weeks.

I looked over the top edge of the paper and saw the pattern was a little different: two plain-clothes men were taking up station not far from the police officers, who didn't appear to notice them. If they hadn't in fact been plain-clothes men the officers would have noticed them and moved them on.

Mirror.

A similar pattern change. He was short, slow-moving, and alone. He came to within fifty yards of the Mustang and then went back to the intersection. I didn't think he was plain-clothes or F.B.I. because he didn't look like that.

21:50.

Ferris had told me to report by phone on the hour at hourly intervals but he never gave me anything useful so I made some enquiries about James K. Burdick, Secretary of Defense, since he was the most interesting man among Finberg's acquaintances.

Now I was sitting here wishing to Christ I could get on a plane to New York and take over the Zade surveillance because that was the other thread, the one that hadn't snapped, the one that could snap at any next minute because Kobra had told us before not to get in their way.

Mirror.

The slow-moving man passed the telephone box again, looking behind him twice in the next fifteen seconds. His image was wrong for an official service operator but he'd undergone basic training. He had noted the Mustang and the fact that I was inside it. He was keeping within the necessary distance of the telephone box and glancing behind him the necessary number of times per minute to ensure that if anyone tried to get into the box he'd be there before them. I assumed that he didn't have to make a call on the hour – in nine minutes from now – but had to make a call when something specific occurred: the arrival of the Secretary of Defense outside the hotel.

I didn't think it was a bracket situation where he was surveying for any form of assassination attempt although information is always information and when he reported Burdick's arrival he could be triggering any one of a hundred chains of events.

Two identical black Cadillacs turned the corner of the nearest intersection and came towards the hotel entrance, slowing.

At this distance I wouldn't be able to identify Burdick with certainty but the image of the man getting out of the leading Cadillac compared very well with the seventeen photographs I'd studied at the newspaper office. Also he outranked every other guest at the convention dinner by a wide margin and the four uniformed officers were now standing slightly more upright and the two plain-clothes men were turning their heads in a slow sweeping rhythm.

The party of five men crossed the pavement from the leading car into the hotel and I got out of the Mustang and walked back towards the telephone box.

The man inside was talking but I couldn't hear what he was saying. I walked fairly fast, with the paper under my arm. Every one of the twelve cars parked between the Mustang and the first intersection was empty and there were no cars parked along the other side of the street. The man had walked here, turning this corner. He wasn't interested in me. He'd seen me sitting at the wheel of the Mustang but it hadn't meant anything to him: his basic training was narrow focus and all he could think about was obeying orders and his orders were to make a signal when James K. Burdick arrived at the hotel. If the man had been police or F.B.I. or any trained service operator he would have done one of two things: he would have come right up to the Mustang to check me or he would have kept out of my driving mirror.

I reached the corner.

Note two people leaving blue Chevrolet and walking south.

Note patrol car heading in this direction from the next intersection.

Note light-haired girl walking north on opposite side.

Fine rain beginning.

Three cars stopped at the traffic lights, this side; two cars stopped at the lights the other side. A cab went through on the green and the lights changed and the patrol car slowed and prepared to stop.

The traffic lights would govern my sequence of actions, then. There was nothing I could do about that.

Red.

The rain began jewelling the green spring leaves above the pavements and drops fell, darkening the ground. There was no need to note consciously that wet stone is more slippery than dry: the body would adjust automatically.

Green.

One of the cars opposite turned south and the other north. On this side two turned north. None of them stopped at the hotel.

Wait.

Assuming it was a genuine case of cardiac arrest I suppose Finberg had been overworking or had been under the strain of what he knew. Or the strain could have been greater than that: he had vital information and had decided to reveal it and knew the consequences would be heavy and when the time came to make his revelation the stress factor rose to fatal levels.

Assuming it was suicide under the guise of cardiac arrest and using some discreet form of cyanide the same considerations were valid: as the time came for making his revelation the stress factor rose and he swallowed something.

Discount possibility of homicide in those high-security environs.

Red.

Four cars pulled up and the patrol car began moving.

The man was still in the box.

Police don't like people standing at corners in the proximity of a place where security is mounted so I turned and
walked north towards the telephone box as if waiting to use
it. If they were alert to the situation it would appear normal.

A slightly worrying factor was that if the girl saw the
occurrence she might scream and the patrol car might still
be within hearing distance and I didn't want any trouble
because there wasn't time to have Ferris get me out of it.

Consider abandoning.

The police observer was checking me as I opened the
paper. The patrol car didn't slow.

The light-haired girl was walking slightly quicker because
of the rain. Jeans and a mackintosh and a music satchel.

The two people walking south were out of sight and there
was no one else between the two immediate intersections.

The man came out of the box and began walking towards
me.

I looked down at the paper.

The time was telescoping to a narrow band of three or four
seconds and I reviewed the situation and it was like this: the
girl was almost abreast of me on the opposite side of the
street and her head was down because of the rain. The
patrol car was fifty yards away to the north and if the girl
happened to scream it would be heard and the driving
mirrors would pick up the occurrence. Given another two
seconds the situation would change and the girl would be
too far ahead to see anything and she wouldn't scream.

But the man was only one second away from me and we
were walking towards each other so I decided not to risk
anything and just turned round and walked back towards
the intersection, slowing until he came abreast of me.

This would have alerted him despite the fact that he
didn't know I was the man he'd seen sitting in the Mustang.
Compensation was provided by my now being in a vulnerable position with my back turned slightly towards him and
both my hands visible on the edges of the newspaper. In
case this wasn't sufficient I swung very fast and obliquely
and took him low and brought medium force to the neck as

137

he came down quietly and my right hand cupped his head to stop it hitting the pavement.

Armpit-holstered .22, knife, no wallet, no papers, no cheque-book, no identification of any kind.

When I walked back to the Mustang the girl was halfway to the hotel entrance, hurrying because I supposed she'd washed her hair and didn't want to get it wet.

'Where are you?'

'Kennedy Airport.'

Pause.

He was listening for bugs.

That meant he wasn't in one of our safe houses and he wasn't in a hotel so where the hell was he? I couldn't ask. It's all right to be at an airport but not all right to be in a place where you've got to listen for bugs.

'Time check,' Ferris said.

'03:12.'

He paused again.

I couldn't tell what was worrying him.

All he'd said when I rang him at 22:09 last night was *get into New York*. He hadn't asked for a report or anything. I suppose the Finberg thing had shaken the network badly.

The rest of the passengers from Washington were still coming past and I watched them. I was fairly confident about security but you've got to watch everyone, all the time, wherever you are: then when you notice the same type showing up in two or three different places you know he's watching you.

'Did you get anything?' Ferris asked.

'That's a pretty odd question.'

'No,' he said, 'I'm all right.'

Fair enough.

If he'd been talking under duress or in the presence of a third party he would have answered: 'It only *looks* an odd question.' So whatever was worrying him it wasn't that.

'Yes,' I said. 'The Secretary of Defense had a tag on him last night at 22:00 hours.'

'What sort?'

'I'd say it was someone from a local cell or someone working for a bigger organization, probably blind or at least without any specific rdv's or cut-outs. Routine training, smaller than a hit-man, bigger than a peep. Gun carried but a lot of trouble taken to remain unidentifiable in case of arrest. His job was to signal when the Secretary of Defense arrived at the Quaker House Hotel and he did it by telephone.'

In a minute Ferris said: 'All right.'

He sounded very tense but I didn't make any comment or ask any silly questions: if your director in the field isn't tense most of the time it means you're not getting warm.

The last of the passengers went past and I memorized them, concentrating on those walking by themselves.

'All right,' Ferris said again. 'You know the objective for this phase.' I began listening very carefully. 'I want you to take him over without letting the other two know.'

'Two?'

'The third one's just been hospitalized in Bellevue. He's in intensive care.'

Shown his hand.

This was conceivably why Ferris sounded so worried.

'For Christ's sake get me running,' I said.

'Yes.' Another brief pause. 'The objective is in Room 23 of the Lulu Belle Hotel on Broadway and West 69th Street. As soon as you feel you've got full control I'll call the other two off. Questions?'

Couple of dozen but none that I could ask. London was probably in a flap over Finberg but Ferris wouldn't tell me that: it doesn't do the man in the field any good to know the network's got the shakes. My report on Burdick's tag could have been vital or useless and he wouldn't tell me that either unless it would help me to know. What I had to do now was go after Satynovich Zade and leave the rest to Ferris.

'No questions.'

05:17.

The place was at the end of a long alley where a group of dustbins stood under one of the three lamps. The cop on the beat had gone past twice since I'd arrived and I kept out of his way. Ten minutes ago I'd located one of our people: he was sitting in a parked VW on West 69th with a long-distance view of the Lulu Belle entrance. The road was up at that point and he was tucked in alongside some machinery in a roped area and I passed across his line of vision only once. He would be using field glasses.

Five minutes later I saw the other one: the pale blob of a face in the corner of a pool-room window. The place looked abandoned and had a padlock and chain across the doors and Ferris must have paid him inside through one of our people in place as an intermediary.

The set-up amounted to a bracket: the only part of the Lulu Belle that neither of them could see was a blank wall at the rear and they could see each other at a distance of some sixty yards with a fairly wide signalling vector if the VW had to move around. They wouldn't have had to re-arrange this setup since the third man had been got at, because they'd have been working three-hourly shifts, but it was a good deal more dangerous now. He must have been exposed in some way at his base or en route, or the remaining two wouldn't still be manning the peep: the zone was extremely small and they would have been flushed.

I went back twice to the blue Dodge Charger and moved it a few yards, taking half an hour to work out the optimum station and going on foot from the corner of Broadway and West 69th Street to the next intersection south. I was very restricted because I had to move around without being seen by the two peeps or seen too often by the cop on the beat, but even at this pre-dawn hour there were one or two bums on the street and a group of winos lying in a doorway thirty yards south of the hotel entrance. I don't think it would have been possible to find an effective station without this degree of camouflage.

With the amount of sleep I'd taken in transit from Taiwan to Washington I was good for at least twenty-four hours before performance diminished, and the concussion in Phnom Penh had left me with no after-effects. The only difficulty about the take-over would be to signal Ferris that

I was in control of Zade and that could only be done when he stopped moving again. Until then I'd have to run the surveillance in conjunction with the other two people and try not to let them see me.

That could be extremely sensitive and of course dangerous.

Ferris wouldn't normally have gone after a disinformation ploy: it was an ideal, not an essential. But Kobra was running hard and determined to drive any surveillance into the ground before they made their rendezvous: they'd killed three men and put a fourth into hospital and brought Control to the point where he was being pressured to call off the mission and Ferris had been brought in from Tokyo to do two things in New York.

One: to lock me on to Satynovich Zade and keep me with him all the way to the rendezvous.

Two: to let it be thought that the two people now surveying him had lost him beyond any hope of picking him up again.

This was logical. In given circumstances one man can stay with the objective more easily than a dozen: his image is smaller. At the point of locking on the final surveillance Ferris wanted to make it seem that the reverse had happened: that all surveillance had now stopped. The disinformation component was a refinement: the take-over zone was extremely hot and one of us could be picked up and killed out of hand as in Milan, Geneva and Phnom Penh: but at any phase the Kobra people could try a straight snatch and grill whoever they took, and the disinformation would come up during the interrogation: Zade had been irretrievably lost.

05:43.

First light was touching along the roofs of the buildings.

A work gang had gone past in a truck two minutes ago and I prepared for a sudden rearrangement of the set-up because the VW would have to move off when the road works started up for the day.

The telephone I'd picked was on the other side of a small drug store near the end of the alley, two minutes' walk from the Lulu Belle Hotel. Ferris had told me to signal at ten

141

minutes past each hour, leaving the exact hour interval for the other two.

The cop was still the same one, working the midnight-to-eight.

There was no sign of the opposition.

But they were here.

The deadline for the Kobra rendezvous was close. They hadn't run this far and this fast as a delaying action: they'd done it in an attempt to run our surveillance into the ground. They would zero in to the rendezvous the moment they were satisfied that the field was clear and when Ferris called off the last of the tags and left me in control, it would look like that.

05:49.

Two men.

They hadn't been there before.

I was at the Broadway end of the alley that ran alongside the hotel and I saw them when I checked the south vector. They were keeping to the dark where they could: in the patches of shadow thrown within doorways and in the cover of the hoardings where building was going on in the daytime. They moved about quite a lot but after five minutes I saw they had a focus.

Note. Review. Formulate.

Formulate what action to take if and when they came. Work out escape lines. Control the situation to the point where there was nothing they could do without counter-action or a get-out.

That was ideal but of course you can't always do it because you don't always know the terrain well enough to use it for your defence and you don't always know what support they can call on when you select an escape line and find it blocked.

It was a good suit I'd bought for the interview at the White House and in this area it looked a little incongruous and they could be a couple of muggers.

I didn't think so.

There was a slight problem because the obvious escape lines were along Broadway and 69th Street but if I moved towards them from the alley I would have to cross exposure zones and I'd been avoiding them for the last thirty minutes. These zones were the open areas directly opposite the front of the hotel, where anyone in the street could be seen from any one of its windows.

The danger was that the two men *could* in fact be a couple of muggers. If I could be certain of this, there was no problem. I was ideally placed for a lure situation and if they followed me down the alley I could deal with them out of sight.

But I couldn't be certain, and if I assumed they were not muggers but hit-men from a Kobra cell I could take escape action that would expose me to actual Kobra surveillance in the area and that was what I'd been taking so much trouble to avoid.

It was a question of identity.

They were still moving.

But nothing had changed: I was their focus.

I waited.

Half a minute later the cop passed between their station and mine. He didn't check them and that could mean they were local and would therefore have nothing to do with Kobra. It was a clue to their identity but not reliable and I began worrying.

Milan. Geneva. Phnom Penh.

Gut-think: discount.

The darkness was composed partially of light. The actual sources of the light – the street-lamps – were blinding to the eye and left the shadows almost black in places where doorways were deep and the hoardings threw an angular pattern. I had sufficient cover to use but couldn't reach it without showing my direction.

A Yellow Cab passed between the buildings, sending a wash of light along the walls. The two men turned their backs until it had gone. This was quite a professional move but not all that sophisticated: it was a street-crime skill and it didn't identify them as trained operators.

They were facing forward from the doorway again and watching me. I didn't think there was much chance of identifying them until they came close and if they came close it could be too late because if they were operationally trained they'd know how to kill.

Harrison. Hunter. Chepstow.

Gut-think: ignore.

They moved again, one going north and one south along the opposite pavement. In ten seconds they were out of sight because I was a few yards into the mouth of the alley and was therefore blinkered beyond a thirty-degree vector.

I listened for them.

Nothing.

Nothing close.

A ship on the Hudson.

The rattle of a cab.

Silence again.

Then their footsteps.

I walked halfway down the alley and turned round.

From this position I could assess their approach and if I thought they were professionals I could turn again and get out of the alley at the other end.

They became visible, their silhouettes moving against the back-lighting of the street behind them. They came quickly but were not running. There was a certain discipline in the way they walked. I couldn't see any sign of a weapon and certainly neither of them was holding a gun: their silhouettes were sharp and I could see their hands swinging freely as they walked.

They looked confident and I now assumed they were professionals. Their quick footsteps were taking on a strange echo and it alerted me: they were closer than they looked. I turned and began my run but stopped dead when I saw the two other men coming the other way.

11

Zade

The sky throbbed.

I lifted the bottle. It took all my strength.

The bottle was empty.

Light flared on the glass, blinding me. It came from the lamp.

The tall lamps burned in the sky, searing my eyes.

The man beside me stank.

My feet were in the gutter, one sock half off.

'Shit, man, git your ass outa here.'

'Shuddup,' I said, 'or I'll smash you.'

He stank of alcohol and vomit.

I lifted the bottle again, moaning.

'Shit, man,' he said.

He thought there was wine in the bottle, thought it was his.

'I'll smash you to a pulp,' I said, 'if you don't shuddup.'

He was dangerous.

He could get me killed.

My head throbbed and the sky throbbed.

But there wasn't any blood. Not enough for them to see.

Tyres squealed faintly at the intersection.

I saw one of them coming again, and lifted the bottle.

Consciousness began gaining now, faster, because of the danger.

He came past, walking steadily. I watched his feet.

His feet were at eye-level.

If he looked down, that would be it.

Finis.

His heel into my face: *finis.*

He stopped.

I looked up at him obliquely, squinting, my eyes almost shut against the blinding light, the bottle blazing. I didn't recognize him: he was one of the four who had been in the alley. One of the three still alive.

And he wouldn't recognize me either, I knew that. We'd all been moving very fast and it had been half dark. But he'd see, if he looked down, that my clothes weren't filthy and torn. He'd see other signs that I hadn't been lying here for months, night after night for months, dying the way I wanted.

But there was nothing more that I could do except wait. My present position was as vulnerable as it had been before in the alley but that was academic. Fire, frying pan, so forth.

The organism had looked after itself without my having to do any more thinking. I'd done the necessary amount of thinking first and then given the instructions to the organism and it had taken over. With two of them coming at me from each end of the alley there'd been no point in waiting till they closed on me at their own pace. The only chance lay in immediate and very aggressive action and I had made my run flat out, choosing this end of the alley because the street at the other end had exposure zones that I wanted to leave alone.

I didn't know if the two men behind me had started running: it didn't make any difference because I was going so hard that they wouldn't gain on me. The strength of the opposition had now been halved and there were only two people to deal with. They'd both stopped and were waiting and I think one of them was pulling a gun as I reached them.

The techniques of unarmed combat taught at Norfolk are based partly on karate. I have only used them twice to save my life, once in Warsaw and once in Hong Kong. In those instances there was only one adversary. Here there were two. There is nothing new about the primordial components of speed and surprise: they are essential to any attack, by whatever technique. Two further psychological components come into play when life is actually threatened: the instinct to survive, and the ability to relax and allow the primitive animal to perform in its own right.

In civilized society the will to take life is seldom conscious.

Most murders are committed by relatives or close friends of the victim and the motivation is subconscious, an expression of rage, jealousy, humiliation, so forth. The need is not to kill but to relieve the psyche of its stress, and to do it in the quickest and surest way available.

The animal will do it consciously in order to survive.

There is no name, at Norfolk, for the extended techniques based on classic karate. Most of them are psychological and the most effective is this ability to relax and leave the animal to protect itself: not by defensive tactics but by the most implacable ferocity. In brief it might be termed the invocation of blood-lust.

There is probably a spin-off involved: the instillation of fear in the adversary. As I reached the two men I was an animal totally committed to killing them and I would believe that my whole body projected a degree of menace that would give them doubts.

Doubts at the instant of lethal combat can be critical.

Basically I used the *tobi-mae-geri* and was in the air with my feet at the knife-edge angle when I crashed into them. The man on the right died immediately and this was to be expected because I am right-handed and since it wasn't possible to aim a specific blow at both of them I aimed it at this one and he had no chance. The most effective weapon I had for the other man was my left knee, the leg doubled, because it isn't possible to perform the *tobi-mae-geri* with both feet: the body has left the ground and the balance has to be maintained.

I don't think the knee connected. But the momentum was there and the animal had killed only one of its adversaries and its life was still in jeopardy and it wanted to go on killing and I felt my left foot strike into softness before I landed and there was a clatter of metal and someone moaning as I span and bounced, hitting the ground and getting up and going headlong out of the alley, the organism still performing at peak effectiveness and thinking for itself as I dragged my collar up and my tie off, sliding across the pavement to where the winos were huddled in the bleak light of the lamps, one shoe coming off and then the other as I

147

dropped across the gutter where the empty bottle was lying.

The thing had been done half-consciously and without rehearsal, but habit and experience came into play and issued some of the instructions during the six or seven seconds available before the other two men came from the alley in a headlong run. In a situation where there is no time to hide, the routine action is to change the image and make the new one conspicuous.

I raised the bottle again, shutting my eyes.

He went on standing there.

He was sweeping the whole street visually, checking the doorways and every other site for cover. I thought I heard the other man calling something from the opposite pavement. He didn't answer.

A vehicle went past, heavy, a truck or a bus. Its lights brightened against my closed eyelids, then faded.

'Gimme that goddamn juice, you – '

'Christ sake shut your mouth,' I said, 'you son of a bitch.'

I rolled over and tried to keep control of the situation, wanting to know things: where were my shoes, how much blood was visible, so forth. My shoes were in the gutter and I was lying on them, concealing them; there was very little blood visible but as I rolled over I let my sleeve cover it because it was fresh in colour and they would expect me to have been grazed when they'd seen me crash on to the ground.

Through my half-closed eyes I watched his feet, his shoes, the sharp edge of his heels.

He could do it without any problem.

A crushing strike downwards.

Executive deceased.

We've all got a rough idea of the way we'd like to go when it gets too hot to hold. For most of us it doesn't work out like that, although Delacorte managed it last year on the end-phase of the Bulgarian thing when he took his Mercedes through the frontier at Svelingrad into Turkey, straight through the bloody barrier flat out at a hundred and ten miles an hour with the tank on fire where they'd shot him up with a sub-machine-gun and the stuff still coming at him from the guard post – finished up like a sieve but his director in the field was there at the rendezvous and got him out and found the stuff on him: military installation lay-outs, airfield preparedness schedules, Moscow directives and fifteen long-run tapes of the Sovinformburo breakdown of the tactical manœuvres operation, the whole beautiful bonanza right in London's lap.

That's the way we'd like to go, when we've got to.

Not lying around with the drunks in the gutter without even a drop left in the stinking rotten bottle –

Steady.

Waiting for a crushed skull and nothing to show for it, the mission run into the ground because –

Steady. You've got to sweat it out.

Easy to say.

But it's got to be done.

Think. Shoes out of sight and one sock half off to make it look like a potato heel, dirt on my face and my hair roughed up: was there anything I could do to emphasize the image? Not a lot. Roll over another inch or two and get the light off my face because it hasn't got the yellow pallor, the drained look of the man lying next to me.

Roll over and moan a bit, give a moan. You're a drunk and your head's full of booze. *Work* for your living. Work for your life.

The bottle rolled in the gutter. One of the others woke up and cursed and someone told him to screw himself and he shut up but it was good cover, first-class cover.

The man hadn't moved.

He was watching the street.

Two cars went by, one of them with the emergency light flashing and the siren beginning to howl. Then a truck, with its wheels bouncing over the bumps near the intersection.

Now the man moved.

I watched his feet.

He was going back to the alley.

Someone was talking and now I could hear a sudden sharpness come into his tone.

'Hey, Harry. Chuck's had it.'

The man's feet disappeared into the alley and I rolled over and got up and staggered along the pavement, passing the doorways and keeping close in case I needed them, my shoes in my hand because when you break cover you leave nothing behind you.

Except, when it's unavoidable, a few spots of blood in the gutter.

'What happened?' Ferris asked me.

I was twenty minutes overdue on the call.

'They put a bracket on me.'

'How many?'

He wasn't listening for bugs this time.

'Four.'

'What about your face?'

He meant could anyone recognize me again.

'It was half dark.'

'Did the objective see you?'

'No.' The objective was Zade.

He was getting his priorities right: there was still a chance to lock me on and he wanted to know how difficult it was going to be.

'Where are you?'

'West 69th Street. A pay phone.'

In a couple of seconds he said: 'The objective's on the move.'

'Oh Christ, when did – '

'Don't worry.'

'Listen, I can't – '

'Shut up.'

So I did that but it wasn't easy because I'd just blown the tag and it shouldn't have happened and I was beginning to think I couldn't handle this one and that brought the sweat out more than anything else.

Be positive.

I'd let them throw a wall in my face in Cambodia and now I'd –

Be positive and remember that a mission can be difficult.

'All right,' Ferris said, 'have you still got your transport?'

'No.'

'Why not?'

'I can't go back into the area.'

'What kind of trouble was there?' he asked rather quickly.

'I've bloody well told you — they put a bracket on me and – '

'Information. Just information.'

Ferris is good at pulling you up when he knows you need it.

'It was just a case of getting out,' I said, and rested my head against the acoustic panel. 'So I got out.'

'I see.'

He knew I'd give him more if there was anything more to give but he didn't want a running commentary because one get-out action is like the next and there's nothing to talk about afterwards.

Some of the bruises were starting to throb and my shoulder felt wrenched, try telling him that.

'I had to terminate,' I said.

'Oh did you? How many?'

'One.'

'D'you need smoke out?'

'No.'

'What's your condition?'

'Stunning – how's yours?'

Meant I was operational and that's all he wanted to know.

'Very well. Get to the Hertz office on West 71st Street and I'll have some transport lined up. The objective is at a diner in Queens and we've still got one man on him. Give it another go and this time see if you can take him over. Questions?'

I needed a clean-up but there wasn't time. I needed some new clothes but there'd be no stores open yet. Maps, cash, cover were still intact.

'No,' I said.

He gave me the Hertz address and where to find the diner.

'You'll need to be quick,' he said and hung up.

He was taking a newspaper from the box outside the Varig

Airlines section of the check-in area. The first coin apparently didn't work because he hit the box with the flat of his hand and tried again. Nothing happened so he put another coin in and this time it was all right and he pulled the paper out and let the glass lid slam back.

Five ten, lean, thick black hair, long arms, feet splayed a little as he stood by the box. Leather jacket zipped halfway up to a polo neck sweater. Panda sunglasses, thick gold chain around the neck, two heavy gold rings. Bronzed, general attitude relaxed.

Satynovich Zade.

I watched him from inside the Hertz Cougar at a distance of fifty yards. He couldn't see me even if he were looking for surveillance in this area because the sun was 09:16 hours high in the south-east and the reflection off the windscreen would blind him to anything behind it.

I listened to the engine cooling. It had been a fairly exacting run from the diner in Queens to Kennedy Airport because I'd had to assume three elements: Zade, the Bureau tag and the Kobra protection cell. I couldn't just fall in behind the leader because until we were within three miles of the airport we hadn't followed any of the main routes to the downtown areas and I didn't know if the Kobra cell was in front of me, behind me or both. The only suspect had been a Corvette with two men inside but they'd peeled off and stayed out of sight and didn't come up in the mirror. The only thing to do was put the Cougar through a series of doubling-back patterns whenever I could skin through on the amber and that had called for a lot of acceleration bursts and close control of the brakes and the whole car smelt of a hard run as I sat here watching the objective.

The Bureau tag had been using a dark blue Pinto and it had gone now. I'd seen him get out and go across to one of the phones and talk to Ferris for thirty seconds; then he'd got back into the Pinto and driven away. The objective was now solely in my hands.

Ferris had told me he'd still got one man in the running and he hadn't told me what had happened to the other one and I didn't want to think about it now. Later I'd have to.

Zade moved, opening the paper and glancing at it and folding it as he went into the airport building. I was out of the Cougar at the same time.

This was a hellishly sensitive phase and I tried not to think about that either because at this moment I could be moving through an opposition surveillance zone and there wasn't anything I could do about it. I believed Zade had got here from Queens without a protection cell because I hadn't seen any evidence of one and I could be wrong.

There were two reasons why I didn't want to think about the second man who'd been watching Zade at the Lulu Belle Hotel: Ferris wouldn't have simply called him off, and that meant he'd either been got at by Kobra or Ferris had been ordered by London to dispense with him as a disinformation tool and neither eventuality would have been pleasant for him.

The thing was that I was now locked on to the objective and the field looked clear, and Zade's destination could be the Kobra rendezvous.

The check-in area was crowded when I got inside the building. 'Porter, are you free?'

'Can't help you right now – '

'Here's fifty.'

'Okay, what do I do?'

'That man in the queue at the Varig desk, black hair, leather jacket, dark glasses – '

'Sure, I got him.'

'Hang around close to him and find out where he's going – I want every detail you can get – his name, flight number, destination, single or return. Another fifty if you get it right.'

I moved away and found easy cover in the crowd and did some fast checking close to Zade and extended the field progressively. It was impossible to be certain but I did the best I could. Half the people in the queue with Zade were South American Indians and there was no one I'd seen before since I'd arrived in New York.

Zade was now at the desk and the porter stayed close to him, bending over some of the baggage lined up for the scales and looking at the labels, half-turned away from Zade and working rather well: good agent material but don't let it go to your head, buster, don't get into this game because it's strictly for freaks.

I stayed where I was until he came away from the desk and began looking for me.

'He's going to Belém on Flight 238, coach class.

'All right, we'll keep moving. Single or return?'

'Goddamn it, I forgot to – '

'Never mind. What's his name?'

'He's a Mr Zane.'

Close enough. The professional terrorists in the international class don't use a cover name: they're too proud of the ones they've built their reputation on.

'Listen, I'm going to the Varig desk and I want you to keep him in sight. The other fifty's still waiting for you but not if you lose him, understand?'

'Well okay, but I could lose my job if I don't look after those people down by the – '

'I'll be ten minutes.' The queue at the desk had dwindled. 'If I'm longer than ten minutes you get double.'

I booked first class because that would allow me to go aboard before Zade and use the toilet for cover while he came through the forward compartment. Once in his seat he wouldn't come forward and since I'd be first off the plane when it landed I could set up the surveillance and take my time.

'Have a nice trip, Mr Wexford.'

'Thank you.'

The porter had moved out of sight but I'd seen the direction and found him at a drinking-fountain near the gift shops.

'He's right over there, mister.'

'Yes, all right.' I turned my back and used the window of the coffee-shop to keep him in view. He was standing at one of the telephones, looking around him as he talked. I gave the porter his fifty and told him he was off the hook and went over to the gift shop and bought a plastic rain-cape and put it on. I'd cleaned up a little in the men's room at the Hertz office and seen in the mirror that my suit had in fact been ripped at the shoulder and one knee when I'd done the get-out thing in the alley: good cover for a drunken bum but inconsistent now with the image of a first-class passenger on Flight 238.

Zade was on his way to the departure gate and I followed him through the X-ray and used one of the telephones in the Varig bay while he stood at the windows looking out. He had my image in reflection but I wasn't concerned because I couldn't board the aircraft without his seeing me and he didn't know who I was.

Ferris came on the line.

'Kennedy Airport,' I told him.

Slight pause. Possibly he'd been thinking the Kobra rendezvous had been arranged for New York and now he knew it wasn't.

'All right,' he said.

I gave him the info: Zade, Belém, flight number, so forth. When I'd finished he asked quickly:

'What time are you boarding?'

'Five minutes.'

He was thinking again: this was giving him a lot of work to do.

'Clear field?' he asked next.

I said I thought so because I'd been checking the whole time since I'd followed Zade into the bay and I'd drawn blank on two counts: no one here was watching Zade and no one was watching me.

'You think this could be a jump feint?'

'No,' I said.

Zade was too big for that. I knew something about his style and he preferred working solo, as I did, and if there were any peripheral footwork to be done he got someone else to do it and when he booked a seat for Brazil that was exactly where he was going.

I don't think he was holed up in the Lulu Belle Hotel on Broadway in order to pull his travel pattern together while his protection cell tested for ticks: he had a reputation for getting through half a dozen girls a day when he was under operational tension and the Lulu Belle had been a characteristic port of call on his way through the city.

'We haven't got anyone in Belém,' Ferris said. 'Our nearest man is in Recife.' He gave me the address and asked for a repeat. 'You think the objective might be in transit there?'

'If he is, he didn't book right through.'

'Oh bloody hell,' he said quietly and I knew what he meant. Most of the South American countries need a visa and medical certificate with smallpox on it and a subsistence attestation and anything up to four passport photos and Ferris was going to have to get them for me in New York and do it fast enough to make sure I didn't lose Zade at Belém Airport.

I wondered if he could do it. The Travel people in London are first class but if the director in the field has to use local facilities there's always a risk and you can blow a complete mission with a suspect border-franking if you're forced into frontier-jumping by the opposition: it's one of the objects of making a feint.

'Listen,' Ferris said, 'Brazil is a signatory to Interpol.'

'Fair enough.'

But it doesn't always work and he knew that.

'What about signals?' I asked him.

'Through the consulate. Booth Building, Avenue 15 de Agôsto.'

Repeat.

'I've got two minutes,' I told him. The boarding call was coming over the speakers.

'I think that's everything.'

He sounded rather vague.

Ferris is never vague.

'What happened,' I asked him, 'to that other tag?'

There was time now to think about that. I still didn't want to, but there was time.

'He was called off,' said Ferris.

'What the hell for? You had both of them running when –'

'Orders from London. He – '

'Listen,' I said, 'I want to *know*.'

Brief pause.

'It's not your concern.' His tone had gone cold. 'You are now locked on to the objective in a clear field and you know what to do and we expect you to do it. Questions?'

Quite a lot but he was right: it wasn't my concern.

In any given mission London knows as much as there is to know: as much as Briefing can get out of their files and as much as Signals can get out of their network and as much as Codes and Cyphers can get out of their computers. London gets all there is. But they don't pass all of it on. They give the director in the field precisely as much as it's essential for him to know; and out there in the field where the pattern is changing rapidly from phase to phase the director uses his own discretion as to how much his executive needs to know in order to work at his full potential.

The executive is a ferret. They put him down the hole and he doesn't ask any questions that don't concern him. All he's got to do is stay alive and come up with the goods and the only way he can do it is by trusting London. If they don't tell you everything you've got to believe it's for your own good and eventually your own salvation.

'No questions,' I said.

The line went dead.

'Would you like something to read?'

'Please.'

New York Times.

This was the edition Zade had bought.

He was sitting twelve rows behind me in the coach class: I'd gone into the forward toilet and swung the catch and shut the door against the lever, using one eye at the three-millimetre crack until I picked up his image as he passed through the front-end compartment.

Since we shall be flying for most of our journey over water, so forth.

The whine of the reactors increased and we began moving across to the runway.

I knew what they'd done with the tag. The other one.

Those four men on Broadway and West 69th Street had been local hirelings, like the man reporting on the Secretary of Defense in Washington. Two of them had still been in fit condition when Zade had left the Lulu Belle Hotel and they might have given him mobile protection on his way to the diner in Queen's: I didn't know because I wasn't there. But I'd been there when Zade had driven from the diner to the airport and there hadn't been any protection and there still hadn't been any protection at the airport itself and I could think of only one reason.

London had in fact used the tag as a disinformation tool.

The girl with the limpid brown eyes was showing us how to put on the oxygen mask when it dropped out of the panel.

At the diner I'd signalled Ferris I was locked on to the objective. The tag in the dark blue Pinto was still working but Ferris couldn't call him off because the only way to do that would be by asking me to tell him and I couldn't do it: there was to be no contact. So the Pinto had been with us to the airport and when the man had reported location Ferris had called him off and I'd watched him go.

The field was at that time clear.

But except for the Pinto tag it had been clear since we'd left the diner and it shouldn't have been.

Somewhere in the area where the executive isn't concerned, Control or Ferris or our man in Washington had rigged a bug or bust a code or in one of a dozen ways had found out that Kobra were getting worried and were ready to snatch and interrogate if the chance came: and the chance was given them. The disinformation had been pushed across to the Kobra intelligence and they'd believed the field to be clear and they'd dispensed with any protection cell for Zade at some time between his leaving the hotel and reaching the diner.

A disinfo tool doesn't always survive. Statistics at the Bureau put it at fifty-fifty. But it's no good thinking about that sort of thing or you'll jar the nerves and finish up making mistakes.

We were standing at the end of the runway.

'May I get you something to drink?'

A lock of dark hair swinging as she leaned over.

'Some milk.'

Suggest 100 mg daily.

London must be getting bloody-minded about this one. But that tag hadn't been sacrificed out of hand: Egerton was controlling the mission and his work was always calculated. He'd pushed the opposition to the point where they'd started counteracting in Milan and Geneva and Cambodia and then he'd pushed them to the point where they were so worried that they were ready for disinformation and he gave it to them, despite the cost.

From New York and into Brazil the single remaining executive was to have a clear field and open access to the Kobra rendezvous and Control had provided them. The rest was up to the executive.

The sound of the jets lifted to a scream and the brakes came off.

I began drinking my glass of milk.

12

Lagofondo

'Where are you from?'
  'London.'
  'London England?'
  'Yes.'
  'Never bin there.'
He took out a cheroot and bit the end off.
  'Wanna smoke?'
  'No.'
  'Keeps the bugs out.'
He gave a sudden loud laugh, for no reason, and lit the cigar.
  'Your first time out here?'
  'Yes,' I said.
I was thinking about Satynovich Zade.
  'You ain't no tourist, I guess.'
  'Shipping agent.'
  'With Booth Line?'
  'A subsidiary.'
The last time I saw Satynovich Zade was at Belém Airport and if I didn't see him again then the whole thing was wiped out. Extended surveillance is always nerve-racking but when you have to do it during the end-phase it induces a kind of numbness. Extended surveillance is when you're tagging a man and find out he's got a fixed destination, and instead of keeping him in view you decide to jump ahead of him into his destination and wait for him there. He's still technically under surveillance but it's extended, not constant.

There are a lot of advantages: you avoid the risk of his discovering you in his immediate area and you give yourself time to signal base or change your image or simply catch up on sleep. The obvious disadvantage is that you're relying on his going to that fixed destination and he can change his mind and you've lost him for good.

'You get anything to eat down there?'

'Yes, I had time for a hamburger.'

'At that joint? Then you got the ears and eyeballs thrown in for free!' He gave another loud laugh.

I watched the two King KX 175 Navcoms.

This was the end-phase and normally I wouldn't have let Zade out of my sight but I'd had to: the authorities at Belém threw me straight into quarantine for twenty-four hours while the objective walked away. Ferris knew it might happen and he got at the local police through Interpol and they put a tag on Zade and that was how we knew he'd booked out on Panair do Brasil Flight 540 in two days' time. The destination was Manaus, on the Amazon. We'd missed the Loide Aereo flight by three hours because of radio trouble and there are only three flights a week from Belém to Manaus at this time of the year.

So we were running the objective on extended surveillance and it had a numbing effect and I wished Chuck Lazenby would stop talking.

'You know something? That jungle's goin' to eat up that whole damn place one day an' all you'll see is the trees, like it was before.'

There was a blinding flash and the windscreens went opaque as we hit the wall of rain.

'Okay,' Chuck shouted, 'here it comes!'

He pulled a knob and the windscreen wipers started waving around but the force of water was too strong and they stopped halfway.

The instrument panel blacked out as the next flash came and then started glowing again and I took a few readings. This was a Twin Beech and the avionics were basic but adequate – the two King Navcoms, an A.D.F., a Narco transponder, Century III autopilot, a D.M.E. and a ten-year-old R.C.A. radar unit – and they were behaving normally and stayed illuminated when the next flash lit up the cockpit. The altimeter was at a steady ten thousand feet.

'It's okay when it's kinda yellow-coloured,' Chuck called out. 'When it turns white it means it's real close.'

He blew out cigar smoke and adjusted the throttles.

Ferris had found him for me. Ferris had worked non-stop for thirty-six hours and I don't think anyone but a first-class director in the field could have done it and that was why Control had pulled him in from Tokyo for the Kobra mission. He brought my forged papers with him from New York and spent half an hour talking icily to the Immigration officers, hinting at 'obstruction' and 'incompetence' and using the Interpol connection until they got the message and let me through.

He also switched my cover because of the Burdick situation: the journalist image was no longer appropriate and I was now a shipping agent's representative looking for small-boat charter franchise along the Amazon between Manaus and Itacoatiara.

'Gonna ship a little water,' said Chuck. 'She always does. You know what they stuck this windshield in with? Horse shit!'

A trickle was beginning along the left edge of the panel and I kept my legs out of the way. The windscreen wipers were now on the move again and we could see patches of cloud whipping past.

The Burdick situation was now very interesting.

Ferris had seen the same report in the *New York Times* as I had, and Satynovich Zade had probably been on the lookout for it when he'd bought a paper from the box outside the Varig Airlines area at Kennedy.

Yesterday Pat Burdick, daughter of the Defense Secretary, left Washington for the isolated river-village of Lagofondo near the Amazon in Brazil, with a small party of fellow-adventurers and two experienced guides. 'It's to be an entomological field study,' she told reporters before she left, 'and I guess the bugs out there in the jungle ought to be pretty impressive. It's also to get me away from the intense political atmosphere here in Washington for a while, because I've been finding it very confining and – you know – claustrophobic.' There was no truth whatsoever, she added, that there was any rift between herself and her family. For security reasons the names of her companions are not presently being revealed.

A flash lit the cockpit again and then the din of the rain

on the windscreen stopped abruptly as we ran into clear weather. The pale blue ring of Saint Elmo's fire vanished from the propellers and the full moon drifted above the sky-line.

'Easy come,' said Chuck, 'easy go!'

He got out another cigar and lit up.

'Was that a bad one?'

'They're all bad, if you wanna worry. Me, I shut my eyes till I'm out the other side.' He laughed noisily and blew out a cloud of smoke.

The second report in the newspaper had been a syndicated piece on the Defense Secretary's brief speech at the Quaker Hotel in Washington on the increasing need for sophisticated armaments. In the last few lines of the report it was stated that 'Mr Burdick was seen to be suffering from the strain of his many recent engagements.'

Ferris hadn't picked this up because he'd been working the clock round. I didn't know if Zade had noticed it. By itself, it wasn't significant.

'I been runnin' the night-mails a couple of years now, you know that? Start at nine at night, finish around four in the mornin', maybe five.'

'You must know Manaus pretty well.'

'Sure do.' He cranked his seat up an inch and adjusted the soiled belt. 'Like I say, that place is goin' to get eaten up by the jungle one day. Industry's dying, 'cause they won't take the export tax off of electrical goods, an' what else've you got? Bit of rubber, maybe some gold in the mines, animal trapping. Listen – ' he took the cigar out of his mouth and jabbed it in the air – 'that place is a thousand miles from the nearest city an' there's no roads in or out, y'imagine that? Okay when the rubber boom was on, but now there's no real money around any more.'

'No tourists?'

He jerked his red crew-cut head to look at me. 'You kiddin'? You know what the Brazilians call this jungle? The Green Hell – I guess you must've heard that.' He pointed with his cigar again, downwards. 'We run outa gas or blow an engine or what the devil an' we go down there an' can't

163

get up again, that's it – you know what I mean? The trees'd just close over this crate like we'd never existed.'

He went on for a while and I thought about Burdick.

In Washington Ferris had told me that Robert Finberg was the only man in the United States who knew about Kobra and knew about our counter-operation but we now assumed Burdick himself had also known and was using Finberg as his representative. We also assumed that at this moment Burdick alone knew, and that with half a dozen major agencies including the F.B.I. and the C.I.A. at his disposal he was keeping strict hush.

Ferris had told me nothing beyond that. London may have told him nothing beyond that, or he might know some of the background but felt it wouldn't concern the executive. Fair enough, but a ferret can think.

Theory: somewhere among the networks of international intelligence an agent had run slap into some highly explosive information – someone like the late Milos Zarkovic – or they'd asked Zarkovic to bring it across to the West. It had been for the eyes of the Bureau only and it had personally concerned the U.S. Secretary of Defense. He could have called in the C.I.A. and he hadn't: he had asked the Bureau to handle it for him with no one else involved and to handle it with the highest possible discretion.

Facts: I'd discovered a tag on Burdick in Washington. He had used his rank to bring me out of Cambodia. His daughter was on an insect-hunting expedition along the Amazon but not on account of a 'family rift'. He himself was seen to be suffering the strain of his 'many recent engagements'.

These facts taken separately were not significant. Put them together and it didn't seem terribly illogical that Satynovich Zade was now on his way to the Kobra rendezvous somewhere along the Amazon.

Question: how much were they asking of James Burdick? It wouldn't be money.

'Oh holy cow, we got some more shit comin' at us!'

Chuck adjusted the mixture handles and I saw the flame from the port exhaust change to a bluish pink. Ahead of us the broken stratus deck was beginning to pile up into thunderheads.

'How far are we out, Chuck?'

'Huh? Twenty minutes, I guess. Take thirty, through that stuff.' A distant streak zig-zagged across the mountainous dark of the clouds. 'Don't mind flyin' through it but I don't like landin' in it, know what I mean?'

I said I did.

We began going down and I watched the altimeter, already feeling the warmth of the lower air. Manaus was three degrees below the Equator and the humidity was in the eighties at this time of the year and the man in the outfitter's in Belém had suggested light-weave tropical kit and I'd dumped the New York suit into a rubbish bin together with the rain-cape. There'd been time to book out on the same Panair with Zade but we'd have risked blowing the mission and losing the executive because this was the penetration phase and I had to go in very close to the target and the target was Kobra and the Kobra people were now ultra-sensitive about surveillance: their operation was almost certainly centred on the entomological study group along the Amazon and they would be wary of strangers, so I had to jump in ahead of Zade and establish myself as a new image instead of a passenger who'd followed him in from Belém.

'Jesus, look at this!'

Rain hit the windscreens with a white explosion.

Chuck adjusted the set and I heard Manaus Approach Control come in, clearing him down to two thousand feet.

I sat back and went over the mass of data Ferris had given me to study in Belém: the layout of Manaus, location of consulate, airport, police headquarters, so forth. I'd dumped the set of maps when I'd got the essential topography into my head because I was going to present the image of somebody who knew the place well: somebody in other words who hadn't followed any of the Kobra cell to Brazil.

I didn't know if the Pat Burdick party were in Manaus itself or somewhere along the river so I'd gone over the outlying terrain rather thoroughly. It consisted of two elements:

the river and the jungle.

Okay 9 Whisky, please turn left heading 200.

Water was trickling again down the side of the windscreen.

Three very bright flashes in quick succession.

'An' screw you too, baby!' Chuck shifted the cigar to the other side of his mouth and cranked his seat down an inch.

The starboard wing dipped suddenly as I looked past the pilot's head, and the moon lifted out of sight above us. The altimeter was down to a thousand as we intercepted the final approach course a mile out with the airspeed on 90.

The rain had eased and visibility looked workable but I stopped reviewing the local data and noted the angle of the door-lever and the disposition of the fire extinguishers and made a few mental practice runs with the seat-belt release because Chuck was a bit worried and not talking any more.

Bright flash.

The thunder was still rolling when we began going in with the first of the approach lights flicking out of sight below the fuselage.

Gear-down light on.

Flaps at full.

500.

9 Whisky, you are cleared to land.

'Roger.'

200.

Another flash lit the cockpit.

I could feel the heat of the tropical night seeping into the cabin. A haze of lights drifted past.

100.

One bounce.

The blades of the ceiling fan droned above my head.

I could smell creosote on the moist air, or something like creosote; maybe it was the stuff in the little bowls: they'd lifted the bed and stood its legs in the little bowls and then poured the stuff in, almost to the brim. The boy at the desk downstairs had said it was against the centipedes.

I opened the 8 × 50's a fraction on the fulcrum and refocused. Chuck Lazenby had told me where to buy them after we'd got into Manaus. The trouble was they misted up every thirty seconds and I had to keep wiping them.

Chuck had said he'd earned a crate of beer for bringing the Beech in through that storm and I'd spent half an hour with him getting some more data on the environs while he got slowly drunk: the flight in had worried him more than he admitted.

In the circular field of vision I could see their heads, below in the courtyard. Sometimes they disappeared as they moved, then came back into view: the foreground images were complex and consisted of the Indian screen across the lower half of my window, the uprights of the veranda and the leaves of the fan-palms in the courtyard. With the lowering sun throwing oblique light across the hotel I needed this much cover to haze out any glint from the lenses.

There were five men down there, and a woman.

The girl sat more or less in the middle of them.

Satynovich Zade had come through on the noon plane, still with no baggage. I saw Ferris a few yards behind him but we made no contact at any time: he was booked in at the Hotel Amazonas. He stayed at the airport long enough to see me lock on to Zade and then got a taxi.

Zade was one of the faces I had in the 8 × 50's, blurred and merging with the leaves. He was sitting next to the woman, very relaxed, his dark glasses occasionally swinging upwards and turning slowly to scan the first-storey verandas. At these times I kept the binoculars perfectly still.

We had come the four miles to Lagofondo in separate boats from Manaus harbour. I had told the Indian boy to keep half a mile distant because the risk of Zade's getting lost was now almost nil: the terrain on each side of the river was thick jungle where according to Chuck Lazenby only a lunatic would go on his own. On the river, nearly seven miles wide in this area, the small-boat traffic provided adequate cover.

Lagofondo was at the neck of a tributary: a cluster of water-front cane-and-thatch dwellings along the steep bank where the jute reeds had been hacked away to make room, with a banana grove and some farm buildings and a church. The hotel had been a German mission house during the rubber boom; it had started to rot when the slump came and had then been repaired and was starting to rot again.

A mosquito whined close and I waited for the silence, then hit the side of my head, bringing blood away on my fingers. I put the field glasses up again.

They were sitting in the shade of the palms: everyone here sat in the shade. The thermometer in the hall had been at 103° when I checked in, and the boy at the desk said it was cooler after the rain. An hour ago I had been sitting in the courtyard myself, talking to a Dutchman who was here collecting Indian artifacts for a mail order line he was running in Canada. I hadn't once looked at the group of people on the other side of the fountain: I didn't want to see them but I wanted them to see me, to establish the image. Zade and another man had been drinking pisco sours and the rest had asked for mineral water. They had talked now and then, but with an effort, and always led by Zade. They had talked about the Amazon and its insects, mostly in English with strong accents.

Sometimes I had heard the soft frightened tones of the girl.

I watched her now. She was centred in the field of vision: pale, fair haired, sitting perfectly still and looking up at the others only when they spoke directly to her. The woman spoke to her more often than the others. Her name was Shadia.

I moved the glasses.

They had that vague familiarity of faces seen before only in photographs: I'd seen the photographs in London and Ferris had shown me some more on the plane between Los Angeles and Washington four days ago.

Sabri Sassine: undercover operator for the Turkish *Dev-Genc*, released from gaol in the Argentine. Carlos Ramirez: mercenary terrorist, explosives expert. Francisco Ventura: freelance saboteur and sometime Black September assassin. Ilyich Kuznetski: another freelance with the Simplon Tunnel bombing on his record and a gaol shoot-out in Rome. Satynovich Zade: currently wanted by the Dutch police for a political assassination reportedly undertaken for the P.L.A.

I didn't know who the woman was.

I knew who the college girl was.

She was sipping some water as I watched her.

The woman was talking to her now but I couldn't hear the words intelligibly. The accent was Polish. I moved the field glasses and studied her again, wiping the condensation off the lenses and steadying them with my elbows on my knees. I am a bad judge of people's age but she looked thirty-five. Sun-tan, auburn hair hanging loose, very pale blue eyes that hardly ever moved: when she wanted to look at something she turned her head, in the way of a cat.

Possibly she had been taken on as a chaperon for Pat Burdick but these men were terrorists and if they wanted to search the girl they would do that and if they wanted to rape her they would do that: I didn't think the woman was a chaperon. More probably she was the current partner of one of the men but in half an hour's constant surveillance I hadn't seen who he was: she hadn't touched any of them, or sat particularly close. Ten minutes ago Zade had said something to her in Polish and she had cut in quickly, turning away, and there'd been a short silence among the group.

I moved the field glasses again to watch Ramirez.

Above my head the fan droned rhythmically: the blades were out of balance and the electric motor was vibrating with each revolution. It produced a warm draught, but the sweat went on running down my face and steaming the lenses.

I wondered again what they were asking of the Defense Secretary.

He would know by now. They would have presented their terms.

The fact was that Burdick could have called in security or investigatory or counter-espionage agencies and he hadn't done that and I could see only one obvious reason: he'd been ordered not to. If this were the standard hostage-and-demands situation then the United States Secretary of Defense was at present under the orders of the five men down there:

in the courtyard, so long as his daughter was alive.

There was of course a difference in the standard pattern but it didn't affect the situation as such: in this case the hostage hadn't been kidnapped. Pat Burdick was studying insects along the Amazon with a few companions and probably writing home and probably sending photographs as evidence. Only two people had known the truth and one was Finberg and he was dead. The other was James Burdick.

This difference in the standard pattern was crucial. If the group had seized their hostage and concealed her whereabouts there would be nothing Burdick could do for them: the F.B.I. and the counter-terrorist department of the C.I.A. would have been mobilized and the group's demands would have been made public and Burdick would not have been *allowed* to meet them.

The demands wouldn't be for money. They would be for something only Burdick and a few men in similar positions could supply: military information, arms, technological data, access to ultra-secret documents or blueprints or designs. Pressure to supply them, in whole or in part, could be applied to the Defense Secretary *only if he alone knew* that his daughter's life was in jeopardy and that these demands were being made.

According to the Bureau intelligence, passed to the executive by his director in the field, Burdick alone knew.

London doesn't pass out disinformation to the people in the field. It doesn't tell you much but when it tells you something then you can believe it.

The glasses were misted up again and I lowered them and wiped them with the corner of my handkerchief. I could feel a swelling on my scalp above the ear: the blood on my fingers had been my own, drawn out by a female mosquito. There hadn't been time to ask for malaria shots but the incubation period would see me through the mission if the chances of survival were good enough.

I didn't think they were.

This was the end-phase and there was the target: the Kobra rendezvous. When I reported to Ferris in a few minutes from now he was going to throw me the final directive and I knew what it was.

I steadied the field glasses again. The right shoulder was still inclined to ache if I kept it still too long: it had taken most of the impact when I'd hit the ground in the alley in New York. One of the group – Sassine – was moving about restlessly and I wanted to keep them all in sight in case anyone thought of coming up here to my room. They shouldn't do, because security was total: they'd never seen me before and I'd made no specific surveillance of them except from my room and behind adequate cover. But I had believed security to be total when the wall had blown out in Phnom Penh.

Note in passing: James Burdick could say nothing to anyone because his daughter's life was in hazard. The converse must also be true: his daughter had been warned that if she tried to leave the group or seek the help of the police she would bring about her father's killing.

I watched them for another fifteen minutes and then signalled Ferris.

Code-intro. No bugs.

I made my report and he started putting questions: did it look as if any exchange were to be made here in Brazil; did it look as if they were waiting for other members of the Kobra cell; did it look as if they felt on top of the situation they had created; so forth.

No, no and yes.

He was silent for half a minute.

'They've still got the road up,' he said at last.

'Have they?'

Directive. He'd been in signals with London.

'This is really quite big. Quite substantial.'

Egerton's word for it.

I began worrying.

The phase had only just opened and there wasn't much I could do: to get as close to the target as this I'd had to present a frank image and rely on cover and this was very limiting. There hadn't been time to get any leverage, any kind of counter-force that we could apply against the group as a whole: Satynovich Zade was clearly the top kick and I'd obviously go for him as soon as I could arrange something workable but it'd have to be a hundred per cent effective because a stalemate wouldn't be good enough – they still had the girl in their hands.

I thought I could get at Zade and keep him alive and use him to argue with but it might take hours or even days because a lot would depend on luck.

'They told me,' I said, 'that it was substantial. What are you trying to do, for Christ's sake – put the fear of – '

'There's nothing to worry about,' he said.

I shut up.

It had just sounded so bloody silly to remind me the mission was 'substantial' because Egerton used that kind of word where people like Parkis or Sargent would say 'hot-war level' or 'Minister's priority' or whatever term they picked on to express something that was going to make a lot of waves, win or lose.

But Ferris doesn't ever say anything bloody silly and he'd just told me he'd been in signals with London through the consulate in Manaus and London had instructed him to remind me that we weren't on just another field exercise and that meant they wanted me to do something difficult, and what Egerton really wanted me to understand was that it was going to be worth it.

Not in terms of any reward, of course: apart from a living wage and a bit extra for roses for Moira we don't ask any reward for doing something we couldn't live without doing even though we know it's going to kill us in the end. Egerton meant in terms of making the necessary effort.

Bloody London for you: they think that when you've finally got the target in your sights and you're set up to go in and get the objective you're either too dead-beat or too ready to chicken out if the going gets rough.

Gut-think: not precisely true.

Egerton was a worried man, that was all. The red light was on the board and he was sitting up there in Signals with his legs hooked over that crate of stuff they hadn't unpacked yet and his shoes covered in clay from down there in the street and he was developing purpose-tremor: with the executive on the target and 'substantial' considerations in the balance he didn't want anything to go wrong. So he'd sent his little ferret a shot in the arm.

'I'm not worrying,' I told Ferris.

'Of course you're not.'

Ramirez had moved and I watched his head vanish and reappear beyond a gap in the leaves. I wasn't using the field glasses because I had the phone in one hand and wouldn't be able to control their movement: any terrorist in the international class is constantly sensitive to surveillance and will catch the glint of a lens if care isn't used.

'Just give me a directive,' I said.

I didn't want to stay on the phone too long because that group down there could split up at any minute and I'd need to keep track of them as long as I could.

'Yes,' I heard Ferris saying. 'We want you to get the objective for us as soon as you can do it safely.'

'The girl,' I said.

He didn't answer right away. I could hear something like static from his end: he was probably in the wireless room at the consulate, and not at the Hotel Amazonas. Conceivably he was getting stuff direct from Control while he had me on the line. I didn't know, and I wasn't going to ask because if he wanted me to know then he'd tell me.

'No,' he said in a moment, 'not the girl. We want the whole group.'

In a couple of seconds I said:

'You want the whole of the Kobra cell.'

There are always a lot of repeats when a major directive is being put on the line, especially when it's being done on the phone. It's not a time for mistakes.

'The whole cell,' Ferris said, 'yes.'

Another mosquito was whining faintly near my head, but I didn't think, for the moment, about swatting it.

'Alive?' I asked Ferris.

He answered straight away because he'd expected the question and had already got a directive on it.

'That's immaterial. But if you can get the girl out, everyone would appreciate it.'

13
Shadia

'The damned creature was twenty feet long, can you imagine?'

Van de Jong broke some bread.

'Who came out of it?' I asked him.

He'd come to join me for dinner at my table and it suited my book: he was a compulsive talker so I didn't have to listen, and he provided good cover. The solitary image is always suspect.

'They *both* came out of it, of course! He does it for the tourists, when there are any. Listen to me – the anaconda does not crush its victim. It merely throttles it. So all this fellow does is to keep the coils away from his throat. In any case, man is not its habitual prey, so it is just confused when a man comes to wrestle with it, you see.' He gave a laugh, showing a gold tooth. 'But it is fun to watch. You should see it. I will take you tomorrow.'

The Kobra cell was across the room: the five men and the woman they called Shadia. The Burdick girl was sitting in the corner with someone on each side of her. They were eating, but seemed more to be waiting.

The Indian boy came to our table again.

'*Vôce precisa alguma coisa?*'

'*Nada. Tudo está bem.*'

We were eating *paiche* with *farinha* and de Jong was on his third rum punch: he had so far made three jokes about the ulcer I was using as an excuse for not drinking.

The Burdick girl looked pale in the light of the oil lamps. She didn't talk very often but sometimes I could make out a few of the words. The woman was asking her about life in an American college and the answers were token and desultory: 'It's okay, I guess,' and 'you can get into a whole lot of subjects,' that kind of thing. The Kobra policy was consistent: it was public knowledge that Pat Burdick was on an expedition in Brazil with selected companions, and she could even be seen there if anyone were interested. The conversation I had so far overheard was about the Amazon, insects, and American college life: all subjects appropriate to the cover. The party wasn't keeping to its quarters upstairs, but was eating openly in public, and I assumed that if anyone went over to the table in the corner and said excuse me but aren't you Pat Burdick she would say yes, I am.

I didn't intend to do that.

'It is different with those damned piranhas, my friend. Have you seen them at work?'

I said I hadn't.

It had taken me a long time to analyse the data inherent in the directive Ferris had given me. London doesn't tell you more than you need to know for your health but it can't stop you forming your own conclusions.

'They are not so big,' said de Jong, 'but when they are in a feeding frenzy they can pick a hundred-pound animal down to the bones, can you imagine?' He speared his fish steak with his fork. 'Of course, I suppose we avenge ourselves!' His laughter was attracting some attention among the group of animal trappers near the bar, and someone laughed in response. He seemed to like this, and raised his glass of rum.

The big ceiling fans stirred the air above our heads, and sent the fly-papers twisting. The nights were cooler here: the thermometer by the desk was down to 97° and they'd thrown open the double doors to let the air in through the mosquito screens.

Conclusion 1: Since Ferris had instructed me to knock out the Kobra cell, termination being optional, it was obvious that any physical threat to the Secretary of Defense could be dealt with. Pat Burdick must have been told that if she tried to escape or call the police her father would be killed and in most hostage situations the captor means what he says. But if I could knock out Kobra it would amount to outside intervention even though the girl hadn't asked for it, and the Bureau must be covering the Defense Secretary in some way.

Conclusion 2: This meant that I could in fact get a message to the girl, to the effect that if she could escape, her father would be safe. But there was a risk and London hadn't told me to do that. Ignore.

Conclusion 3: The Defense Secretary was in constant touch with London and would know that London had someone penetrating the Kobra operation and had obviously asked for his daughter's life to be spared if that were possible. But I believed that even if the Defense Secretary were not involved, the Bureau might have set up the Kobra mission in any case.

Corollary to Conclusion 3: Regardless of the Burdick involvement, London wanted Kobra and they wanted Kobra with that brand of calculated desperation that would keep a human computer like Egerton at the signals console in Whitehall till he dropped dead of fatigue, the brand of desperation that had knocked out one agent after another in Milan and Geneva and Cambodia and New York in order to leave one man alive in the end-phase to do the job.

'That is why my mail order business is successful, you see.' De Jong slit open a papaya with his knife. 'I give them the real thing, and they know it. The jewellery is crude but it is *genuine*. Look at this!'

He began throwing small objects on to the woven cloth.

I heard the telephone at the desk begin ringing.

'Dyed bones and teeth, fish scales, caiman scales, seed pods, stones. Aren't they attractive? Wouldn't *you* be tempted to buy this kind of thing if you saw examples in your own mail box?'

Said I would.

I had looked across at the woman several times during the past half an hour and she had twice found my eyes on her. She was young and sexually aware and would expect the distant attention of any man in the room and I was duly giving her mine. The second time she didn't look away and I'd finally turned my head to hear what de Jong was saying.

'I suppose you know what this is? It's a blowgun dart. And I suppose you know what they put on the tip when they mean to kill. Every schoolboy knows.' He pushed the pointed sliver of bone across the cloth towards me.

176

The telephone had stopped ringing.

'Curare,' said de Jong. 'Of course when I sell these things through the mail there is nothing on their tips – I need live clients, not dead ones!' He laughed loudly and got an echo from the group of steadily-drinking trappers near the bar.

One of the boys was on his way across to the table in the corner.

'You know something? The C.I.A. is in trouble right now for stocking these gadgets, can you imagine? But they use sodium cyanide. You know what they call the gun? A "nondiscernible microbionoculator". Where is progress, my friend?' He raised his glass of rum.

Zade and Kuznetski were leaving the corner table and taking Pat Burdick with them to the lobby, the boy leading the way. It looked pre-arranged. The three others remained at the table with Shadia. I would have given a lot to follow them out after thirty seconds' interval but that would be fatal.

There was a brief exchange of voices in the lobby and then I heard footsteps on the stairs, hurrying. They were taking the call in one of their rooms. My watch read 21:17 but that didn't mean the call hadn't been arranged to be made precisely on the hour: in a remote village on the Amazon a delay of seventeen minutes would be routine.

In Pat Burdick's frightened eyes there had been the light of hope as she had passed our table. She might not know the terms of the deal but in any case they wouldn't mean anything to her because she was young and she didn't want to die and she wouldn't care if these people were asking an entire squadron of nuclear bombers in exchange for her life. But even if she had enough pride to tell her father he must expend her if that was the only way, she wouldn't be allowed to say it. Zade would have rehearsed her and he'd be there beside her.

Daddy, you must do whatever they tell you.

Van de Jong pushed another artifact across the table.

'Now look at this. Isn't it charming?'

Nobody else had left the dining-room.

Ventura, Ramirez and Sassine were looking casually

around them, their glances passing across our table and moving on. Shadia sat watching me, perfectly still.

'I get them from the garimpeiros, when they come down from the goldfields across the Xingu River. I don't know where *they* get them, but I would say it was from the prostitutes up there. Don't you think this one is charming?'

I looked down at it, away from Shadia's light blue gaze.

It looked like some kind of nutshell, with apertures carved into it, after the fashion of Chinese trinkets. It appeared to be filled with coarse, springy hair.

Daddy, they won't hurt me until midnight. Then they say they're going to start hurting me. Can't you do something?

'Of course I don't sell these to my regular clients.'

He gave a confidential laugh, showing his gold tooth.

Shadia watched me.

I looked down again.

The shell was painted gaudily on the outside, in bright childish colours.

'There was quite a demand in Copenhagen, until they got bored with them. Now I sell through the adult bookstores, in Canada.'

If you still love me, Daddy, please do what they tell you. Please.

Question: what would James Burdick *not* be prepared to do?

'It's amusing,' I nodded to de Jong.

'One thing I guarantee.' He leaned towards me and the beads of sweat on his pink face gleamed in the light of the oil lamp. 'It comes from a woman. The men are too proud of themselves!'

I assumed that Pat Burdick was the go-between. In most cases of hostage-and-demand the captor handles the communications but in cases where he knows his business he will leave the hostage to make the appeal directly, usually over a telephone or sometimes on tape. This is logical because the demands are usually made to a man – almost always the victim's father – and if he receives threats from another man his male aggressiveness comes into play and he considers himself challenged and will sometimes try to brave it out and urge the police to go in fighting on his behalf.

I had sufficient respect for Satynovich Zade to believe he was handling this operation professionally.

Daddy, they say I won't ever see you again.

In my trade we don't take things personally or if you want to put it another way we take things about as personally as a pilot does when he drops his bombs. But when I killed Zade it would be with a sense of satisfaction.

'Take it. I give you the damned thing!' said de Jong.

He threw up his pink hands, laughing generously.

Shadia turned her head a degree to look at him, then looked at me again. It occurred to me that the cell had been making enquiries into the guests here: there were probably fifteen or twenty in the hotel. Their first question to the staff would concern the time of arrival here of each guest. I had arrived on the same day as Zade and there'd been nothing I could do about that.

'Thank you. It's a charming souvenir.'

I put the thing into my pocket to please him.

There were voices upstairs suddenly, and the men near the bar stopped talking and looked at the ceiling. For a moment the whole dining-room was quiet, then people began talking again. In five minutes Zade and Kuznetski came down again with the girl and crossed over to their table. She had been crying, but was making an effort to appear normal, and I don't think anyone would have noticed it unless they'd been watching her closely.

Flat white light came against the windows and a few people turned their heads and looked away again. In a moment distant thunder rolled.

'Have you been here when there is a storm?' asked de Jong.

'Yes.'

He wiped his pink face dry.

'I tell you something. This is the most poisonous climate in the entire world, it has the most poisonous insects and the most poisonous reptiles. But people come here. I come, and you come.' He drained his glass. 'This place has something, yes?'

'Yes. Something for everyone.'

The rain roared incessantly on the roof.

Light flared white in the room through the slats in the shutters, silvering her body for an instant. She said something but it was lost in the drumming of the thunder overhead. The building shook.

Then there was the warm light of the oil lamp again, glowing on her tawny skin and the mass of body hair as she writhed on the bed with her long legs, reminding me in colouring of a tiger lily because she was heavily freckled, reminding me too of Marianne of the Villa Madeleine, because they both wanted the light on, and everything to be slow.

Shadia said something again, speaking in Polish with the Varsovie accent and laughing a little, perhaps afraid of the storm. She wanted me to put it here, and here, as she moved restlessly on the bed for me, her sweat slipping.

'I like it like this,' she said, 'with the storm.'

She was afraid of it. And probably of nothing else.

I remembered her now.

When Fogel had fired at point-blank range into the faces of the two *Deuxième Bureau* men in Paris last year there'd been a woman involved, a native of Poland who had joined the new extremist group being formed in Athens. She had trained as usual in the Palestinian guerilla camps, in this case with the Japanese Red Army units. The only place in Europe where she refused to operate was Germany, and she would have nothing to do with the Baader-Meinhof group.

She was typical: restless the whole time and never stopping to enjoy a new sensation before we went on to the next. Nothing could satisfy her because she couldn't wait, couldn't give it time. I'd known these women before: they're afraid of letting go, and in the end the male streak in them sends them out into the streets with grenades to prove their point that they can't love and so they're going to hate.

She spoke in English sometimes against the drumming of the storm.

'Oh my God, darling.'

Nothing that meant anything.

Fierce light and almost immediate vibration as the thunder banged.

These were the more dangerous moments: when I couldn't hear anything but the storm. At these moments I watched the door.

She had been wandering in the courtyard, around midnight, knowing I would see her because I had to pass that way to my room. Van de Jong had been trying to talk me into becoming a part-time representative in his mail order business because I travelled quite a lot and seemed interested; it was excellent cover because his voice carried, and we had talked till twelve.

'Now,' she said in Polish, 'this time *now*.'

But of course it didn't work.

The force of the rain rattled the tiles overhead. The hotel was perfectly square, its four sides surrounding the courtyard; and the Spanish tiles sloped at a low angle, sending the flood of water into the guttering and forming cascades through the gaps where it had broken.

'Slowly,' she said, out of breath.

But her long hands were still restless and unsatisfied. Later she'd find more release in the orgasmic flash of a grenade.

The thunder came and I watched the door again.

Because this was a Venus trap.

'Oh darling,' she said in English, 'oh my God.'

The door was locked but there wasn't a bolt.

They might have a key but it wasn't material: they would need approximately the same amount of time to open the door with a key as to smash it inwards. I had estimated from three to four seconds for them to reach me from the passage outside, including the opening of the door. That was long enough but only if I stayed alert.

Her thighs twisted again under me.

'Where was this?' I asked her.

In the glow from the oil lamp the tattooed number showed blue on her skin.

'Auschwitz,' she said.

'You were only a child.'

'Yes. Four years old.'

Light flashed and this time she cried out and I held her close so that she'd feel less afraid, my feelings ambivalent and impossible to relate: she was a female of the species and we were making what kind of love we were able and I wanted to protect her from the storm, but I would put the chances at fifty-fifty that she'd brought me in here to get me killed.

'Oh my God, darling.'

She seemed to think this was an English idiom.

In the tropical heat of the room she smelled fresh and magnificent, the animal scents pouring from her body. If it weren't for this I would have been useless to her because the libido was having to compete with the forebrain and the forebrain was concerned with a possible threat to life. I didn't think she would have brought an unknown male to her room because she was bored with the members of the Kobra cell or because they were bored with her frustrated carnality, driving her to take anyone available. Nymphomania is a common mechanism of women terrorists, often expressed in lesbianism but not always; and Shadia could simply be on a sex trip tonight, trying to relieve her tensions: the cell was in touch with the Secretary of Defense and some kind of rendezvous might have been agreed and the most dangerous phase in this situation is the rendezvous. James Burdick could draft in a regiment of marksmen to the point of exchange and they knew that.

But I preferred to assume this was a Venus trap.

They can work both ways.

'How did you bruise your shoulder like this?'

'In a car smash,' I said.

'Where?'

'London.'

Normally the trap is one way because the woman – or sometimes the boy – doesn't know anything classified: the object is simply entrapment. But Shadia was more than the routine bait: she was informed and had access to almost limitless intelligence within the Kobra cell, or they wouldn't have needed her at the rendezvous.

She lay quiet, jerking a little when the next flash came,

then lying still again. The rain was a steady roaring: we couldn't see it because of the shutters; it could have been anything, a thousand drummers.

'Are you here for a story?' she asked me, close to my ear.

'What sort of story?'

'I mean are you a journalist?'

She spoke in Polish all the time now.

'No. I'm a shipping agent.'

'Of course. They told me.'

Three seconds.

'Who did?'

But *don't* sound too interested because you don't *mind* people asking questions about you.

'The manager.'

Pass off.

'He's a very good chap – he's given me a lot of advice about the shipping situation. Apparently the Booth Line's got it pretty well sewn up.'

'He is a nice man, yes. With that wife – have you seen her?'

'Yes.'

'Oh God, what a face!' She paused. 'Maybe if I asked him, he might – ' she used her fingers on me and the bed shook to her low laughter.

Flash.

The thunder took a little time now. The sound of the rain seemed less.

I watched the door.

'I thought you were a journalist,' she said.

There wouldn't be any specific action I could take because they wouldn't come singly but in the three to four seconds available I could reach the knife and swing her in front of me, the point at her throat.

She didn't know I'd seen the knife. It was in the top drawer and I'd left the drawer an inch open because the handle wasn't easy to pull. She had been a few minutes in the bathroom, earlier; it was only a paper knife but adequate.

'Why should I be?' (Why should I be a journalist?)

She let it go but came back to it later and took it the whole way, letting out information and feeling it for the response, then letting some more out, like a thin-drawn line: the American girl was 'quite famous' and she and her friends were 'looking after her' and didn't want any journalists snooping around, so forth.

For ten or twelve minutes she worked within the precise confines of the Kobra cover released to the press and made only two small mistakes: she didn't ask me how I'd arrived in Lagofondo and invite a slip; and she didn't ask me if I'd booked ahead at this hotel. She could have passed off both questions in a loose ad lib context: they'd had trouble getting seats on the Panair plane; and the hotel had tried to give them double rooms because there were no singles left; or any one of a dozen variations.

I filled in as necessary: I thought they were a linguist group because I'd overheard some of their conversation in the dining-room (because that was why they'd taken their meals there: to be overheard); it would be a pleasure to meet the quite famous young American girl (appropriate interest theme); my firm had an option on a small-boat charter operation in Bermuda and I might be called out there at any time (gratuitous but useful as projected cover: I would have to leave here when Kobra did, and might do it overtly at least as far as the first airport in transit.)

In the absence of data I was assuming two things and both could be wrong and one could be fatal if wrong: that the exchange of the hostage wouldn't take place in Brazil, and that she hadn't brought me here to pin me for killing but to tap me for information.

'It's going away,' she said, 'the storm.'

'Yes.'

She moved again, throwing her long hard body across mine and covering my face with her hair, talking incessantly in her own tongue, goading herself to the edge of frenzy in the heat of the night and lying still, in the end, lying still with the tears streaming in the glow of the lamp.

'I hate you,' she said.

'I know.'

184

'Do you know why?'

'Yes. The thing is,' I said, 'you won't let yourself.'

Then the phone began ringing.

The moon was behind cloud and it was almost totally dark and I didn't see the thing until it sprang up with a screech right in front of me with one of its wings hitting my face as it took off.

I lay perfectly still for ten minutes, listening for any sounds from below. Faint voices rose but their tone hadn't changed: they assumed it was normal for a buzzard to screech in the night. The bloody things were black and they roosted on the tiles and I'd known that and I should have been prepared for them and I wasn't.

I began moving again, testing each tile before I put my weight on it. Some of them made slight cracking sounds as my movement displaced them, and I stopped every time it happened.

The doctor hadn't arrived yet.

Within twenty minutes I judged I was above the room where they were talking. I couldn't tell whether they were in Pat Burdick's room but assumed they were not; I couldn't hear Shadia's voice and further assumed she was in the girl's room, keeping her company until the doctor came. When the phone had rung she'd got off the bed and taken it a little distance so that I couldn't hear the caller's voice. In a few seconds she'd hung up and got her bath robe and left me without saying anything.

It had been too dangerous to try getting close to the Kobra quarters because the corridors were open to the court-yard and without visual cover so I phoned a complaint through to the desk about the noise people were making and the man at the switchboard said the little *Americana* was ill with a fever and the *médico* had been summoned from Manaus.

I moved again on the tiles, lying on one side and resting my ear on the baked clay surface. The voices were no louder because there was too much space between the overlapping curves; but I could hear occasional words, some in Polish and a few in poor English with a Spanish accent: Ramirez. From what I'd seen of the Kobra cell, Zade was the leader and Kuznetski his second in command. Ramirez was specifically a technician, as an expert on explosives; Ventura appeared to be the least disciplined member of the group and I'd heard Zade cut him short once or twice in the dining-room when he'd begun straying from the conversational subjects appropriate to their cover. Sassine talked very little but I didn't have the impression that he was intimidated by either Zade or the group as a whole: I put him down as a slow-burn operator who preferred listening and assessing what was said. Shadia had given nothing useful away when I'd been in her room but she had the reputation of being a ruthless and dedicated activist and a formidable adjunct to any task force; I suspected she had joined the group on account of some sexual involvement, probably with Zade.

I turned and lay on my back, cupping my hands backwards in front of my ears and resting my elbows. By 02:13 I'd picked up and put together a dozen phrases, mostly in Polish and probably spoken by Zade and Kuznetski; and it was clear that some kind of crisis had arisen and the inference was that it concerned Pat Burdick's fever.

At 02:13 a Volkswagen arrived outside the front of the hotel and I heard the doctor being shown to the room below the part of the roof where I was lying. He began speaking in Portuguese but had to switch to English when they didn't understand.

Various routine questions, some of which I heard distinctly because he spoke slowly for them: how long had the young lady been in Brazil, were there any symptoms of fever, aching of the bones, vomiting, before arriving in this country, so forth.

He stayed for twenty-five minutes and soon after he left I could hear Zade's voice speaking into a telephone: he became angry and lapsed once or twice into Polish; then I thought I could hear the fainter voice of the Burdick girl, answering rapid questions. From a sharp word here and there in Polish I understood that a call had been made, or was to be made, to Washington D.C. By the tone of the voices there was some degree of dissension about this.

I went on listening.

Above me the stars were enormous in a clearing sky, and to the south the moon drifted in layers of light cloud, sending pale illumination along the rooftops. Not far to my left I could make out a black squat form jutting upwards: this was the habitual roosting place of the buzzard and it was prepared to accept my presence so long as I didn't go too close again.

More voices from below, several together: a heated discussion concerning 'schedules', 'hospital', 'charter service', 'nursing', and various other less informative words. Manaus was mentioned two or three times, and Washington once.

Then a new phase began: the voices almost died away and there were the muffled bangs of doors and the click of catches. A tap was run for a few seconds and then shut off. A cistern was flushed. The general impression was of haste and I began crawling across the humped tiles to the far corner, where the vines ran from the roof to the communal balcony below.

There was no direct access to either of the windows of my room and I had to walk along a dozen yards of the exposed balcony but they were too busy over there to mount any kind of lookout. The hair was still intact across the join of the door and the post, and I went inside with only a token degree of caution because no one could have got in through either window without my hearing them from the roof. I closed the door but left it unlocked because I believed the Kobra cell was professional, or at least composed of professional individuals, and there were some gaps in their thinking that worried me.

There were still a few things in the suitcase I'd bought in Belém and I distributed them on the chair and the dressing table and left the case on the stand with the lid open, because they'd sent Shadia to check me out and that meant I was suspect and if I were suspect they ought not to leave the hotel without making sure where I was. The bed had only a sheet on it but I rolled up one of the Indian rugs and made a forty-five-degree kink in it and put it under the sheet, bunching the pillow and pulling down the mosquito net to cover the bed.

This was routine and my movements were directed mostly by habit, reinforced by experience and training: to leave this room without attending to these details would be like driving a car through a surveillance zone without checking the mirror.

The bathroom looked acceptable and there was nothing missing; the shaver would be in deep shadow if the light were put on in the bedroom so I moved it six inches: a shaver is the last thing in the bathroom a man forgets because it's a lot more expensive than the toothbrush and the other things. One of the taps was dripping and I left it like that because false impressions are furnished with small details designed to misinform the enquirer at the subliminal level and at that level the sound of a dripping tap is a sign of occupancy.

I stopped to listen. None of the doors on the other side of the courtyard had opened yet: I would have heard them through the bathroom ventilator. I could hear two voices, one of them carrying more than the other, though both men were trying to speak quietly. Zade and Kuznetski.

Theory: Kobra had been waiting for the Secretary of Defense to agree to their terms and arrange the rendezvous for the exchange: Pat Burdick, safe and unharmed, for whatever commodity or facility was demanded. It was unlikely that they would ask James Burdick to come to Brazil, even on the pretext of visiting his daughter during her expedition, because his duties were exacting, and knowledgeable people would be surprised at his sudden absence. Possibly Burdick had been putting up some degree of resistance but had now broken because he believed his daughter to be ill; and the exchange had been agreed on: it was to take place as soon as possible and in the United States, possibly in or near an isolation hospital with tropical medicine facilities.

Theory, not assumption.

Assumptions are dangerous.

I had assumed for instance that when one of the doors was opened on the other side of the courtyard I would catch the sound through the bathroom ventilator, but as I turned to go back into the bedroom I saw the crack of light widening across the floorboards.

I stopped.

The movement of the latch had made no sound: they had taken great care with it. I didn't know if they'd taken the second key from the board in the hall and had been prepared to use it, but that made no difference: I'd left the door unlocked because the gaps in their thinking had worried me and I had wanted to make it easy for them to check on my whereabouts.

The crack of light became a band, tapering from the door towards the bed; it was thrown partly by the lamps outside and partly by the moon. The shadow of the intruder was slowly taking shape as the door was inched wider by infinite degrees.

Tidal breathing, the lungs filled.

The drip of the tap.

If they turned to look in the direction of this sound, simply because it was a sound and possessed associations, they would look straight into my face.

Consider *immediate* action.

Wait.

Because they were not yet inside the room and couldn't at the moment see me and when they had come far enough to see me they would experience a half-second of shock and would require another half-second in which to react and that would give me time to move.

Without turning my head I looked at the mirror on the dressing table and saw that it formed a blind angle from here to the door: all I could see was the diaphanous whiteness of the mosquito net covering the bed. The shadow forming across the floor was distorted by the angle of contact and it was recognizable only as that of a human being. The door was not yet open more than five or six inches but I noted that the left hand was on the handle.

None of the Kobra cell were left-handed.

Inference: weapon.

The incoming data was increasing rapidly as the light

from the balcony flooded softly across the mosquito net, reflecting a diffused radiance. The shadow was taking on form.

The scent of *huile de citron*.

Shadia.

She used it against the mosquitos and its lemon sharpness had been on her skin when I was in her room earlier.

The door was now open ten or twelve inches and stopped moving.

Wait.

But consider taking Shadia hostage and trying for a stalemate. It was possible, practicable, and dangerous. But it was not less possible than other moves, and not more dangerous. I think it was the opportunity that looked so attractive so I decided against it.

I listened to her breathing.

The air was perfectly still and she was controlling each breath, but I heard it, and heard the excitement in it. Her shadow was moving, a short linear form bringing in a new component. It was some kind of gun and the muzzle was highlighted by the diffused glow in the room: I would have said it carried a silencer.

This would be the moment.

Later could be too late.

If she saw me now I would have the use of that one final second because her gunhand was against the door and she'd have to move the whole of her body through a right angle before she could take aim and fire. If she moved extremely fast I could finish up running into the first shot at zero range but the risk was calculated and I decided to accept it and began relaxing the leg muscles to whip up the circulation prior to tension.

Empty the lungs slowly. Refill.

Somewhere in the moist air a mosquito whined thinly and we both heard it. She believed that only she heard it. She was keeping absolutely still.

I watched the muzzle of the gun steadily: that was the sole focus of danger and I mustn't let it out of my sight even when I hurled my body against it.

She was within a few feet of where I stood and I could smell the recently-known scent of her body, subtler than the sharpness of the lemon oil.

Final review of situation: she hadn't come here to stand in the doorway and leave again without searching the room and when she began searching the room she would see me and shoot to kill. She was waiting only to make sure that the figure under the mosquito net was still sleeping and in a few seconds now she would move fully into the room.

Findings: it was logical to take her now.

Various sensory data presented itself: my right foot was within an inch of the bathroom doorpost and I would use that to initiate the spring; the muzzle of the gun was approximately waist high and I would go for it with the right hand while the left hand dragged at the door to expose her to the subsequent phases of the attack; the diffused light was sufficient to bring me accurately on to the primary target (the muzzle of the gun), and the brighter illumination from the balcony would give me all I needed to make the necessary movements once the gun was controlled.

Peripheral considerations: she might have time to cry out and for that reason I should make the secondary target her throat; she might drop the gun if I didn't control it before her fingers came open in shock; one or more of the Kobra might come on to the balcony across the courtyard before I could gain conclusive dominance, and I should therefore go in very fast indeed to the primary and secondary targets and use the remaining momentum to pull her bodily away from the door.

In the last few microseconds before any physical action the mind enacts it first, leaving the blueprint for the nervous system to follow. This was happening now but I wasn't conscious of it. Consciously I was tensing the diaphragm, blocking the breath and bracing the right foot against the doorpost.

But she began shooting before I could move.

14

Mantis

In extreme danger the senses are very alert and I could hear the whine of the mosquito loudening, either because it was coming closer to my face or because the muffled explosion of the first shot had left the eardrum desensitized and hearing was now coming back.

Phutt.

Two.

The muzzle of the gun scarcely wavered.

I watched her shadow.

If her shadow moved, I must move, and faster.

Phutt.

Three.

The mosquito net shook again, and was still.

This was why excitement had sounded in her breathing.

She held the gun with great steadiness.

Phutt.

Four.

Her shadow was misshapen on the floorboards: her arm looked grotesquely thin, reminding me of a praying mantis.

This was what she hadn't been able to do when she was with me. It was what she'd never been able to do, with any man.

Phutt.

Five.

Orgasm.

The mantis devours its mate, following copulation.

My spine crept.

In my trade we are frequently a target, and when we are quick or lucky we live to remember, and learn to be even quicker next time and to hope for more luck. But our very proximity to the bullet and to death lends an almost banal reality: there's nothing for the spirit to dream on, in the potential smashing open of a skull by a hurtling object.

This was different.

I wasn't there.

I was some distance away from the target of murderous intent, even though that target was myself. As if removed from my real body by some altered state of consciousness, I was a mere observer, a witness to my own dying; and it occurred to me, as the bullets went regularly into the mosquito net, that this was the mechanism of the voodoo killer who sticks pins in the effigy of his victim.

By small degrees I felt drained of life as each bullet smashed into the bed.

Phutt.

I hate you.

Six.

I know.

The reek of cordite was on the humid air.

In the silence her breath was trembling.

The mosquito whined faintly in the room.

In a moment she went away, closing the door.

'Information,' he said.

I listened for bugs.

'We're blown,' I told him.

There was another silence.

Ferris thought fast but he never spoke fast.

I waited.   'Where are you?'

His tone was under a lot of control: I'd told him the mission was blown and he knew I wouldn't say a thing like that for a giggle.

'Manaus Airport.'

I could see the plane as I talked to him. It was a DC–6, one of the three listed in the Amazonas Airlines flight schedules, and the departure board had it down for 04:20 today.

My watch read 04:07.

It was a four-engined propeller aircraft: Amazonas Airlines was a shoestring outfit flying animal trappers, gold miners and Indian jute farmers from Manaus to Belém and back.

One of the engines was now being started up.

'All right,' Ferris said.

He meant talk.

'The girl has a fever. They're flying her out in thirteen minutes from now.'

'Where to?'

'Somewhere in the United States, as far as I could learn.'

'Washington?'

'I heard it mentioned but I don't know in what connection.'

The four-bladed prop of the second engine, port side, began turning.

'Do you think they're moving to the exchange point?'

'Yes.'

He was listening carefully and I watched what I said: if I'd *known* they were moving to the exchange point I would have said so and he understood that.

This looked like being the final signal of a blown mission and if there were anything to be rescued we didn't intend throwing it away on sloppy communications.

'How did you get to the airport?'

'I took the hotel jeep.'

'Did they know about that?'

'No. Listen, for Christ's sake, I can't – '

'Don't worry – '

'If London thinks I'm going to waste time – '

'Relax.'

But he said it like a whiplash.

Sweat ran down my sides and I looked across the tarmac again at the DC–6. The second engine was running now, pouring out a stream of unburnt oil towards the group of passengers.

London's terribly fussy about private property and if you're stuck for transport you're meant to call a cab or Avis or someone and hang around while the objective slips the hook and leaves you with a blown operation and I do *not* know why those *bloody* idiots can't see the problem of the executive in the field when – all right, relax, he's right, relax.

Sweat it out.

Third engine running.

Eleven minutes to go.

And all Ferris could do was worry about letting the hotel know where to find their bloody jeep. I'd left two hundred-cruzeiro notes in the glove pocket and a scribbled note so what more did anyone expect me to –

'Would they recognize you if they saw you?'

'Of course they'd – '

'Easy,' he said.

I shut up.

This wasn't very good. If that aeroplane took off in ten minutes from now the Kobra cell and their hostage would be on board and there wasn't anything I could do about it. I couldn't believe I'd blown the whole operation so easily as this, but I'd better start getting used to it. They were going to walk away and I was going to watch them do it.

'Can you delay the take-off?'

'Of course. But it wouldn't do any good.'

You can always stop a plane taking off at the last minute and there's a dozen ways of doing it – start a fire, call up and say there's a bomb on board, so forth – but in normal circumstances it's an extreme measure and too clumsy to give you more than a few minutes' advantage. In the present circumstances it would blow the mission sky-high instead of letting it die a natural death because this was a group of international terrorists we were handling and at the first sign of anything unusual they'd close up and start using their guns on the first target they could see and from that point onwards the situation could explode into fatal dimensions and the first one to die could be Pat Burdick.

The *only* way to control Kobra was to do it quietly, without their even knowing.

'The next plane out,' Ferris said on the phone, 'is at noon tomorrow.'

I knew that.

I didn't say anything.

They'd got number 4 running and the slipstream blew a sheet of newspaper across the tarmac and I watched it, and didn't see it.

All I saw was Egerton picking up the yellow telephone.

Yes?

Signal from Ferris, sir.

Well?

They've blown Kobra.

The newspaper drifted upwards again in the rush of air, and caught against the railings by the emergency bay.

And Tilson, sipping his tea in the Caff.

Who was operating that one?

Quiller.

Good grief, I've never known him miss.

We all do, old boy, in the end.

Exhaust gas blew past me from the DC–6.

The next plane out was at noon tomorrow and the night plane had already taken off for the coast: I'd heard it when I was with Shadia.

'By the way,' I said, 'they think I'm dead.'

'Oh do they?'

But it was shut-ended.

It was the perfect cover, and she'd handed it to me when she'd stood there in the lamplight pumping six slow shots into the shape of the rolled-up rug on the bed, firing blind through the mosquito net but making sure, taking her time, working from the head and down along the spine to the coccyx. The perfect cover.

But I couldn't use it.

'There's no way,' Ferris asked rather tightly, 'of going aboard with them?'

'No way.'

I could see them from where I stood, waiting at the departure gate and checking everyone in sight. They thought I was dead but they'd recognize me and realize there was a mistake and they'd rectify it and this time they'd make sure.

'Can you think of anything,' Ferris asked me, 'that I could do?'

'No.'

I'd already thought about it and there was nothing. I'd

thought of a hundred things, and there was nothing.

Ferris couldn't get here before take-off in nine minutes and even if he could get here it'd be no go because he'd come into Manaus from Belém on the same flight as Satynovich Zade and Zade would recognize him and if he tried to follow the Kobra group they'd know it and deal with him. Ferris was in any case the director in the field and his function was totally different from the executive's: he was here to run me from phase to phase and keep me in signals with Control and provide me with access and cover and directives, and if the opposition wrote me off or I became missing or overdue on a rendezvous then Ferris would remain in the field where London could find him. In any mission the end-phase can blow wide open and the director can go through half a dozen executives and finally bring in a hit for Control, regardless of cost.

The executive is dispensable; the director is not.

I looked at my watch.

04:12.

'What about Interpol?' I asked him.

'No,' he said. 'Not twice.'

The rules are quite explicit on this: London can use Interpol at its own discretion but the director in the field can only make one appeal to its services unless a signal permits it. The Bureau doesn't exist and if too much contact is made with other services the involvement deepens and becomes dangerous: Ferris had asked for Interpol's help when I was holed up in quarantine and the local police had co-operated; but if we asked them again they'd start taking an interest and they'd want to know who this group of Europeans were and finally they'd want to know who *we* were and we couldn't tell them. And there was only a hairline between that point and a breach of security.

Further: the United States Secretary of Defense had called on the Bureau for an ultra-secret operation, exclusive of the F.B.I. and the C.I.A. and therefore exclusive, by definition, of the Brazilian police.

The four engines of the DC–6 gunned up a degree and then fell to idling. Movement came towards my right and I looked in that direction and saw the passengers being led across the tarmac to the plane.

04:13.

One of the major functions of the local director is to think for his agent.

'Ferris.'

'Yes?'

He knew what I was going to ask.

'Have you got a directive for me?'

At this moment the Kobra mission was still running.

'No.'

Then it stopped.

15

Ghost

Noise.

Darkness.

The noise deafening but the darkness not total.

Vibration beginning as the power came on. Increasing vibration.

I couldn't see my watch. Its digits were luminous but it was out of sight and I couldn't bring my hand down. In any case time wasn't significant: the Amazonas Airlines DC–6 was down for take-off at 04:20 hours and that would be the approximate time now because the engines were hitting peak revolutions and the wheels were rolling.

Very little was visible in my immediate environs: vague dark shapes, the gleam of a highlight on metal, nothing more. Below me the rubber-streaked surface of the runway was slipping past mesmerically, the streaks becoming a blur in the faint glow from the exhaust flames.

Estimated ground-speed seventy.

The roaring was infinite, quelling the senses: the ears being deafened, vision seemed impaired, and I believed it was growing darker. Perhaps it was. During this phase I could do nothing except wait and hope to survive.

Estimated ground-speed a hundred and twenty plus.

Errant and abstract thought: a noise like this could bring the sky down. Thunder must sound like this in the instant of its inception.

The runway was now blurred to the point of looking perfectly smooth, and the last chance of changing my mind had gone: if I dropped to the ground now the spinning tonnage of the twin wheels would leave a sudden red smudge along the concrete.

I hadn't told Ferris what I was going to do. There hadn't been time.

My right foot was slipping again and I pulled upwards,

feeling the electrical conduit flex critically under the strain. The problem was to keep my body arched against the curved top of the wheelbay, giving me a chance of escaping the wheels when they slammed home and locked. This was the only place where I could hope to survive: right at the top and right at the back, lodged against the transverse flight-control cables and their rack of pulleys. The engine-control cables ran fore and aft above my head and I had to remember they were there and keep clear of them. I had also to remember that if I lost purchase and grabbed for any handhold available, the flight-control cables were within dangerously easy reach and my weight on them could disturb the aircraft's trim to the point of crashing it.

The vibration was easing.

Easing.

Lift-off.

The flick-flick-flick of the runway lights, falling away.

It was going to happen now and I was suddenly exposed to the last-second thought that I'd got it wrong: there wasn't enough room in here. The landing lock was going to fold on the fulcrum and the oleo strut was going to swing up and bring the wheels with it, their huge tyres spinning and their weight forced into the bay by the hydraulics, slamming home as the doors came together below.

There hadn't been time to measure anything, even crudely. There'd only been time to look upwards and assess the chances and I'd done that and I'd thought the chances were good but at that time I'd been on the ground and in no immediate danger and now I was jammed into a death-trap and when the wheels came up they were going to crush me against the bulkhead and the only thing I knew for certain was that it was going to be quick.

Lights falling away.

Then darkness below. The jungle.

There hadn't been time to tell Ferris what I was going to do because I hadn't known I was going to do it till a few minutes before take-off. This flight and the night-mail service were the only traffic movements between dusk and dawn and there was a skeleton staff at Manaus and I'd had the choice of a dozen pairs of mechanic's overalls in the ground crew locker room, together with the ear-mufflers. The baggage-trolley had gone out past the emergency bay and I took a lift at the rear end where the driver couldn't see me.

The electrician had been busy with his gear and the checker was talking to the navigator through the flight deck window when I'd looked into the wheelbay and made the decision. To vanish into the wheelbay of a DC-6 takes approximately three seconds and kids do it in Cuba and some of them survive.

It's easier when you don't think too much.

You have to believe there's going to be enough room when the wheels come up and you have to believe you can go on holding on like this with the open doors leaving you poised above the surface of the earth at a lethal height if you lose your grip and drop and go on dropping. You have to –

Mechanical movement beginning.

I couldn't see the wheels: they were well aft of the bay. All I could see in the light of the exhaust flames were the hydraulic cylinder and the two long coils springs and they were moving now, working in unison.

Darkness began rising.

Keep yourself braced.

The jungle below had the faint sheen of moonlight on its leaves and the rising darkness was the black rubber of the tyres as they came swinging forward and upward, blotting out the ground. They were immense and I dragged a breath in and arched my spine and felt the sharp heads of the hose-clip screws digging into my shoulder as I pulled upward against the conduits and waited, hearing the faint scream of the windrush in the roaring background. The wheels were still spinning and I could feel the sting of stone fragments as they were flicked away from the ribbed treads by centrifugal force.

Keep braced and don't weaken.

Then there was sudden and total darkness as the strut locked home and the doors of the bay came together, shutting me in. I hadn't imagined that this degree of sound could increase but the three-thousand-horsepower radial engine was immediately forward of the wheelbay and the closing doors had trapped its sound, confining it, until its volume swelled to a vibration inside the skull.

Into this constant thunder came a higher note that alerted me to unconsidered hazards but for a moment I couldn't identify its source. Conceivably it was an alarm buzzer sounding somewhere above my head but it wouldn't be heard from the flight deck and I discounted it. My right foot was trembling and heating up and the faint whine was diminishing gradually and I took a better grip on the conduit and raised my foot an inch and the sound stopped at once: the heel of my shoe had been in contact with one of the tyres and they were still spinning and I was warned.

Don't drop.

If I dropped I wouldn't live: the wheels would flick me against the forward bulkhead and jam my body there with their momentum.

But I was tiring now.

Noise fatigues the organism. So does fear.

I was afraid.

There was no action to take. I had to do nothing, in order to live, except hold on and try not to think. The wheels would lose their rotary inertia within minutes but I didn't know how long I could force the muscles in my hands to remain contracted with the fingers hooked over the conduit or how long it would be before the conduit broke away from its clips and sent me down. Once the wheels had stopped spinning I could drop across them and rest but if I did it too soon it would be fatal. It was a matter of time.

Euphoria.

A sense of twilight.

The noise roared far away, in the caverns of Nirvana.

Watch it.

A sense of floating, of life adrift in weightlessness, of deep and eternal peace.

Three great swans flew across the aching dome of infinity, and were caught in its vortex, spinning. The sky cracked like an egg.

Get out of this. Pull yourself out.

Consciousness flickering, like a loose light-bulb.

Colours swirled, ebbing and flowing to the theta rhythms of hypnagogic sleep. The sun burst, and the birds turned black and struck horror in the psyche.

Pull up and pull out. Move.

My hands floating in the –

Move for Christ's sake or you'll –

Adrift in the streaming depths of Lethe, where –

Move your hands, hit something. Feet, kick something. Pull out.

Heart thudding.

Darkness, the real thing, and the engine roaring.

I kicked and floated back the other way, nearly losing the sense of reality as the clouds drew down and blinded – *watch it, pull out!* Kicked again and floated to the right, and I knew now what was happening: I was lying prone across the enormous tyres and when I kicked at the bulkhead the force was turning the wheels and they were swinging me across in an arc against the firewall.

Consciousness was painful: the organism was being born again into the deafening storms of reality and in the confusion the forebrain was trying to function, desperate to get its messages through to the motor nerves.

Please note that you are lying on the wheels and when the undercarriage goes down you will automatically drop into space.

I didn't register the significance of this because the euphoria was still fogging my head; but I realized that I was in the conscious state, with the beta rhythms taking over. There had been oxygen deprivation and this was the hangover and it was unpleasant: headache, nausea, shivering.

Tried to stand up but of course no room so I grabbed at things to steady myself, physical orientation necessary, but *watch it*! Cables, don't grab at the cables or you'll crash the whole bloody bazaar.

Something was trying to get through. Some kind of information.

My head lolled and brushed the conduit and the ear-muffler went askew and the roaring came through my skull like a freight train and I pulled the thing back over my ears.

My weight had shifted and I swung back on the wheels, hitting the firewall. The noise was worse here because the engine was on the other side, so I swung back to the rear end of the wheelbay and bruised my arm and felt the pain pushing consciousness into the open, as if I were coming out of a tunnel.

Information: we were probably going down, and the oxygen was increasing; hence my return to consciousness. I couldn't think why we were going down but I hoped we *meant* to do it and we weren't doing it because I'd been hanging on to those flight-control cables.

Discount unreasonable fears: it felt as though we were in stable flight conditions, inclined nose-down by ten or fifteen degrees. But something urgent was still trying to get through and I didn't like the way my head was still fogging. My hands were cold but there was no icing anywhere: the metal conduits were perfectly dry. The air temperature at ten thousand feet above the Amazon in spring would be somewhere about 45° and the heat of the radial engine would raise that considerably. After an hour's flight, the conditions –

Time.

Check the time.

07:20.

This was the warning that had been trying to get through. It was a three-hour flight from Manaus to Belém near the Atlantic coast and we'd been flying for that period of time and the distinct nose-down attitude of the aircraft plus the return of oxygen availability meant that we were probably approaching Belém Airport.

The final piece of information was very urgent indeed but I didn't have time to look at it because something gave a metallic click below me and a rush of air screamed through the wheelbay doors as they started to open and the tyres began dropping away and I grabbed for the conduit, my fingers clawing and not finding it, clawing again and touching the skein of control cables – *don't* – as the mass of rubber began rolling forward and the air howled into the bay.

I felt the conduit and pulled upwards, kicking my weight

off the wheels as they went down. Daylight was flooding in and I caught a glimpse of water shining below as I found some kind of a purchase for the heels of my shoes, pulling hard on the conduit and feeling it buckle but hold. With the dazzling light after the hours of total darkness there came the heat of low altitude, and the faint brackish smell of the ocean as we swung in a wide circle, settling lower with the engines idling and the landing-gear down and locked.

I looked for new handholds in case the buckled conduit tore the clips out of the panels under my weight: the wheels wouldn't be coming up again into the bay and I didn't have to mould my body into its roof. As the DC lowered from the sky there would be no abrupt shifts of mass but when the wheels hit the runway my weight would increase critically for a few seconds and I felt for handholds strong enough to take the strain. Then I looked down at the network of city streets and the estuary's bright water, five or six hundred feet below.

Pain was beginning in the ears and I pinched my nose and blew back. The heat was increasing and the sweat started coming to the skin. Onset of thirst.

Final approach.

I couldn't see the runway because the forward bulkhead concealed it from sight; but the first of the approach lamps were sliding below, unlit but glinting in the morning sun. I was now straddled across the bay with one foot on each door-stay and my hands on the two lower conduits. The slip-stream spilled inwards, tugging at my overalls.

The dead weight of the aircraft lowered over the next thirty seconds and then the power came on for the touch-down and I saw concrete immediately below, its scarred sections becoming a blur as the distance closed. For a moment everything seemed held in suspension as the insubstantial air cradled the mass of the machine and supported it; then a shudder came as the main wheels hit the runway and the hydraulics took the shock. The conduit under my left hand buckled and tore away from the two nearest clips and I was swung sideways and hit the bulkhead with my shoulder as one foot lost its hold on the door-stay and I floundered, feeling the vibration as the main wheels bounced and touched down again and rolled, taking the weight of the machine as the nose-wheel made contact, forward of where I was clinging.

I was swung off-balance again and felt the conduit pulling away before I got a new purchase with my feet across the door-stays. The concrete was a blur of colour immediately below me and I could hear the heavy tramping of the tyres as their ribbed treads flexed under the weight of the aircraft. Dark ribbons began showing up in the blur as the speed came down, and the tarred expansion joints between the blocks sketched a slowing pattern of lines. Dust and stone fragments blew into the wheelbay, thrown up by the nose-wheel and caught by the turbulence of the propeller.

I heard the rough hiss of the brake-shoes as they clamped into the drums and brought the speed down, sending my weight forward until I hit the bulkhead, burning my arm against the oil-drain pipe before I could steady myself. Under the heavy deceleration I could see the streaks of burnt rubber showing clearly now on the concrete, until the last of the blur was gone. The power came on again and I felt the machine swinging to the left, its weight flexing the oleo struts as it turned and gunned up slightly towards the parking bay.

Ears very painful and I blew again with my nose blocked.

The faint cry of a sea bird.

Wheels rolling.

The sound of the engines dying.

Brakes again, pitching me forward.

Rolling.

Stop.

I leaned there for a minute with my eyes shut. The early sunlight threw the shadow of the propeller across the tarmac beneath my feet, and when I opened my eyes I saw the blades become still. A service vehicle was on the move somewhere, and I could hear voices. I stayed where I was, waiting. In three or four minutes the fuel bowser swung towards the mainplane on my side and I heard the clang of the doors as they were thrown back from the pump unit.

I dropped to the ground.

Nearly fell: question of sea legs.

There was a long screwdriver holstered in the leg-pocket of the overalls and I pulled it out and checked a loose cowling button. If anyone had seen me drop from the wheelbay they would assume I had climbed into it a few minutes ago.

'Who are you?' Short fat mechanic, head on one side.

'Douglas Aircraft inspector,' I told him.

'Nobody told me.'

'Do they tell you everything?'

I checked the oil-cooler frame and told him there was a buckled electrical conduit inside the wheelbay that needed looking at.

'You'll have to tell Carlos,' he said, and began helping the refuelling crew at the bowser.

I walked away from the aircraft, leaving the sunglasses and the ear-mufflers on my head. The leg muscles had been under strain since I'd regained consciousness and I felt none too steady. On my left, fifty yards or so away from where I walked, the passengers were being led towards the building. I turned my head only once to make sure the Kobra cell was among them, then kept on towards the maintenance sheds.

'Where are you?'

'Belém Airport.'

There'd been a twenty-five-minute delay and it'd got me sweating badly because there wasn't a lot of time left to decide what I had to do.

'How did you get there?' Ferris asked me.

'Wheelbay.'

He paused again.

'What's your condition?'

'Operational.'

He didn't ask me to repeat that. If I were half dead he'd expect me to say so.

The phone I was using was at the end of a maintenance hangar, and I was watching the TWA Boeing as I talked. A few minutes ago another mobile television unit had gone across the tarmac from the main gates, with a cameraman already at work on the roof.

'What's your local time?' Ferris wanted to know.

'08:55.'

It was an hour later here than at Manaus.

'Are you still locked on?'

'Yes,' I said.

The sound of sirens was coming in again from the highway, and I could see the intermittent light of an emergency vehicle. Everyone seemed rather excited, but I would have thought the South American countries were pretty used to this sort of thing.

'All right,' Ferris said.

He meant he wasn't going to put any more specific questions because he'd got the basic data and now he wanted information.

'They've struck some kind of problem,' I told him. 'From what I could put together in Lagofondo, I think they're making for the States, but I shouldn't think they've got visas and they'll need some pretty authentic medical certificates. The thing is they've seized a TWA Boeing and a couple of minutes ago they ordered two aircrew to go aboard: presumably pilot and navigator.'

I stopped to let Ferris think about it for a while. It would also give me time to work something out if I could. I didn't think there was anything I could work out. The whole thing looked terribly shut-ended and I stood here baking in the direct heat of the sun with the sweat running down and a lot of slow-burn angst in my soul, because I'd followed those bastards all the way here and now they were taking off again and I couldn't hope to pull the same trick again because I wouldn't get through the police lines and even if they let me through I couldn't get into a wheelbay unseen and even if I could get into a wheelbay I'd freeze to death at thirty thousand feet.

Ferris was quiet.

'The whole of the Kobra cell is now on board,' I said, 'and they've got Pat Burdick with them. The police have got the aircraft cordoned off but they can't actually do anything useful. That's all I've got for you. Sorry there's no jam on it.'

In a couple of seconds he asked:

'Do you think they're going to take off?'

'Yes.'

'When?'

'Soon.'

He paused again.

'All right. Details.'

'TWA Flight 378 normally scheduled Belém to Miami. Boeing 707. Normal departure was 08:45 and the ETA is 11:15 Belém time, 09:15 Miami time.'

Ferris answered a little more quickly now. 'The aircraft is fuelled up and ready to leave, then?'

'Oh yes.'

'They didn't flush you, of course.'

'No.'

He paused again.

The siren was loud now and I saw the patrol car swing across the tarmac and pull up near the television unit. The man with the camera swung the thing half-circle to cover the people getting out of the patrol car in case they were official negotiators.

'What do you intend doing?' Ferris asked me.

I suppose it was a compliment, really, for him to assume I had any kind of answer to this one. There was of course an answer but it wasn't very subtle, and I didn't feel like spelling it out for him because he might order me not to do it.

'I think I'll have to go aboard,' I said.

From this distance I could see three people standing at the top of the flight steps but couldn't identify them for certain: the two outer figures were holding what looked like sub-machine-guns and the one in the middle would be Patricia Burdick. I didn't think they could have got any weapons that size through Manaus Airport: they must have a contact in Belém and they'd phoned him before they left. These people were internationals and if they'd decided to move to the United States they wouldn't have left anything to chance.

Ferris had been thinking it over. Now he said:

'All right. I'll keep track of the plane.'

'Do that.'

He asked if there were anything else and I said no and we hung up and I stood there for a minute wiping the sweat off my face and feeling a bit queasy because this could get me killed.

Then I took off the overalls and put them on a bench with the ear-mufflers and walked across the tarmac till I reached the police cordon. I now recognized Satynovich Zade and Carlos Ramirez at the top of the steps with the girl between them. Ramirez was shouting to the group of police negotiators in Portuguese, asking again for a doctor to go aboard and look after the hostage. He promised repeatedly that the doctor would be regarded as a 'brave humanitarian' and would come to no harm whatever happened.

I saw a small man pushing his way through the crowd with a bag in his hand, and decided I ought to start parleying.

I cupped my hands.

'*Satynovich!*'

I didn't want to talk to Ramirez because he might be limited to Spanish and Portuguese and if the police understood what I was saying they might take me for a friend of the terrorists and arrest me and that'd be strictly no go.

'*Voce émédico?*'

He was a captain of police and his hand had gone to his gun.

That's right, I told him, I was a doctor.

I cupped my hands again.

'*Satynovich! I want to talk to you!*'

I used Polish and hoped none of the police understood.

Zade had turned his head and was looking straight at me.

He wouldn't expect anyone to speak to him in Belém in his own language: their contact would be Spanish- or Portuguese-speaking and Ramirez would be the go-between. Zade was turning to him and Ramirez now looked across at me.

In a moment he began calling to the police in Portuguese,

ordering them to let me pass through the cordon.

They didn't want to. On principle they didn't want to do anything the terrorists told them, which was natural enough. A lot of shouting went on and I looked around for the nearest press group. A European was hanging from the side of a television van, trying to angle up a shot with the police captain in the foreground and the group on the flight steps beyond. I called out to him.

'*Vous êtes Français ou quoi? Sprechen Zie Deutsch?*'

He looked across at me.

'Bit of both, actually.'

'Listen, do you know who that girl is? The hostage?'

'American, isn't she?'

'She's the daughter of the U.S. Secretary of Defense.'

'Jesus Christ! So that's – '

'Listen, get on a phone to Washington and tell him where she is and never mind about the bloody pictures.'

He was coming down from the side of the van.

'You're so right,' he said and got a quick shot of me in case he could use it later. 'Which side are you on?'

'Go and find a phone – you've got it exclusive.'

I wanted James Burdick to know the score because if that Boeing came down anywhere in the United States he'd want to be there. Forty-five minutes ago the Kobra operation had been running as a fully secret hostage-and-demand action and Pat Burdick had been insect-hunting along the Amazon with a group of friends but the situation had now changed radically: the girl's fever and Burdick's reaction to the news of it had either driven or panicked Kobra into the open and in seizing the Boeing they'd gone public and from this point onwards they'd be making their stand against the combined strength of the F.B.I., the C.I.A. and whatever law-enforcement, counter-espionage and anti-terrorist organizations could be brought into the field.

That wouldn't make it more difficult for Kobra, as long as they held Pat Burdick. But it would infinitely increase her danger.

Ramirez was shouting again.

In thirty seconds, he announced in Portuguese, he and his

companion would open fire on the crowd unless that man there were allowed through the cordon.

The police captain had been holding my arm. Now he released it.

He didn't believe I was a doctor.

'*Um dia,*' he said, '*você pagavá, você e seus amigos.*'

Then he gave an order and the cordon let me through and I walked across the tarmac under the hot sun, my right foot trying to buckle over because the heel of the shoe had been worn away by the tyre of the DC–6.

Satynovich Zade hadn't yet recognized me: he had known only that someone in the crowd not only spoke his tongue but knew his name and he wanted to find out who it was. He was still standing at the top of the flight steps as I climbed them, and when I was halfway up he stopped me with a jerk of the machine-gun. I took off the sunglasses and looked up at him.

His own eyes were still concealed by the smoked lenses, so that I couldn't see their expression; but I noticed his mouth give a slight jerk as he recognized me.

'She didn't succeed,' I told him carefully in Polish.

Then I caught movement and looked higher, beyond him, and saw Shadia staring down at me with her face dead white.

Zade had been keeping the sub-machine-gun aimed steadily at my heart, and now I saw his finger go to the trigger.

'Don't do that,' I said.

The sun was reflected on his smoked glasses as he stood above me with his head perfectly still. It looked as if his eyes were blazing, but of course it was just the reflection.

This was why Ferris had taken his time thinking about what I'd said, when I'd told him I was going aboard: it wasn't a terribly good move and I'd probably get killed; but something had to be done and if I could do it and get it right it'd mean a lot to that bastard Egerton. There was of course the ghost of a chance that I'd get away with it, and that's all we ask, when despite all we've done there's nothing more we can do to save the mission, when the only choice is to abandon it and try to live with our pride or make the final throw and hope for the only thing that can get us through: the ghost of a chance.

I watched his finger.

'Don't do that,' I told him again. 'I'm working for Burdick, didn't you know? That gets you another hostage for nothing, and you can use me to negotiate the exchange. So don't throw away good material – you might be glad of it later.'

He didn't move.

Shadia had gone inside the aircraft.

Pat Burdick looked down at me but I don't think she was taking anything in: her skin was yellow and her eyes dull and I could see why they'd wanted a doctor on board.

Carlos Ramirez watched me with his gun steady.

Zade watched me, his finger curled.

I heard the cry of sea birds in the distance.

Some kind of aircraft landed and reversed thrust, sending out a rush of sound that diminished slowly.

I watched his finger.

It'd be a quick pressure, then off again: with shells that size he only needed one shot to blow me right off the steps.

'Work it out for yourself,' I said. 'It makes sense.'

There wasn't anything else I could do now, because I didn't want to oversell the idea: it'd look as if I were worried. It was his decision to make, entirely his decision, with nothing on my side to help me. Except the ghost of a chance.

16

Boeing

'I told you,' I said. 'It makes sense.'

He didn't answer.

I watched the reflections in his sunglasses.

He kept very still.

Sunglasses are effective in two ways: they disguise the face and they conceal the thoughts in the eyes of the wearer, and in a poker-type situation that can offer a critical advantage.

I couldn't see what he was thinking.

'Find out,' he said at last, 'where we are now.'

He was talking to Shadia, not to me.

She turned away and I watched her reflected back view in his sunglasses as she went forward to the flight deck.

We were still over the ocean: the glare still lit the mouldings above the windows. I hadn't been told anything but I assumed Zade would try for Washington: Flight 378 was originally scheduled for Miami so it would carry enough excess fuel.

Shadia came back.

'We're a few minutes north-east of Miami.'

'All right,' Zade said.

She looked into my face for a moment before she turned away and went aft to where Pat Burdick was lying on a tilted seat. Sometimes during the flight from Belém I'd found Shadia staring at me from a little distance, as if she still wasn't sure what had happened. I think if I'd suddenly sprung up with a fiendish cry she would have passed straight out. I don't use a gun so my experience with them is academic but I suppose when you pump six killing shots into someone's body it must do something to you as well: there must be a kind of rapport between you, in the giving and receiving of so much hate. For several hours Shadia had believed she'd killed me and when she'd seen me standing there on the flight steps at Belém it must have been psychically traumatizing.

'Do you think he would take your advice?' Zade asked me.

He meant Burdick.

'Yes, he would.'

We spoke in Polish most of the time, but he tried out some weird English phrases now and then to impress me, though I hadn't actually heard them used before. We sat facing each other: he was on the inside seat of the front row in the first-class section and I was on the steward's jump-seat. I'd been searched and everything and they'd calmed down during the flight, though Zade and Sassine were still rather nervy and I had to watch what I said or they'd begin firing questions at me and I didn't want to tell them some of the answers.

Kuznetski was the quietest: his dossier had mentioned something about scientific training in Prague University and he was probably some type of bent boffin. He'd only spoken twice during the flight out of Belém and now he was sitting alone, preoccupied.

Sassine was across the aisle from us, reeking the place out with pot. Zade had told him to shut up a few minutes ago and Sassine had come off his high in a swallow dive. I'd noticed on other occasions that when Zade said anything, people really listened.

'Then you can advise him not to make any trouble for me,' he said, watching me with his sunglasses.

'I don't think he wants to do that.' I leaned forward. 'He wants his daughter back with him, and I'm ready to advise him to do precisely what you say. From my personal observation that is the only way he can save her.'

I tried to sound like a smooth Civil Servant, using that bastard Loman for a model, because the showdown might involve a modicum of close combat and I didn't want these people to think I was any good at it. Similarly I was trying to persuade him that the Defense Secretary was also a pushover because a determining factor in any confrontation with an adversary is the degree by which you can get his guard down in the preliminary stages.

'You have had contact with Burdick?'

'Yes,' I said.

I hadn't.

'So you know what we are demanding from him.'

'Yes.'

I didn't.

He looked away from my face at last, turning his dark head to the window. I could now see part of his left eye, but couldn't judge the expression at this angle: he was just staring into the distant sky.

'We know that Israel has the bomb, and we know that the United Arab Republic is building one. That is the key factor in the imminent Israel-Egypt accord, already outlined by Kissinger.'

I looked beyond him to the pallid face of the Burdick girl. Dr Costa was sitting alongside her: he was the short man who'd been pushing his way through the crowd at Belém: the 'brave humanitarian'. I hadn't known, until now, how slight her chances were.

A group like Kobra wouldn't come together from the ends of the earth to acquire a single nuclear bomb. They'd want more than that: fifty or a hundred of them.

'Yasser Arafat published his manifesto in *Al Thawra*, two months ago, in Beirut.' His head swung back. 'Did you read it?'

'I read the *Newsweek* interview.'

'Good. That is *his* manifesto, and it is *my* manifesto. We may not be able to prevent the proposed Israel-Egypt accord, but we can prevent some of its consequences. Have you met Yasser Arafat?'

'No.'

'If you met him, you would follow him. I can do nothing for Poland, but I can do something for Palestine. You understand?'

'Of course.'

He was on a liberation kick and he was sincere about it and therefore dangerous: the political terrorist is the man who could create new and better worlds if he could express his dreams with intelligence; having none, he can only express his frustration.

I leaned forward again, wanting to know things.

'But you said that the bomb is the key factor. Do you mean – '

'The bomb is *always* the key factor. In the ultimate show of strength, that is the form of strength that is shown. Surely you know that.'

He looked up as someone came off the flight deck: I heard the sliding door hitting the stops. I turned my head and saw Ventura. They'd been taking it in shifts to mount guard on the flight deck and Ventura had been there for the last twenty minutes. He was a narrow-chested man with a bald head and slow wet eyes: he looked like a disinterested assistant in men's haberdashery but he had killed Hunter in Geneva and he would kill me when the showdown came unless I could pre-empt him.

Zade moved quickly and I felt the power in him as he swung past me. The sliding door banged shut behind them and I changed my seat so as to face forward. Sassine went nervously for his gun but I didn't take any notice because he was as high as a kite and his reactions were notably slow: I could have got his gun and shot Zade or Ventura or possibly both as they came back from the flight deck but Kuznetski and Ramirez were behind me now and so was Shadia.

Sassine seemed ashamed of his show of nerves and crossed his legs and pinched out his reefer and put it in a tin box marked 'Aspirin' in Czecho-slovakian and began talking rapidly about the paradoxes of political history and the undercurrents of popular thought and their influence on the world revolutionary scene in terms of pseudo-neo-Fascism and its abortive attempts to achieve liberation for the élite. One of the port engines cut out and came back on power while he was talking but he didn't notice it.

Behind him, farther along the aisle, Ramirez was watching me with one hand on a sub-machine-gun, and I saw him glance to the window. Sassine went on talking and I assessed his potential for creating difficulties: I thought Zade would probably have trouble controlling him when it came to the crunch. He was a thin, hollow-eyed man in his twenties, haunted by things he had done or perhaps by things that had been done to him, and I believed he would put a bullet into Pat Burdick's head and my own as well if he thought it would be politically correct.

The engine cut twice more, coming back each time, and five minutes later Zade and Ventura came back from the flight deck and stood talking in urgent whispers in the catering area forward of the passenger section. I couldn't hear anything they said.

Sassine was recommending the advantages of what he called 'socialistically-oriented referenda' as a means of 'reaching the proletariat' without disturbing the 'mass-media syndrome' when the port engine cut out and stayed out. The background noise was diminished by one quarter and was noticeable even to Sassine.

Zade and Ventura had stopped talking and were moving forward again when the flight deck door banged back and the pilot stood there, a tall mahogany-faced type with four gold rings on his sleeve and his cap on the back of his head. He spoke directly to Zade.

'Okay, you better get this. I'm the captain of this ship as long as she's in the air and I want to tell you something in case you didn't happen to think of it for yourself. We have one engine out and it can happen again so I'm going to take her into the first place that can give me clearance, and if you don't like it you can shoot me right between the eyes and you've got a hundred and thirty thousand pounds of junk going through the air at thirty thousand feet and it's doing five hundred knots and she's all your baby, know what I mean? You think that guy in there can take her down? He's not a pilot, he's a navigator and he couldn't land a goddam bicycle. I realize you've got the biggest ass in the ball-park so I thought I better just tell you the score.'

He turned and went back to the flight deck and slid the door shut with a bang.

The Boeing was in a wide turn and drifting lower.

My watch read 12:31 and I altered it to 10:31 provisionally: I didn't know which airport we were going into but it wouldn't be far from the time zone for Miami because we'd overflown it.

Zade and Ventura were on the flight deck and the door was open but I couldn't hear any voices. Kuznetski had come forward to ask Sassine what was happening, and Ramirez was squatting on a front-row seat in the coach class section with a sub-machine-gun across his knees and the other on the seat alongside. When Sassine came back to talk to him I moved down the aisle to where Dr Costa was looking after the girl.

Shadia was with them and I couldn't say everything I needed to say but the main thing was to keep Pat Burdick's morale up in case she had to look after herself while I was busy.

'How are you feeling, Pat?'

'I'm okay.'

She was lying back on the tilted seat looking up at me with dulled eyes, but managed to smile.

'You know I'm here to look after you, for your father?'

'I didn't know.'

Her eyes showed a flicker of interest now.

'I've talked a lot to these people, and they've told me that whatever happens they've no intention of harming you. We're going to reach a working agreement with your father, some time today, and then you'll be free to go home.'

She went on looking up at me, frowning a little against the reflected light on the ceiling.

'Are you just kidding me along?'

'No, I'm not. You don't need any false reassurance – you're too tough for that.'

Dr Costa took the pad off her forehead and dipped it into the bucket of ice and squeezed it out and put it back.

'I don't feel very tough. I feel really spaced out, over all this. Do you know what they want from my Dad?'

'Yes.' Because Shadia was listening. 'And it's nothing he's not ready to give them, in exchange for you.'

I pressed her hand and straightened up and looked at Costa and he came back along the aisle to talk to me.

'How bad is she?' I asked him.

Shadia hadn't followed us. I think she didn't like to come too close to me, possibly because she was superstitious: with part of her mind she saw me as someone who'd come back from the dead.

'She needs to be in a hospital,' Costa said.

He was short and rumpled with soulful brown eyes that spoke of devotion to a dozen gods, whichever could get his attention first. He smelt faintly of herbs.

'What's your diagnosis?'

He shrugged.

'It could be blackwater fever, or it could be yellow fever; the symptoms are much the same in the early stages.' He looked up at me dolefully. 'Do these people mean what they say?'

'It depends what they say.'

He looked along the aisle.

'Poor child. They say they will show humanity. Where will they find humanity?'

I turned round a little so that I had my back to Shadia: this wasn't an intelligence cell but she might have had training in lip-reading somewhere along the line.

'Dr Costa, have you given any sedation?'

'Sedation? Oh no, she – '

'Don't give her any. If you can give her stimulants without doing any harm, you should do that.' He broke in but I stopped him. 'I might not have long to talk. I don't know what's going to happen but I want to get the girl out alive if it's possible. She might have to run, or look after herself in an emergency. If I can give you any warning, I'll do that.' I moved again, walking back with him along the aisle. 'I'm quite sure we can all reach a peaceful agreement as soon as contact is made with the other party.'

'But of course.'

The aircraft was still settling and when I looked through the windows I could see a control tower and the roofs of buildings and then a whole row of military jets with U.S. Air Force markings: the pilot had obviously put the fear of Christ into Zade and persuaded him there was an emergency and this was the nearest airport that could take us. I suppose he thought the best place to land a bunch of terrorists was at an Air Force base and that was a logical thought: the moment the Boeing touched down it'd be surrounded by enough fire power to blow an aircraft-carrier out of the sea. But I wasn't too happy because the thing we'd all have to avoid was a shoot-out because in a shoot-out there wouldn't be many survivors.

10:34.

Timing was now important. I didn't know if Ferris could do anything for us at this stage: there might be a short-wave transmitter at the airbase he could use for talking to London but I didn't know if London could do anything for us either. This was the end-phase and in the end-phase of a typical penetration job it's usually the executive in the field who has to complete the mission without anyone's help: it's in the nature of the operation because he goes in alone and he's got to get out alone for the simple reason that that is what he's for.

Ferris would be here in two hours: I'd worked with him before and I knew his style. The minute we'd stopped talking on the phone when I'd called him from Belém he would have got on to the Secretary of Defense direct and asked for a pick-up in Manaus, and Burdick was capable of ordering an unmarked military aircraft to go and get him. This Boeing had been on the plot tables ever since it had taken off and Burdick would know it was now landing.

He would be here sooner than Ferris.

We were reversing thrust and I leaned against the bulk-head between the coach and first-class sections until the deceleration eased off; then I went forward and spoke to Kuznetski.

Zade had said that the bomb was the key to international power politics and of course he was right but he was here for more than one of the bloody things and they couldn't expect to get away with a shipment.

'I hear you studied at Prague,' I said to Kuznetski.

He turned to look at me. He was holding himself in a lot, and only his eyes showed his nerves; he didn't look a typical terrorist, if there is such an animal: he'd set up the Simplon Tunnel operation and shot his way out of gaol and all that sort of thing but he didn't look like a dedicated revolutionary; he looked as if he liked the technicalities of violence as distinct from its political excuses.

'Yes,' he said. 'I was in Prague.'

'In '69?'

He watched me quietly with his nerves in his eyes.

'No.'

'I was there in '70, on one of those exchange things. You've got a doctorate in physics, haven't you?'

His shoulder hit the edge of the bulkhead as the Boeing swung off the runway and gunned up a little, but he didn't take his eyes from my face.

'No. I have a degree.'

'What were you doing?'

'When?'

'In Prague.'

He hesitated, wondering whether to answer.

I heard voices from the flight deck now, and radio static.

'I did some revision techniques on deuterium moderators,' Kuznetski said. 'I was with Dr Schwarz.'

He seemed to be waiting for some kind of answer.

'Are you going after your doctorate?'

Again he waited, watching me.

'Perhaps.'

We could hear the pilot clearly now.

' – *And if you think you're going to get me to take this goddam bird up again on three engines you're crazy!*'

I now noticed that Kuznetski was slowly going pale.

'Satynovich,' he murmured, 'is a wild man. He makes me afraid.'

'You should choose your friends more carefully,' I said, and went back along the aisle, hitting a seat-squab as the Boeing swung again and slowed under the brakes.

Then we stopped, and the long wait began, as it had to. This was at 10:41.

Zade stood with one booted foot on the navigator's seat,

staring through the windscreen.

In the last few minutes a nervous tic had started to jerk at the corner of his mouth. His physical control was adequate but he lacked the nerves to back it up and when he spoke there was a tremor of rage in his voice.

He was listening now to the distorted tones from the radio. *I repeat my offer to replace your hostage personally.*

James K. Burdick, U.S. Secretary of Defense.

He had arrived by military helicopter ten minutes ago and was speaking direct from the control tower. When Zade replied his voice was hoarse and the sibilants were accentuated.

'The hostage remains with us.'

His psychology was sound: he knew that Burdick would do more for his daughter's safety than he'd do for his own.

Half an hour ago at 11:04 the F.B.I. had opened up communications via the tower and two-way radio: they were headed by a small group of men standing on the tarmac below the tower and I could see the glint of the chrome aerials as they moved about. The man in charge had announced himself as Dwight Sorenson and he had opened the exchange with an immediate demand for surrender and this had provoked Zade into expressing his anxiety in the form of rage.

At 11:09 he had ordered the pilot and navigator off the aircraft, probably because he thought they might become dangerous. They had been told to confirm that Patricia Burdick was indeed a hostage on board and that she was indeed in a worsening condition of fever.

As Zade began speaking again I heard an aircraft landing but couldn't see it because the main runway was at right angles behind the tail of the Boeing. Zade interrupted himself and ordered all air traffic to cease and got an undertaking from the base commander that only emergency movements would be permitted.

The Defense Secretary broke in again.

The material for exchange has been sent for. In the meantime I would welcome a personal meeting with you, and would present myself at the aircraft, unaccompanied.

Zade considered this and said no.

Francisco Ventura was on the flight deck, watching me with his slow moist eyes, a sub-machine-gun in the crook of his arm. He had followed me here when I'd come forward soon after the Boeing had stopped. He didn't worry me too much because I believed he would only shoot on orders from Zade and I didn't intend that Zade should give such orders, because I wanted to avoid a shoot-out.

But Shadia worried me because she'd been standing in the staff area immediately aft of the flight deck for the last twenty minutes, watching me steadily. On the few occasions when I met her eyes I felt she was ready at any instant to fire the heavy-calibre automatic that she held in her slim tanned hand, and not necessarily on orders from Zade. Her expression would have been hard to describe but I would say that she felt I owed her a death and she wanted to take it.

I could hear Sassine's high rapid tones from the first-class compartment, with nobody answering. The aircraft that had just landed was rolling towards the control tower and in a moment I heard its sound die to silence. It didn't have Ferris on board: the earliest he could get here was 12:30.

At 12:21 Dr Costa came forward to ask if the air-conditioning could be turned on. Zade said nothing: he was now standing with his back against the bulkhead, watching the group of men at the base of the tower, his dark face shining with sweat. He had spent the last ten minutes releasing a little of his rage over the radio, telling Burdick that he had broken their agreement to make the exchange as soon as the Boeing had landed. Burdick had said that nobody had known where the aircraft was going to land, and that the material for exchange had been 'difficult to obtain', for reasons that should be 'well understood'. This material, he assured Zade, was now on its way.

Ventura turned his eyes slowly to look at Dr Costa.

'We don't know how it works,' he said.

Dr Costa went away.

At 12:51 James Burdick came on the air again.

The material for exchange will shortly arrive and we need your permission for the aircraft to land.

Zade gave it.

He had been leaning his head against the panelling behind him for the past few minutes, but was still watching the group on the tarmac. I could see something like fifteen unmarked vehicles in the immediate area, most of them carrying antennae.

We listened to the radio exchange between the tower and the pilot of the U.S.A.F. interceptor aircraft as it lowered into its approach path and touched down on the main runway with the roar of its jets slamming back in echoes from the line of hangars.

So Ferris wouldn't be here. The base commander had reserved his right to receive emergency traffic but I didn't think Zade would allow it: the effort he was making to keep control of himself was increasing his tension, paradoxically, and I didn't think it would take a lot to drive him over the edge. I was now certain that this was his first experience of running a hostage operation and he was having to do it in the presence of massive armament that could blow his entire cell to shreds if he made a mistake.

The Secretary of Defense came in again.

We have the exchange material.

Zade leaned away from the panelling, his face loosening slightly as he looked through the windscreen to the group below the tower. Perhaps he'd been preparing himself for difficulties, for a series of deliberate delaying actions that might take away his initiative and force him on to the defensive. I don't think he'd believed he would be so successful.

Sassine and Ramirez had come into the staff area to listen.

Burdick was speaking again.

No problem is now envisaged. You have Paul Wexford on board with you, and he has my permission to fetch the material and deliver it to you personally.

Sassine had heard the message and came on to the flight deck.

'Let me go and get it,' he said. His eyes were shining.

Zade knocked him down and I noticed how fast Sassine

went for his gun: it was in his hand as he crashed to the floor. He wouldn't have used it against Zade: it was just his instinctive reaction to attack. I noted this point because when the time came to do something it'd be dangerous to underestimate anyone.

'Get the flight steps,' Zade said over the radio.

He was looking calmer: the tension had been mounting in him over the last hours and Sassine's behaviour had been getting on his nerves.

We heard the motorized trolley nearing the aircraft on the port side, bringing the steps.

'Get the girl up here,' Zade said.

Ventura moved past me.

'Wexford.' Drops of sweat fell from Zade's chin and his breathing sounded painful. 'You're alive because you offered to be the go-between. You'd better do everything right.'

On his way to the main door he stopped, listening to the faint whimpering noise from the toilet. The tap was running into the basin and I suppose Sassine had lost some teeth and was to some extent shocked back to normal cerebration. Zade moved again and swung the door open and pushed me on to the steps and for an instant I remember hoping that none of the F.B.I. men out there was working himself up into a state of target-attraction: from the movements on the tarmac I estimated there were twenty or thirty marksmen with the main doorway of the Boeing in their sights.

'Hold her upright,' I heard Zade say behind me.

At the bottom of the steps I looked up and saw Pat Burdick in the doorway, supported by Dr Costa. She had a hand to her eyes because of the bright light but Zade pulled it away so that she could be recognized. Behind her was Ventura and the snout of the sub-machine-gun was pressed into her back.

I walked across the tarmac.

The main group of security people was a hundred yards from the Boeing and as I neared it a big man with a two-way radio slung at the shoulder came forward to meet me.

'Wexford?'

'Yes.'

'I'm Dwight Sorenson, heading the F.B.I. team.'

'Good afternoon.'

Ferris was here and I was going to ask him how he'd managed it but it wasn't important: they must have flown him from Manaus into the nearest airfield from the base and used a helicopter, since they couldn't rely on Zade's allowing an emergency landing.

The man talking to Ferris was grey-faced with sleepless eyes.

'I'm James Burdick,' he said.

'Wexford, sir.'

'How is she?'

He was looking beyond me to the aircraft.

'Dr Costa would like her in a hospital as soon as it can be arranged. She's fully conscious and not under drugs.'

He looked down, then at Ferris.

'What's the situation in there?' Ferris asked me.

Sorenson stood close, listening.

'I can only give you my opinion,' I said in a moment. 'I'd say they're prepared to kill their hostage out of hand, if we could show them we had the initiative.' I looked at Sorenson. 'If you kill them, you'll kill her. There are six of them in there so they can take turns to sleep.'

A voice sounded on Sorenson's radio and he listened for a second and then shut it down. 'You mean that so long as we feel obliged to supply food and water they're ready to hold out for just as long as they want?'

'For days, yes. Or weeks. Of course there's a breakoff point.'

I didn't look at Burdick.

He was watching me.

'That doctor hasn't indicated my daughter is in any immediate danger?'

'No. But if she's to remain in there much longer we'd have to set up what would amount to field medical facilities and in my opinion they wouldn't allow that.'

'There's no way,' the F.B.I. man asked heavily, 'you can go back in there and drive those people out under our guns?

I have fifty marksmen deployed.'

The Defense Secretary turned away slightly and I had the feeling they'd discussed this idea and couldn't agree on it.

'There'd be no point,' I said. 'They'd bring the girl with them and even if you picked off the six of them simultaneously without touching her, one of them at least would live long enough to shoot her at close range.'

Burdick was moving away from the group and Ferris gave me a signal and I followed both of them across the tarmac until we were out of earshot. The briefcase under the Defense Secretary's arm was a security model with four straps and a centre lock and provision for a wrist chain. This was the form I'd assumed the exchange material would take and that was why I'd talked to Kuznetski.

Burdick stopped.

'Are you willing to go back into the airplane, Mr Wexford?'

'Yes, sir.'

He held out the briefcase.

'This is the material they asked for.'

It was difficult to tell him.

'They've got a man there with a degree in atomic physics.'

His tired eyes went dead.

'Kuznetski?' Ferris asked.

'Yes.'

None of us spoke for a while.

From here I could see some of the marksmen ranged along the roof of the main building. Others were deployed in unmarked cars at regular intervals, their dark barrels poking towards the Boeing: these would fire last of all and only then if the situation became fluid and mobile. A dozen Air Force vehicles stood near the end of the main hangar and a group of uniformed officers were talking together, some of them with field glasses raised to watch the aircraft.

A Sheriff's Department helicopter stood just beyond the emergency bay with a pilot leaning against its door and an Air Force man talking to him, and I could see two D.P.S. vehicles over by the tower, their lights still rotating.

There was very little noise. The sun was fitful behind high

cloud patches and the ground wind sometimes whipped the lanyard of the flag against its pole, over the main building, making a ringing sound because the pole was metal.

Mentally I wasn't too occupied. I'd done all the thinking there was to be done and the situation hadn't changed because the Defense Secretary was carrying the material I'd expected him to be carrying: Zade had come here for nuclear arms and they were in this briefcase in the form of blueprints and equations. It was known that the P.L.O. had the technical capability of producing medium-yield weapons and all they needed were the designs and that was what Zade had asked for and wasn't going to get: because Burdick couldn't let him have them.

They should have known that.

All Burdick had been able to do was to bring his daughter back on the soil of her homeland and close to him, and then hope for a miracle.

I didn't have one for him.

Nobody had.

'I was in signals,' Ferris told me, 'with London.'

They'd taken their bloody time, I thought, finding out about Kuznetski. Not that it mattered: a man like Zade would know his operation depended on the expert evaluation of the material for exchange, and if he hadn't brought Kuznetski he'd have brought someone else.

'So what does London say?'

Ferris looked at his feet.

'It's over to you.'

I was listening carefully. The final directive Ferris had given me from Manaus was to go out for the Kobra cell: the life of Patricia Burdick was an incidental factor. So the mission had ended here. Kobra had to be eliminated and that could now be done, as soon as someone gave the signal. It didn't have to be me. It would have, finally and perhaps after days of bitter and useless negotiation, to be James Burdick. He would be given the exclusive right, presumably, of condemning his daughter to death.

I glanced at him. For the moment he seemed to have forgotten us: he was just looking at the ground, his tired eyes narrowed, the wind moving a lock of his greying hair. I didn't think he had any constructive thoughts in his mind: he'd lived with this thing for days on end, and nights on end, and he must have considered every possible solution, and drawn blank.

I looked away from him to Ferris.

'London says I've got discretion?'

'Yes.'

'Total?'

'Yes.'

I turned back to Burdick.

'This man Kuznetski,' I said, 'is probably quite good. How good are those designs?'

His head had come up and he hadn't immediately understood what was being said to him: he'd caught it about halfway.

'Oh.' He looked at the briefcase. 'Not good enough for an expert to read.' He raised his head to watch the Boeing. 'These people are terrorists, and terrorists aren't normally very intelligent. So I thought maybe they'd just – ' he gave a slight shrug – 'accept this stuff without looking at it too hard. There wasn't anything else I could do, was there?'

'No,' I said.

'But we have to try. Don't we?'

'Of course.'

He was looking at me steadily now. 'I'd like it right on the line, Mr Wexford. You've been in there with them and you know them better than we do. And you don't think there's a chance, do you?'

'No.'

He looked away.

The silence came in again.

A few ideas had occurred to me during the flight from Belém and I'd had enough time to treble-check them for feasibility and none of them had stood up, not one. The only thing left was a technical last-ditch action, with the odds so steep that I'd got it out of my mind.

But I thought about it now because there wasn't any choice.

'Ferris,' I said quietly, 'I want to talk.'

He looked up at me quickly.

'Mr Secretary,' he said, 'will you excuse us for a moment?'

'Of course.'

I walked with Ferris across the tarmac, halfway to the emergency bay. Burdick wouldn't like the proposal and I was going to leave Ferris to persuade him to give me a completely free hand.

'Look,' I said, 'if I'm going back in there I'll need something a bit more useful than that ersatz stuff in the briefcase. I want something I can argue with – something they can understand.'

He was looking towards the Boeing.

'What do you need?' he asked me.

'I need to break their nerve.'

17
Zero-Zero

I went aboard the Boeing at 14:55.

Zade was unarmed, waiting at the top of the flight steps.

Ventura and Ramirez were on each side of him with a sub-machine-gun trained on me as I came up.

Zade took the briefcase from me and went into the air-craft.

The other two lowered their weapons and I followed Zade aboard, telescoping the antenna of the walkie-talkie.

I saw Patricia Burdick at the rear of the main passenger compartment with Dr Costa, and went along the aisle to talk to them.

At this point I had the urge to turn back and get out of the Boeing and stay out, stay alive. But then I would have to live with myself afterwards.

'Your father sends his love,' I said to the girl. 'He wants you to know you'll be home again soon now.'

She stared up at me without saying anything for a moment, as if she were repeating what I'd said to herself a few times to find out if it were true, whether she could trust me.

'How's he taking this?' she asked.

'Very calmly. He knows you'll soon be home.'

Quietly she murmured, 'Sure,' and closed her eyes.

I wondered how much she'd be able to do for herself, if she had the chance; her skin was waxen and wet with perspiration. Dr Costa looked at me with his mournful eyes but said nothing; I thought that inside he was praying, and to the most powerful of his gods.

I moved across the aisle and pulled down the table for the end seat and opened the zip of the walkie-talkie case and took out the bomb and put it on the table.

'Zade,' I called.

I set the dial to 5.

The chronometer began ticking.

Zade looked along the aisle. He'd given the briefcase to Kuznetski, and Kuznetski had taken out the batch of vari-coloured papers and was going through them.

I leaned against the seat squab with my arms folded.

'In five minutes this plane's going up.'

They were all looking at me now.

Zade came slowly down the aisle. He still wore his dark glasses and I couldn't see what he was thinking but that didn't matter because there was nothing he could do about this.

He saw the bomb.

'Carlos,' he said over his shoulder.

Ramirez followed him along the aisle. He was down in the dossier as an explosives expert. I had known that, and would use the advantage.

Zade stood over the seat, looking down.

He'd been patient, so far. They'd taken almost an hour and a half to get this thing for me and I'd talked to Zade with a two-way radio, saying we didn't trust him, we wanted him to bring his hostage to a neutral zone for the exchange, accepted practice, so forth. I'd made it sound genuine, and the F.B.I. had taken over and used all the correct phrases; I thought they'd sold it to him, once, then he'd got worried and said if I wasn't back in the aircraft with the material they were going to start with one of her fingers.

Ramirez stood beside him, looking down; then he instinctively edged away a fraction and I noted this.

Zade moved his hand and I said:

'*Don't!*'

I put a lot of expression into it and he drew back. I didn't have to work up any spurious alarm: I just let it show, so that he'd get the message. Nothing would happen if he picked the thing up but he might go and drop it and it was omnidirectionally percussion-triggered and that would be that.

Zade watched my face. I could feel the blood receding and the first of the sweat coming to the surface and presumably he saw this and stood away slightly, not moving his hands any more.

233

'Ramirez,' I said, and began speaking Spanish. 'You understand explosives. This device – '

'Speak in Polish!' Zade cut in.

'He'll tell you what I said,' I told him. 'I want him to know the precise situation and his Polish isn't very good.' I switched back to Spanish. 'This device is produced exclusively for the Central Intelligence Agency and is made to very exacting specifications. It has an electronic blasting cap and booster and the main charge is composed of ammonium nitrate closely confined to increase the detonation wave, which will reach 14,000 f.p.s. The secondary stage is provided by the plastic case, which is chemically sensitized Composition C–4 with a detonating temperature of 290° Centigrade.'

I was watching his face.

Zade spoke to him sharply: 'What did he – '

'One more thing,' I told Ramirez. 'The device has a protective circuit, and I'd be glad if you would warn Zade on this point. It has a clock arming-delay, two pressure-release micro-switches – here, and here – a mercury tilt switch and a vibrator activator. Please tell your friends that we don't want any undue movement inside the aircraft. Now report to Zade.'

I moved across the aisle and sat on the arm of the end seat. The sweat was a problem now, making my scalp itch and reminding me that I was frightened. It's often a chain reaction unless you can control it: you *know* when you're frightened but you want to *feel* you're at least not showing it and can keep on top of the situation. The reason why the sweat was an actual problem was that I had to keep it off my hands.

Ramirez was speaking slowly to Zade, using an English phrase when he could think of one. His eyes were very serious and I believed I'd convinced him. Most of it was the truth, in any case: there was no mercury tilt switch or vibrator but if anyone picked that thing up and dropped it the Boeing would blow.

It would have been nice to tell the girl not to worry, that we still had a chance. But she wouldn't believe me because

I'd said she was going home soon and now she could see there was a confrontation; and if she believed me the relief would show in her face and they might notice it.

It was very quiet in here now.

The ticking was discreet and fairly rapid and we could hear it when nobody was talking. Ramirez had stopped, and Zade was standing perfectly still, looking at the bomb. He didn't seem afraid of it, but he wasn't the unbalanced type of revolutionary who would take a chance for the sake of blood and glory. If he had been that kind of man I couldn't have brought this thing in here.

The others were farther along the aisle, their faces turned this way. I noted Kuznetski particularly. It was Kuznetski I was relying on.

'Shoot him,' Shadia said suddenly.

I saw her face and I knew I was right about her: she was superstitious. She was frightened of ghosts and I owed her a death and she wanted it.

'We don't need him now, Satynovich.'

His dark head half-turned towards her.

'Be quiet,' he said, and it sounded worse than if he'd screamed it out. I saw her face freeze.

He looked at me.

'What is the object?' he asked me.

'I want the girl out of here.'

'She can go, as soon as we have checked the materials.'

'I don't trust you,' I said.

'I can do nothing about that.'

'But I can.'

He was holding himself very still.

I hadn't known him long but I'd seen the way he tended to use more and more control over himself until he went over the edge. His attack on Sassine was an example: he'd been much calmer just afterwards.

He was now having to increase the control over himself again and I hoped I could get the girl out of here before he broke. The bomb was predictable: Zade was not.

Sassine was also a risk: his head was full of hashish.

And I must watch Shadia.

'As soon as we've checked the material,' Zade said, 'we've no more use for the girl.'

'That's not true. You'll need her as a hostage until you've recalled the aircrew and landed in Mexico or Cuba. Then you might release her, but we don't trust you and we don't want her in Mexico or Cuba: we want her in a hospital as soon as possible. Please note that we have three minutes and thirty seconds left.'

He looked down at once at the dial of the chronometer.

I suppose this was what had taken them such a time: I'd asked them to rig the thing so that the dial was visible.

It had a light rapid tick, the sound of an aviation clock of a few decades ago, with sufficient mass to provide precision. We listened to it in the silence and I watched Kuznetski, farther along the aisle.

'Don't you want to live?' Zade asked me.

'Very much. But I'm prepared to die.'

'So are we.'

'Of course.'

He drew a slow breath and I noted this.

'Then there's no point,' he said.

'Yes, there is. It's a question of nerves.'

'How so?'

'I think yours will break, before mine.'

He smiled. He had quite a pleasant smile.

But the tic had begun jerking his mouth again. I'd seen it before.

'Satyn,' said Ramirez, 'I think you should – '

'Be quiet, Carlos.'

Ramirez knew his explosives and he had the imagination to be afraid of this thing on the table. He wasn't a man to brave it out, as Zade would try to do.

'Three minutes,' I said.

My hands were moving very slowly against my clothes, wiping the sweat off the palms. But it kept coming again. I had to keep them dry, or as dry as I could.

Zade turned away and went along the aisle, Ramirez with him.

'Go on checking the papers,' he told Kuznetski.

'Satynovich, I – '

'Check them.'

'Yes.'

Ventura was leaning against the bulkhead, the sub-machine-gun in the crook of his arm. He felt happier like that, and perhaps pictured himself in the revolutionary pose, as so many of them did.

Sassine began talking and Zade put a hand on his arm and he stopped at once. I saw him light another reefer and put it between his swollen lips.

Shadia was perched sideways on the arm of a seat, watching me as she'd been doing for minutes. The only difference now was that she was holding an automatic, the same model as Sassine's. I didn't know how stable she was. That was the major disadvantage I had to contend with: the situation was increasing the tension to the point where even a normal temperament would become prone to irrationality.

The papers scuffed as Kuznetski studied them.

I couldn't tell what was in Zade's mind. He wasn't just missing the point, I knew that. Whether the papers were false or genuine, we all had to get out of this aircraft within the next two and a half minutes because this thing had a protective circuit and no one could switch it off. If they'd put a manual cut-off switch on it, Ramirez would have seen it.

'Do it carefully,' Zade told Kuznetski and came back along the aisle for a few paces, swinging his head up to look at me.

'You want to know the time?' I asked him.

'I want to know the terms.'

I'd thought he was never going to ask.

'There aren't any terms.'

He stood perfectly still, his black glass eyes watching me. I said: 'Didn't you know that?'

Kuznetski looked up from the papers.

'There must be terms,' Zade said.

'Oh, basically, I suppose. It's your lives for the life of the hostage. Or your death for hers.'

He said nothing.

237

I would say that from this distance he could hear the ticking.

'Satynovich,' Ramirez said, 'I'm not going to – '

Zade swung on him and ripped out a series of words in Polish I couldn't follow: his voice was hoarse, as it had been on the flight deck, earlier. Probably Ramirez didn't understand either: his Polish was worse than mine. But when Zade turned back to me I saw his face was white.

'Two minutes,' I told him.

I heard a murmur from somewhere behind me, in Portuguese.

Dr Costa was praying.

Just in case Zade was missing anything I thought I should spell it out for him. We didn't want any mistakes.

'There are fifty marksmen out there, and when you leave the aircraft you'll walk into a firing squad. Or you can elect to live, and let the girl go free.'

He was silent for what seemed a long time. It was probably for only a few seconds, but seconds were a long time, now.

'Have they guaranteed it?'

'Yes.'

I wished now that I could tell what he was thinking.

Perhaps it was too simple for him: he was looking for something complex. But the only terms were those that governed every hostage-and-demand situation: life for life. He could have accepted them earlier, when the F.B.I. had asked him to surrender. But at that time he saw the Boeing as his refuge: here he would make his stand. He could have held out for weeks, against all argument. Now he could hold out for less than two minutes because that was *my* argument: the bomb.

It was something he could understand.

Before this point was reached, he could have stayed in his refuge, refusing all terms that were offered. But now he had no refuge and it could change his thinking radically. I thought the chances of his opting to go out in a Götterdämmerung of martyrdom were rather high but it was one of the risks that had to be taken.

I'd told James Burdick what I'd had to: that I didn't think there was a lot of hope.

'Satynovich,' Kuznetski said. 'The material is genuine.'

I couldn't think what he was trying to do: he must know the papers were no use to them, genuine or false. Possibly he was working on Zade's mind, as I was, but in a different way.

'You're lying,' Zade said.

I saw Kuznetski get up from the seat and stand with his forehead against the panelling, his eyes closed.

'Sixty seconds,' I said.

I watched the thin blued-steel needle pass across the top marker for the last time and begin its final circuit. I had asked the C.I.A. technician what the margin of error was in the firing delay and he'd told me the action was electronic and zero-zero precise.

There was sweat on the palms of my hands again and I wiped them by folding my arms and sliding the palms against the sleeves, because Zade was watching me. They were all watching me.

Then I heard Sassine begin talking rapidly and when Zade stopped him I turned and looked across the aisle at Dr Costa and spoke to him and turned back to watch the dial of the chronometer.

'Forty-five seconds.'

I said it clearly because there wasn't a lot of time left and they were leaving it late. That was because of Zade, I believed: his personality was able to subdue them, especially Shadia and Ramirez.

I turned my head and looked along the perspective of the aircraft. At this point configuration would have to be noted: I had to see the group at the other end of the aisle as if they were figures cut out of the background, like one of those pictures where people are identified by numbers inside blank outlines.

Zade was standing in the aisle to the left side and he was nearer than anyone else and so his figure was larger. Shadia was on the other side, perched on the arm of a seat with the gun resting on her thigh and her unnaturally pale eyes watching me. Ventura was behind them at a distance of several feet, his configuration carrying the extension of the sub-machine-gun. I couldn't see Sassine: perhaps Zade had hit him again and he was sulking somewhere. Ramirez was almost directly behind Shadia and her configuration made a part of his, because she was sitting and he was standing. Kuznetski was still leaning his forehead against the panelling, behind Ventura.

The configuration I needed, unless something unexpected happened, was the space between them, outlined by their figures and by the panels and ceiling above their heads. It would make things much more difficult for me if anyone moved.

Tick-tick-tick-tick.

The soft quick sound reminded me.

'Thirty seconds,' I said.

Then one of them moved.

Kuznetski.

Zade hadn't seen him yet because he was standing with his back to him. I don't think he'd heard him either, or he would have swung round to see what was happening. Now he heard him, and swung round.

'*Kuznetski!*'

Zade didn't carry a gun but Shadia was there and Ventura and Ramirez were there and one of them swung his machine-gun round in the low aim but that was probably by instinct because those two were the hit-men and would ready their weapons at any sign of crisis.

'*Kuznetski!*'

It was a jungle sound, the cry of an animal.

But Kuznetski had gone. The configuration had changed and he'd left a space to one side. No one had closed the main door when I'd come aboard and he had gone through there, as Sassine must have done not long ago.

It was Kuznetski I'd been relying on to break first, but with Sassine I'd got two for the price of one. I suppose Zade shouldn't have hit him like that.

Tick-tick-tick.

I looked down at the needle.

'Sixteen seconds.'

It felt very close now in the compartment: the air seemed to press against the face. I wiped my palms dry again. When I looked up from the chronometer I saw Zade had half-turned towards me again. I could see by the movement of his chest that he was taking deep breaths: something he'd learned, perhaps, as a means of controlling the nerves. His voice still had a tremor to it but he spoke slowly, and clearly enough to make sure I heard him.

'I am not a man to threaten. You can see that now.'

This was what I thought he might do in the last few seconds. I suppose in a way it was admirable: if I had to choose any of these men as a comrade in some dangerous enterprise, it would be Satynovich Zade.

Tick-tick.

I looked down quickly.

The sliver of blued steel was moving in rapid jerks, each one as precise as the last, and as precise as those to come.

'Nine seconds.'

I looked up again, along the aisle.

No one had moved.

'Let the girl go,' I said.

Zade kept his head turned towards me and spoke over his shoulder.

'If the girl moves, shoot her. If this man moves, shoot him. But the doctor can go. Tell him, Carlos.'

Ramirez spoke in Portuguese and I heard his voice was shaking.

Dr Costa answered him, saying he would stay with his patient.

Then I saw Ramirez turn and walk out through the door of the aircraft.

Zade didn't move his head.

'Who was that?' he asked.

'Carlos,' Ventura told him.

There was no sound of firing. Sorenson had told me that if any of these people came out of the Boeing they would be arrested, providing they carried no weapons.

'What would you expect,' Zade said, 'from the son of a

241

Seville prostitute?'

No one answered.

No one moved.

So it wasn't going to work.

Again it was a question of predictability: the chemical chain reaction that would take place inside the time-bomb a few seconds from now was predictable; the chain reaction within the Kobra cell was not. I'd been relying on breaking their nerve and I'd been relying on Kuznetski to provide the initiative and Sassine had done it for him but only two of them had followed him out. The reaction had stopped there, as if the powder in an explosive compound had been badly mixed.

Shadia watched me still, her sun-bronzed hand on the gun. She was smiling with her mouth but the pale eyes were glass-bright and expressionless.

Ventura had come to stand behind one of the seats, and his arm rested along its back. He stood perfectly upright and perfectly still, and his eyes were slightly defensive, as people sometimes look when they're having their photograph taken in a studio: there was something Victorian about him, and something still of the men's haberdashery assistant.

He and Shadia had a certain likeness: they were thin and quietly-moving people with shut faces and eyes that saw everything and showed nothing. Zade seemed a man of action, a man of iron, with reasons for his actions and some brand of dim political philosophy to push him along; but in the other two I sensed an unnaturalness, the kind of sado-masochistic force that had once sent millions of their fellow humans into the gas chambers. And somewhere in it was also the death wish and that was why they had stayed.

Sweat on my palms. I wiped it off.

Tick.

I looked down.

There was no need to tell them.

A stray thought sparked across my mind: they should have let the girl go. It was all I'd asked.

Final thought-flash: roses for Moira.

I could hear the click of the four-second alarm sounding

but I'd already begun moving and I picked the thing up and aimed for the centre of the space outlined by the solid configurations at the other end of the aisle. The sweat on the pads of my fingers had caused the plastic case to slip a little but I'd allowed for that and it left my hand with an up-swing designed to drop it seven or eight feet behind where Zade was standing because if I could get it to burst at that exact spot a considerable degree of blast would vent through the main doorway and reduce the enormous air pressure inside the fuselage.

Final impressions aural and visual: Zade shouting something and Shadia's gun coming up with the flame burst spreading at the muzzle.

Then I was down on the floor with my head buried in my crossed arms and my legs drawn clear of the aisle. I was thinking about Dr Costa: I'd told him what to do when he saw me pick the thing up and he'd understood. He and the girl were three rows aft of where I was lying and would experience minimally less blast, but it was relative and it would have been pointless to try working out the chances for any of us.

Popping noise: Shadia's gun again.

Then the Boeing shuddered to the shock of the blast and my hearing was blocked off as the detonation wave drove through the length of the fuselage and brought debris with it to smash against the panels of the aft bulkhead.

Someone screaming.

Everything red for an instant and the air burning the throat: a sensation of being somewhere else, spinning in the vortex of some vast cataclysm, with the reason struggling to survive and the forebrain desperate to analyse data. Then memory making its demands: the memory of intentions to be carried out if there were a chance left for us.

Thick smoke billowing and I rolled over and got up and smashed into one of the seats and went down and got up again and lurched to the place where Costa and the girl had been sheltering. But they were in the aisle ahead of me and the rear emergency door swung inwards as he wrenched at the lever and then the girl fell down and I got hold of her and dragged her on to her feet and pushed her through the opening and dropped after her.

The rescue people had positioned something for us, some kind of chute – I'd asked them to wheel up some flight steps but I suppose the height was wrong for the tail end. I hit the ground and saw Costa with the girl, helping her along in a limping jog-trot, then the main tanks blew and we all began running as hard as we could through the fire-foam that was spreading towards us. Sirens wailing, like the cry of the dead.